M

The Gin Girl

River Jordan

Livingston Press
at
The University of West Alabama

In Special Appreciation to: My mother, Lea Thames, for reading *The Four Little Kittens* a thousand times and instilling in me a love for the written word, my sister Sheila Goode for her incredible faith in my destiny. My sons, Nick and Chris, for tolerating with humor the artistic idiosyncrasies of their mother. My cousin Debbie for championing my every cause. Virginia Dixon, my partner in chasing the perfect line, Dr. Yolanda Reed for teaching me to ask the right questions and a thousand layers more. The company of the WFPP for being so smart, talented, funny, and the toughest group of peers a girl could ask for. Wild-man Joe Taylor for bravely publishing this book. My agent, Jill Grinberg for loving *The Gin Girl* at first read. Finally, in great appreciation to the memory of my father who bought my Thesaurus and never, ever belittled my dream. These names are but a shadow of the number who have stood behind this endeavor and of the others who will embrace *The Gin Girl* on its continuing journey.

Typesetting: Gina Montarsi
Cover Design: Gina Montarsi
Proofreading: Josh Dewberry, Liz Drinkard, Daphne Moore,
Jessica Meigs, Jennifer Brown, Glenda Sims,
Roderick Ashford, Tricia Taylor, Deshandra Rash
Margaret Sullivan, Tomeika Walker, Kim Mardis

Livingston Press is part of
The University of West Alabama and
as such welcomes tax-deductible contributions
to support literature. Brothers and sisters, we need 'em.

visit our website: www.livingstonpress.uwa.edu

The Gin Girl

This novel is dedicated to my husband,
Owen Tyler Hicks,
a mighty, mighty, good man.

CHAPTER ONE

The night I had the dream, I was in Memphis. It was unbearably hot, made hotter by the fact that there had been no warning of the coming heat. From the comfortable air of a languid southern winter, to a furnace blast like the dog days of August, we were engulfed by humidity. There arose in the city a communal understanding: we were all being assaulted by the same curse. Strangers would look at each other on the streets or in bars and shake their heads as if to say, "Why? What have we done to deserve this?" But there was no answer forthcoming, although I occasionally suspected it was because of something I had left undone. Something of primary importance, overlooked on my part, for which the entire southern region was now having to pay penance.

To hide from the heat, I sat in front of the air conditioner in my pay-by-the-week motel room, a dingy end-of-the-line where I watched the flowered wallpaper peel while I drank Jack Daniels from a plastic cup. On the weekends I tended bar at a place called Seals. It was easy. I didn't have to look good. I didn't have to make small talk. I didn't even have to smile, and I still got paid enough to get by and drink Black Jack and smoke Marlboros instead of generic. I didn't think as much as I had the time to.

The night that changed things had been a regular night. One filled with regular customers at their regular seats crying in their regular drinks. Occasionally, some new face walked in searching for a bar to call home.

Eventually, all the faces looked the same: drawn and pale with a suggestion of sweat. Some sat huddled away in booths, the seclusion providing a blanket from whatever had driven them out of their lives. Others found solace at the bar, sitting on stools, desperate for conversation regardless of how disparaging or remote mine might be. In their minds, the close proximity of my presence offered at least a hint of hope, like someone who sat outside a church looking in thinking, *Maybe. Just maybe.*

"There are better choices," I wanted to tell them. "Go to Huck's place. He'll remember your name and talk in his loud, shout-the-world-down voice and ring his bar bell whether he gets a big tip or he doesn't. Huck likes a lot of noise. It's all so alive. Go there if that's what you're seeking." But incessantly, they were drawn to the damp darkness of my face because it matched their own. The bar had a manager, Tom Ricks, which meant he also had a regular seat. His was at the end of the bar where he drank scotch with a splash, but as the night wore on, the splash wore off, and he was usually drunk by the time we closed.

I locked the door, counted what little money the register held, and put it in the floor safe. Tom said, "You're a good kid," even though we were about the same age. I said, "Oh yeah, I'm a good kid," and dumped the tips in my bag without counting them. I re-locked the door behind me and started the short walk home thinking about the heat and how it might be my fault. Seals was surrounded by bars of the same type, a few pool halls and a scattering of run-down stores: a women's dress shop from a different era, a tattoo parlor offering body piercing, a T-shirt shop that smelled of incense, and the odd assortment of motels that had been turned into a pay-as-you-go arrangement like mine.

I opened the door to my room, closed it behind me and then sat in the only chair, my feet propped on the corner of the bed, smoking and letting the hours at Seals fall away. From somewhere nearby, a blues riff filtered its way out to the sidewalk, rolled a few feet and died; we were a long way from the gates of Graceland. Intermittently, cars drove past throwing shadows against the walls. The lights ran over and over the tiny closet revealing the few pitiful hangers and the white flash of a work shirt. Even in the darkness, the room looked old and tired and sorry to be alive. It had been so long since I had stayed in one place. For no reason, without explanations, I would leave one city and plow into a new but slight variation on the last. It kept me separate and barren like an estranged, futile fugitive. Now, I had enough miles on me to die. And I felt them. Every year, every inch encroaching with stealth as though death would catch me unaware and succeed when I wasn't looking. I closed my eyes and fell asleep.

*

During the course of those numbing hours, in the midst of the half-world of my mind, I began dreaming. In the dream I was a child, playing on the beach with Joe, catching crabs and turning them loose, collecting shells until our pile grew into a castle, until the castle grew into the world, the salt sitting heavy on our tongues and our skin, and we were laughing like we used to. But in the dream the sky grew suddenly dark and I could see my father calling me, waving as though he were trying to warn me of some encroaching danger. But the wind would take his breath away so that I couldn't hear him. He kept waving and waving. The sky was growing darker, the waves grew angry, the spray from them cold and stinging. Then Joe began sinking as though the sand were eating him alive, the gaping hole of an unseen animal pulling him below the surface. He was up to his waist before I grabbed him by the hands and pulled with all my might, but I was so small and the sand was eating him so fast. It was to his shoulders, and then above his chin. Then with one last desperate look, he was completely gone, and I was crying and digging and digging with a freezing wind blowing cold until I shivered and couldn't stop. Then someone said, "Mary, it's time to come home," and I turned to see my father, but he just wasn't right, and I woke with my heart beating against the silence of the room.

I could still hear this voice hanging in the air, the words running along my skin so that the tiny hairs stood up, and I looked around expecting to see him as I lit a cigarette with a shaking hand. Toliquilah had surfaced.

There is no place in the whole world like the island of Toliquilah. To some people it doesn't even exist, concealing and revealing itself to whom it chooses. To those of us who were born there, it refuses to let us go, as though we are intertwined. And secretly, I know this to be true. We are. I looked at my hands outlined against the darkness, the strength undeniable, the gracefulness surprising, and I saw before me great green vines wrapping around old oak trunks as though, over the discourse of time, we grew together, overlapping one another, the island absorbing the very folds of person, place and thing with a sleepy ease so that Percy Falls, who walked back-crooked and looked at you under the leaves of his lidded eyes, might as well have been one of the twisted oaks that grew in the grove. The same was true for Redbeard Mahoney, who was and still is the largest man I've ever known, like a swamp cypress growing straight up, unbending. Even that ogre of a woman Lolly Eden blended with the island when her teeth became as cracked as her concrete motel.

*

Everyone always understood the affiliation between the living things that moved on Toliquilah and the living things that didn't. Everyone, that is, except my mother. "We aren't Jesus and can't walk on water," she would say through irritated teeth pointed at my father's back. She never spoke of Jesus otherwise and didn't seem to know much about him, but she was quick to point out who we weren't. It was the beginning of a one-sided argument about why we lived in the middle of "dirty water and good for nothing sand."

To my father and me, our home was both mystery and celebration.

My father was a fisherman by trade. It was the second thing my mother couldn't take away from him. The first was me. I was dedicated to big Black Jack, as they called him, although he was not a black man, but he had black eyes and black hair which he refused to cut no matter what my mother called him. He wore it braided way down his back, and his skin was like dark burnished copper. It was one of the most beautiful things I'd ever seen. At some point in her life, surely my mother had agreed.

In the good days, when my father and I possessed the freedom that comes from a life without the constraints of time or demands of schedule, I would sit on his boat for hours as he scrubbed away particles of dead sea or mended a piece of wood, bonding and painting with quiet, strong hands. We didn't speak much because we didn't have to; him being Black Jack and me being his daughter, and us both living the same life, there wasn't much need of conversation. That was our best time, before my mother's diseased spirit slowly poisoned the essence of our lives. And finally, when her sullen anger climbed to an orchestrated pitch, accompanied with shouts and slamming doors, I knew I had to leave. I traveled back just often enough to see the silent deterioration of my father's face and my mother's becoming stronger as if, by the warpness of her shrewd tongue, she was sucking the very marrow from his bones, adding it to her own.

Once, on a rare visit, we waited until she was dead asleep; stole out the back door, holding the screen so's not to slam it; and let the Ford pick-up roll down the driveway without the lights on. Then we stopped at the liquor store and bought the largest bottle of Jack Daniels Black Label they had, my father's choice of brands having blended with his name, and drove on through the grove to the other side of the swamp and out through the marsh grass till the water almost came up through the doors. Then we didn't worry about anything anymore; instead, we sat and watched the moon rising over the shadows of the herons and their huge nests built in the top of swamp trees.

I wanted to ask him, "Why'd you ever marry her? You being Indian and her being contrary, why?"

But he would have just shrugged and took another drink and told me, "There's no such thing as why." So we just drank, and I didn't ask. Then the frogs got loud to the point of crazy. Then they shut up.

We got back just before sunrise, both of us drunk enough to pass out, but we didn't. My father decided to go fishing, and I said good-bye and laid across my old bed without getting undressed, listening to my mother's breathing getting shallower and shallower as she approached the surface of awake.

Three months later to the day, my father died. My mother had him embalmed over the bridge in Clark City where she planned to bury him in the dirt. She picked out a cheap pine box, setting her eyes sideways to get my reaction, but I figured pine would work just fine.

While she wore a black dress and dabbed at her eyes in the funeral parlor, me and Joe loaded the coffin from the hearse to the Ford and drove down Highway 2 over "No-good" bridge, through the grove and right out to the marsh grass till the water almost came up through the doors. Then we lifted the casket, which was heavy for Joe but not for me, and I didn't wonder why, and lugged it over to the cypress trees where we'd rigged up a pine cradle the night before.

It was just big enough to hold the coffin. We put him up there just right so he wouldn't fall out, doused him with gasoline and Jack Daniels and set fire to the whole thing. Then we watched the smoke rise and listened to the pine pop when the fire hit a knot while we polished off the bottle.

We should have gotten into trouble, but by the time anyone put the missing body and all the other pieces together, they were afraid to mention it. I guess they thought we'd be just as quick to do the same to them, dead or undead.

My mother sold the house so cheaply she might as well have given it away. It didn't matter to me. He wasn't in it anymore. Then she moved to Birmingham and lost thirty pounds and married a dentist. That was the last I ever heard about her.

Before she died, my aunt, Black Jack's sister, told me about the night I was born, about how she had been there in the room with my father, about how he watched the way my mother held me, the twisting flesh of her flesh, with a look of both hatred and possession. She said Jack had had a premonition of the years to come and tried to say, "We should never have married," but part of it got choked with revelation, and all my mother heard was "marry."

"Fine," she said, "Mary, it is," so relieved she was that my name wasn't something that sounded more like "moon child of the dog."

*

After my father died, I lived my life in rented rooms like the one in Memphis and between odd jobs like Seals. Then, the night during the heat wave I had the dream, and with my father's voice still ringing in my ears, I packed my bags and headed home.

Between sleeping and sleep-driving, I crossed the "No-good" at four p.m. on Thursday, the seventeenth. It was hot like it is in August except it was February. I hadn't escaped the heat wave but met it in its prime. The air was thick, a substance all its own. You can't walk very fast when the air takes on that shape. You can try, but you can't do it.

I drove down the narrow two-lane and thought about things that had been, never expecting what was to come. Then I lit my last cigarette and drove to Lemuel's to replenish what was left of me.

Lemuel used to have a sign that would light up red at night that simply said, "LEMUELS'S," but a woman he had lived with for seven years got mad and shot it out. That was the year before she took fifty dollars out the cash register without asking and left him.

Lemuel was a crossbreed, but nobody knew what with, and nobody could ever understand a word he said. He had come to Toliquilah a grown man, a long time ago, and bought the old fish shop with some kind of insurance money, somebody had said, and turned it into the liquor store. I opened the door, and with one look he lifted a bottle of Jack Daniels from the shelf, held it to his mouth and blew the dust off the glass before he shoved it in the sack. That was Lemuel's way of doing business.

"How's it goin', Lemuel?" His little black and white television erupted and tried to say something the same time he did, making his answer even more muffled than usual. Then he started mumble-preaching at me, and I pointed behind his head, "Gimme two packs of Marlboro's."

"Gone too long, too late. Joe done gone too, don't you know. Woman next door done took the place. Change name no good. Ain't got but one good arm. Other one long done gone. Now whatchagonnado?"

Then we stood eyeball to eyeball, me trying to decipher and Lemuel waiting for an answer I wanted to ask, *What's going on here, Lemuel? What sleeping creature has awakened? Who is it that calls me home?* But his answers would fall like jumbled bones upon my ears, so instead I said, "You too, Lemuel," and pushed my way out the door to walk across to the water.

I sat on the sand, opened the bottle, and watched the first real sunset I'd seen in a very long time. Home will remind you of where you've been but couldn't care less where you're going. Sitting there drinking Black Jack, watching the stars come out one piece at a time, I didn't care either. I thought about this place which was full of magic and all the places I'd been which weren't. Then I wished I could hold my breath and time would stand still and I'd be in a safe place forever.

It could happen on Toliquilah. Time stopping. I know this because it happened to me once while I was sitting on Black Jack's boat as he was working. He had started to sing a song that rose up from deep within his chest and hung in the air as he moved his hands over the boat hull. I had never known that he knew his native tongue. Perhaps, in some peculiar way, neither did he. And yet on this day, that ancient mystery within himself remembered who he was, where he'd come from and by the power of its being, in some seamless way, halted the earth a moment into stillness. It sounded like a lullaby, and I closed my eyes, leaned my face into the sun, and rocked back and forth until the music finished and faded out across the water.

But time wasn't stopping now. It was pressing on as the night grew darker and the sky became an endless shelter of lights. I lay back on the still warm sand, closed my eyes, and drifted off to sleep.

CHAPTER TWO

The diner, which had at one time belonged to Joe, had a new sign that read "Edna's Place." I assumed it also had an Edna. It was dark inside with the blinds closed, and I had to stop to allow my eyes to adjust. The place was empty with the exception of one comically outfitted matching family in a booth. They sat over in the corner, seriously tracing a map with their fingers.

I could feel the heat lift off my back as I settled into a darkened corner and adjusted my eyes. Edna, or so I assumed, was leaning on the bar with chin in hand watching me without blinking. Then slowly she lifted her huge head and moved in my direction. A mountain of a woman, she uprooted pieces of unseen earth with each plodding step and carried one arm slack by her side. The other arm she didn't carry at all because it was gone. Missing. From the socket. As she approached, I wondered why a slow walking, one-armed woman would want to be in the diner business.

"What'll it be?"

"Burger, fries, and a cold beer."

She let out a breath that she never took in and said, "I don't like frying on Tuesdays," and placed her one hand on a round of hip. I was thinking of, maybe, tuna, but then reconsidered.

"But it's Friday." I said. Then both of us concentrated on the days of the week until Edna replied, "So it is," and moved off to the kitchen. When you only have one arm, it doesn't swing when you walk.

The place hadn't changed so much. It even smelled the same, and I looked up half expecting Joe to walk out from the kitchen, smiling on me and wiping his hands on his apron. The same red vinyl booths lined the walls but were now more worn. I ran my finger in the middle of a rip. I'd thought Joe was crazy to take over the diner, but he did and went on to prove me wrong, adding a long bar and beer taps which was the beginning of the bustling business on Toliquilah next to Lemuel's. On busy Saturday nights, I'd help by pulling draft beers or taking the orders.

His jukebox was still here but not plugged in. He had ordered it from Cincinnati. We'd all laughed when it arrived, but night after night, Joe got busier as blue collar workers from Clark City discovered they could escape close encounters with their wives by crossing "No-good" and becoming regular patrons of Joe's. Then they'd line up and take turns plunking quarters in the jukebox, singing to Merle Haggard or sometimes Alabama. On really good nights, everyone would join in.

Joe managed to have a good place where nobody ever fought or cussed much or got mad drunk. Only once was there trouble when a man and his buddy's wife were on a date and walked in to catch their spouses in a booth on a date of their own. Then it got a little noisy. Joe elbowed me and smiled as if to say, "Watch this," and walked over to where the ruckus was and said something real low that I couldn't hear. Then they all started laughing and Joe bought 'em a round of beers and they sat down coupled up right and finished the night with what Joe called, "appropriate wisdom." He would never tell me what he had said. Joe was like that. He had a way with people that made things easy.

There used to be dollar bills stuck all over the walls and covering the ceiling with funny names and wishes. "Mommy Loves Daddy." "Graduation night." "Great shrimp!" "Way to go, Joe!" They were living proof of Joe's popularity, but they were all gone now, and I wondered if Edna had taken them or if they had been pocketed one by one.

Joe's fish that used to hang over the bar was gone too. I had nailed it up there with him standing back, his arms folded and his lower lip in a Joe pout saying.,"No one'll even be able to read my name way up there, " and me saying, "Everybody knows you caught the thing so what difference does it make?" But it did make a difference, a huge one, to Joe. He had suffered the jaws of hell to catch that fish, at least in his own mind because he was terrified of the gulf, of all that deep water and what he perceived lay beneath in the darkness. "Dead bodies," he said, "and lots of 'em."

We'd have this conversation again and again from the back porch of Joe's house. It was a stilt house on the backside of the island, and when the wind blew, it rocked just like my father's boat. It was close enough to the swamp water that, often, alligators would come up in the backyard. Joe wasn't afraid of alligators and could wrestle them by rolling them on their backs. Then he would put them to sleep. I'd seen him do it a hundred times.

"Why aren't you afraid of gators?" I'd ask him.

And he'd just shrug and say, "No such thing as why," and wink at me like my father would. Black Jack had once, and only once, taken Joe out deep sea fishing "where the big fish are." Joe spent the entire trip out with his knees together and his arms around them as if the tinier he got, the safer he would be as his dark eyes rolled sideways at the water until the whites were all you could see. But once they were out fifty miles and Black Jack got to talking to him and patting him on the back, showing him where to put his feet and how to hold the rod and brace himself, Joe forgot about his fear for just a little bit. And in a great demonstration of God's benevolent kindness, Joe hooked a seven-foot blue marlin and spent the next three hours trying to bring him in. At the end of the day my father pulled the boat to the dock on the backside of the island and made no ceremony regarding Joe's momentous deep-sea journey; instead, he only greeted me with a wink. Joe was all the ceremony needed, standing seasick and weak-kneed and as pale as an Indian boy could get. But smiling.

Years later, one night after Joe closed, a few of us had surprised him with a birthday party. Even Joe's sister, Susan, to my surprise but not delight, was there from Atlanta. She was older than we were and didn't play at the docks nor catch crabs and turn them loose for the fun of it. Once she had tried to explain to Joe that they were Native Americans and not "Indians" and there was a "difference." Then she looked at me and said I was a "half-breed." I went home and asked my Mother what *half-breed* meant, but she just clenched her teeth together and said, "Shut-up." It was a long time until I actually knew. Susan had left when we were kids saying she was "never coming back to this piece of crap island" because she was "born for better things." Which, I guess, she found by tending bar in a strip club making "more money most nights," she said, "than Joe makes in a week." But she didn't look like it. She just looked tired and hungry for something nobody had.

That night we played all Joe's favorite songs on the jukebox and pulled out a birthday cake his mother had baked. It was chocolate with raisins and nuts and white icing because that was Joe's favorite. Everyone but Joe picked out the raisins.

After we had a few beers, we thought about inviting Lemuel over, but his lights were already off, so we didn't. Earl wanted to arm-wrestle everybody, but we told him no, it was Joe's birthday, and nobody was arm wrestling. He said, "Be that way," but smiled when he said it so we'd know his feelings weren't hurt. Then to prove it, he asked Irene to slow dance to Patsy Cline singing "Crazy," and Irene was never a good dancer.

Sometime during the night, somebody had the idea we should all go swimming. Immediately, we all agreed except Joe who followed us trying to be a good sport. Everybody picked on him just enough to show we cared. Even after we stripped down to our underwear and walked out through the waves, we kept calling back saying, "Come on in Joe, the water's fine." He just shook his head and laughed and yelled back, "You're all gonna die," and I knew part of him believed it.

That night there was phosphorous in the water that glowed green wherever we moved. We looked like electric eels and were so mesmerized with ourselves that for a long time we didn't say much but watched our hands and legs underwater or swam close together with our eyes open. Finally, Earl jumped up screaming, "Look Joe, look, we're lit up like a bunch of fireflies."

Later, I climbed out and put on my shirt and sat next to Joe on the sand smoking cigarettes, and I knew he was happy.

The last time I'd seen him was after I'd called one night from a truck stop in Louisville, and he'd said, "Come on home, Mary," and the way he said it made it seem alright, so I said, "O.K." About twenty hours later, I pulled up at the diner. I watched him close the diner and offered to help clean, but my body wasn't up to it, and he could tell. We locked up and went home and sat rocking on the porch with our feet up on the railing, pushing back and forth.

There was heat lightning in the distance, and we watched the whole show while talking about Black Jack and Joe's mama and people we knew that weren't anymore. The inside of the clouds would light up blue and sometimes green like they were being x-rayed. That reminded us of the phosphorous, and we talked about the night of his birthday. Then I got too tired to talk, and Joe put me in his mother's bed and said, "It's good to have you back," before he closed the door.

*

That week I slept late and walked the beach a lot. Then I'd go to the house and just sit rocking on the porch, waiting for Joe. One night I boiled shrimp and ate them with Tabasco sauce and extra horseradish. Joe would peel the shells back with expert fingers and eat them faster than I could talk. His eyes and nose were running like mine because we were both burning up inside. We laughed a lot. I thought coming back would be sad with everybody dead or gone, but it wasn't.

One afternoon, a gator came up in the yard, and for old times' sake, Joe went down and wrestled it to its back and put it to sleep. We sat up on the porch watching for an hour before the gator cracked a lazy eye, rolled itself upright and headed back towards the water.

Then Joe told me about a girl he'd hired to wait on tables some and help behind the bar. Her name was Wendy, and she had red hair. They'd ended up seeing each other to the point she moved in with him, but it didn't work out just right. She was from upstate New York, and when fall came she said she "missed the trees." Besides, she was afraid of gators. I couldn't think of anything substantial to tell him about where I'd been, so we played poker for toothpicks and ran out of beer and drank black coffee with extra sugar. It was the best week I'd had in a long time, and I wanted it to go on without explanation. Without reason.

I thought about staying for awhile because there wasn't a good reason to leave, but then Scrawny Eddie showed up in some kinda trouble and asked for a place to stay. Joe just shrugged and said, "Alright. For a few days." And I knew without warning the seasons had changed. So I made up my mind to leave.

Joe said, "I wish you wouldn't."

But I told him, "It'll be O.K." and left the next day.

After that, I called from Phoenix to tell him I'd seen the Grand Canyon and he should close for a week and come out. I let the phone ring a long time, but he wasn't home.

Now, sitting in the diner staring at the blank space above the bar, I wished I'd had a camera the day Joe came in smiling with his fish. But I didn't, and now the fish was gone. And so was Joe. Shot in the back of the head one night in a parking lot in Clark City. No one had seen a thing. The case was logged unsolved but closed nonetheless, and they buried Joe in the dirt next to his mother.

I didn't come home and steal his body when I heard about it. I was in St. Louis, and he was already buried by the time they found me. But now, I was giving it serious thought.

Edna put the burger down. I pushed it aside and ordered another beer, and wondered where Joe's fish was.

CHAPTER THREE

Saturday morning I woke to the sound of the halyards ringing against the masts. I got out of the car and stretched and sat on the hood with my feet on the bumper and watched the shrimpers as they prepared to leave for the day. They had hardened, sun-dried faces that dared you to say they did it or dared you to say they didn't. Out West they would have been cowboys. In the Rockies, mountain men. But here, they were fishermen and searched for fish with a mixture of belief, superstition and secret spots. The wind picked up, and the masts started singing in double time.

Once, years ago, in Kansas City, longing for something familiar, I had spent the night beneath a flag pole. I closed my eyes and pretended I was on the boat docks of Toliquilah. It had been almost but not quite real enough to lull me into sleep. Today, however, I kept my eyes open until, one by one, the boats pulled away and stray cats came out, searching in between the planks for old bait.

I started the car, directing it toward the swamp, then losing my resolve, I turned and drove back to the grove instead. What we called the grove was the best of in-between. When the wind blew from the east, I could smell the secret, musty things of the swamps and Joe's alligators. When it blew from the west, it carried the taste of salt and wide-open spaces, like my father. Words fell quieter here, nestled by the cushion of the trees filled with hanging moss, and it had always been a welcome refuge from my mother's sharp, unhappy tongue.

Only one bad thing ever happened to me in the grove. He was sixteen and very popular at Clark City High, where Joe and I had to cross the bridge and go to school. We had been considered weird and weren't included in anybody's anything. No groups, no cliques, no clubs. But Jimmy Custler was well liked. In between classes, people would slap him on the back and wish him luck on this thing and that. Then he got into trouble in math class, which meant he was failing and couldn't play football. So Mrs. Stanworth asked me to work with him "just a little to help pull up his grades." I said, "I don't think so," and she said, "You can skip final exams," so I said, "O.K.," and that's how the whole thing got started.

We went to the library after school where I redid all his class work. Then I gave him the answers to his homework, and he drove me home in his father's Impala. When we were alone, he was nice to me, but in the halls, he pretended I wasn't there. It continued like that until the day he said he wanted "to have a look around the island" and drove me out to the grove instead. Then he parked the Impala under the big oak to the left and said, "Since you've been so good to teach me something, I'm gonna treat you to the same consideration." He climbed on top of me while I cried, "No, don't do it," but he wasn't listening, so I took my Coke bottle and came down on the back of his head about three, four, five times, and that was enough. I left him there with blood coming through the surface of his scalp and walked the rest of the way home.

I hadn't known for sure if Jimmy was dead or alive, and I hadn't cared, but two days later he showed up at school wearing a baseball cap that he wouldn't take off for a couple of weeks. That first day, he didn't say much to anybody and nothing at all to me. But by the third day, he started making stupid Indian noises, whooping and dancing on one foot, around and around the hall, and then he stopped and said, "Hey half-breed, why don't you show us how to do a little rain dance?" Then everybody laughed. That's when I learned what half-breed meant. Joe had been standing in the hall at his locker, but he didn't say anything.

Never even looked up.

Weeks later on a Saturday night, Joe and I rode over the bridge in Black Jack's truck. Both of us silent, our lips pressed together in straight lines that stood for something. We sat side by side in the truck watching through Tully's plate glass window as Jimmy played pool with his buddies from downtown, drinking beer that, legally, he shouldn't have had.

Tully Hall, who owned the place, was a retired drill sergeant and had a habit of saying, "It's my place, and I'll run it like I see fit or they can put me in the ground." So he did, and nobody bothered him. He had two huge arm tattoos, one that said "Mother" and the other an American flag. He kept on doing things his way until a heart attack put him in the ground. Word was they buried him with a pool cue in one hand and a gun in the other, but I don't remember who I heard it from.

His wife, Thelma, sold all the pool tables at auction and turned the place into a square dance hall that offered lessons and sold authentic square dance costumes out of the back room. She made good money and later married a man nothing like Tully. I ran into her once at the five and dime that use to be next door to the school. I was waiting on Joe, and she was sitting at the soda fountain on a round plastic stool, drinking a cherry coke and talking to anybody that would listen about how hot it was. I sat quietly down at the counter. She looked me over and then winked saying, "It's hotter'n a June bug on a skillet, Shug. Better get you something to drink." Then she ordered a cherry coke for me and put it on her tab. I liked her right then. More for the "Shug" than the coke even though it was good.

But the night me and Joe sat outside in the truck, it was still Tully's and a pool hall with Jimmy in there drinking and placing bets. Finally, he left, pausing long enough to stop and enjoy his reflection in the glass, running his fingers through his hair until it waved on top the way the girls liked it. Then he turned the corner and headed out back to the parking lot. Joe opened the door and closed it behind him with a gentle push. It made the slightest clicking sound, and I stayed where I was. I watched the open sign go out at Tully's as he crossed the street.

In the distance, I saw lightning followed by the sounds of thunder. The rain was still a good distance away. Just when I couldn't stand the waiting anymore and reached for the door handle, Joe reappeared from the hazy darkness and approached the car without hurry or hesitation. As he closed the door, he tossed a handful of hair in my lap. It included a phenomenally well-known curl.

That night, we stopped in the middle of the No-good where the lightning was moving in closer, drawing thunder with it. The stars were covered with low-lying clouds, and the air was full of electricity as if it wanted to burst open. I had the hair in my hand and held it out now over the wooden railing and opened my fist wide. I cleaned off the remnants of Jimmy Custler by shuffling my hands together in succession of quick claps. It felt like good finished business.

It was late, so we kept my father's truck, and I went home with Joe. He gave me his bed and opted for sleeping on the porch himself. The lightening and thunder were on top of us now. Just before I fell asleep, the first big drops of rain hit the roof like absolution.

The following Monday, Jimmy Custler was back in school wearing a baseball cap, but, this time, for a different reason. And, this time, he didn't make any rain dance jokes. As a matter of fact, he never so much as looked my way again. Not even from the sides of his eyes. Not even when Joe wasn't around, which wasn't often.

Now, Joe wasn't ever going to be around. Joe was dead. But I wasn't. As strange as it felt, I was alive without him, and for the moment, it was good to be sitting halfway in between his world and my father's and right in the middle of mine.

Later, I rented a room from Lolly Eden at the concrete motel. She was a skinny transplant from the woods of Arkansas with more gums than teeth and a mean disposition. Lolly Eden used to chase me and Joe out of her stupid little pool. She looked a hundred years old then, and she looked a hundred years old now.

"How long you keepin' it?"

I had never liked Lolly and didn't think she belonged on Toliquilah. One thing was for certain; Lolly Eden didn't care what I thought.

"Day or two," I said, not knowing the truth.

"Cash up front." She grinned at me in spite of her toothless condition.

Room number eight was at the end of the building. Even in the heat, the old tiles were cool to my bare feet. I turned the air conditioner on high and lay across the bed, listening to the water dripping from a leaky faucet and studying the crack that ran along the wall from the floor to the ceiling. Lolly was the kind of person who fixed things up just good enough to get by.

I lay there until I was hungry and thought about going to the diner to eat, but instead, I watched the room grow darker and darker until I wasn't hungry anymore. Later, I walked over for a drink.

Joe's booth was empty at the end of the counter against the wall, and I slid into it. Two fishermen I recognized from the docks sat at the bar talking, but not loudly. A couple of kids were cuddled up in the booth by the window. The boy had a pierced nose, and the girl wore no make-up. I suspected they weren't staying at Lolly's but were camped out somewhere beneath the trees.

Edna recognized me and brought me a beer. She had put up a sign by the register that said, "No checks. No credit. No kidding."

"You want something to eat?"

"Not now."

"Suit yourself," she said and walked away.

Just then a woman came in. She had red hair and a loud voice. A young boy was with her, and she kept thanking him for something, and he was saying, "No problem," but I could tell it was getting to be.

Eventually, so could she, so she re-applied her lipstick and winked at one of the fishermen, but he wasn't in the mood for winking. She caught me looking, and I looked away, but not before I'd seen what I needed to. I watched faces the way other people watched their backs.

I held my bottle up toward Edna who looked as if she might or might not bring me another one. The kids started kissing as the redhead watched with a jealous eye. Edna threw a piece of ice at them, and they got the point without her saying a word, and then the redhead looked happy and disappointed at the same time. I had watched enough bar fights from the other side of the bar to know women fought the dirtiest, men fought the sloppiest, and, in the end nobody remembered what they were fighting for.

The night grew heavy with a thick fog filling the diner. One of equal substance filled my mind. I kept the beers coming and at some point remember tripping my way to Lemuel's for a bottle of Black Jack and stuffing it in my jacket pocket, then staggering my way back to Joe's booth. I kept looking for someone. Then I'd forget who it was I was looking for. It occurred to me that if I sat long enough in one place, they'd find me and everything would be alright. I leaned my head back against the booth and felt it sway beneath me.

Once, when I was five, Black Jack took me to a fair in Clark City. My mother crushed out a cigarette and said, "She doesn't have any business circulating with the likes of circus people." But Black Jack silently lifted me up and set me in the truck and drove off without another word. By the time we arrived, the sun was setting, the sky growing purple and filled with moving lights from all manner of mechanical means. It was, and probably still is, one of the most magical things I've ever seen. The stars came down and sat on the ground so that we might play with them for awhile. The weather was almost cold, and my father forgot my sweater but later he won a stuffed lion at a shell game at which he could win without ceasing. The smaller prizes had continued to be traded in for those of greater value until we walked away with the largest prize the man had. My father was full of quiet surprises. I clutched the lion tightly and felt my chest grow warm beneath its fur, sheltered from the wind. Later that night, we rode the double ferris wheel, and Black Jack said, "See Mary, you never stop in the same place twice." I watched my tiny tennis shoes rocking next to his feet. My eyes could see the entire fair like a glorious make-believe city in the middle of nothing but dark shadows. The air was filled with the smell of cotton candy and the sounds of sticky children. When the man stopped at the bottom to let us off, my father gave him two tickets and said, "One more time," and the world again grew tiny beneath us as we sailed off into the night.

The booth stopped rocking and I opened my eyes. The kissing couple at Edna's had been replaced by two elderly women. They were wrinkled just alike in all the same places. Same folds sliding gently down their faces. They wore matching red T-shirts and blue jeans and had short round legs that couldn't reach the floor but swung back and forth as they stared back at me. Both of them wore fishing caps with sparkles on the bills. I wanted to ask them where they'd been or maybe where they were going, but Edna walked up with a beer. The sun was coming through the door, and I though it should be night, and then I quit caring what it was.

"You want something to eat?"

"Not now."

"Suit yourself."

I watched the twins eat something with fries. They took the same size bites. The food went down their throats at precisely the same time. Some days they must have hated each other. I was beginning to hate myself. I didn't know what day it was anymore, but I knew I was going down fast.

A man came through the door dragging his foot behind him. I wanted to tell him, "Just take it off like Edna's arm, and you can move along much quicker," but the words didn't come out. He sat sideways in the booth with his foot sticking way out in front of him, and I figured he was gonna trip somebody not meaning to. I half hoped, for no good reason, it would be Edna. Then I thought about her only having one arm to catch herself and decided that wouldn't be fair.

I looked down to find a cup of coffee that I didn't remember ordering. I looked for Edna to bring me a beer but couldn't find her. After a long time I realized the redhead had left, but I didn't see who with. The dead-footed man was still there, and Lolly Eden walked in without seeing me. She picked up an order to go and I wanted to ask Edna what she ordered since she didn't have teeth. Maybe she had some locked up somewhere she kept for special occasions.

Without her noticing, I followed Lolly back to the motel, stumbled into my room, and fell across the bed. I should've stayed but felt there was somebody expecting me at the diner. With a wave of panic, I lurched toward the door, managed to pull it open and step outside. It was dark and I was having a difficult time knowing if I were closer to day or the middle of night. At the moment, I couldn't remember if I had a watch even though I knew I wasn't wearing one.

Somebody was sitting in Joe's booth when I walked in, so I stood by the bar not knowing what to do. I was afraid not to be in the right place at the right time, like I would miss the thing I came for but I didn't know what that was.

At the fair, Black Jack had taken me to a bench next to the front gate and sat down with me saying, "Do you see where we are, right here by the gate?" I nodded yes. "If for any reason you get away from me and can't find me, come sit here and wait for me. Do you understand?" I nodded and we started to go, but he stopped and added, "Just remember, no matter how long it takes, I'll be here."

I finally slid onto a barstool, keeping my eyes on the booth. Edna came by and I tried to motion to her, but she walked right past me. The couple in Joe's booth were finished, but they simply sat looking at their leftovers. Finally, they counted their money over the check, and slowly rose to their feet. I quickly slid into the dirty booth, putting my hand over my mouth because I felt sick to my stomach.

"You want something to eat?"

"Not now."

"You're gonna kill those good looks drinking like that."

This advice from Edna didn't move me.

"Time's going to take care of that on its own."

Once I thought I saw that good-for-nothing buddy of Joe's, Scrawny Eddie, leaning on the bar, leering at me through red, watery eyes. But when I looked again, he wasn't there. I wondered if I was losing my mind.

Ray Charles began singing, "Rainy Night In Georgia" on the jukebox while two cowboys danced together by the bar, but when I looked back, the jukebox wasn't plugged in and the cowboys were gone. Then everybody was gone. The place was empty and the light dimmed, and when I looked up, Joe walked out of the kitchen wiping his hands on his apron, and I tried to get up but couldn't move. He came over to the table and said, "Hello, Mary," as he always did. Then he smiled on me and my heart moved. I wanted to say "Hello Joe," and a thousand other things, but before I could, he was gone.

Edna yelled, "Closing time."

Someone asked about "one for the road." I didn't hear her reply. I ran my finger back and forth in the vinyl rip and looked at the door opening and closing as people let themselves out. Their faces floated up and down, and I realized none of them were Joe's, and they weren't going to be, and then I didn't care about anything anymore. Then Edna was standing next to me.

"It's closing time."

I shook my head no. It wasn't closing time till twelve. I kept my finger in the rip to keep from falling out of my seat.

She stood for a long time as if in the process of making a decision.

Then with a heavy sigh, Edna slowly lowered herself onto the edge of the booth. I didn't have to look to know that her feet were swollen and hurt to walk on. Maybe she should take them off too.

"Look here," she paused and lowered her voice into something softer, "Look here, you're not gonna bring that boy back by staying drunk and watching for him to walk through that door night after night."

"I'm all that's left." I wanted to scream, but it wouldn't come out. I clenched my jaw and started ripping tiny pieces of red and dropping them to the floor under the table. I never took my eyes off her face. I could only look her in the eyes and shake my head and keep my fingers busy working the vinyl farther along the seat.

Then she got up with a grunt, adjusting her weight on her feet and walked off to the kitchen. I kept ripping. After a while, she came back with two short glasses half filled with brown liquid. She gave me one, took a drink of hers and threw something on the table.

"Was a package deal. House and bar. Seems his sister just wanted the cash. That's to his house," she pointed. "Ain't nobody there." I tried to look at the thing she'd laid down. It was silver and attached to something white. I stopped ripping and took a sip of brown from the glass. It smelled like roots and was hot and bitter all the way down. She continued talking, but I hadn't heard her.

"Whatchasay?" the words came out rough against my throat.

"I sleep in my room in the back. Don't have use of the house." She tapped her fingers on the table and took another drink. "Tell you what, you help out here some, I let you stay for free." She tapped the white thing saying, "but I can't pay you nothing," as she kept her hand on it. "You make a tip, you can keep it, but I can't pay you nothing at all." With that she shoved her hand toward me. The white floated towards me, dipping and diving out of sight. Just as another wave of nausea hit, I pushed forward and grabbed hold.

I stumbled back to the motel, opened door number eight, and for the third night in a row, as I later surmised, passed out in my clothes. Only this night, my fist was so tightly clenched around Joe's key, my palm almost bled.

CHAPTER FOUR

The next days were spent with me getting used to Edna and Edna getting used to me. I wanted to do things Joe's way, and Edna wanted to do them the wrong way, and that caused a few minor problems. One night after work, I plugged in the jukebox while I was cleaning and started playing Buckwheat Zydeco the way we used to. Edna moved faster than I had ever seen her to unplug the thing. Then she made it perfectly clear by saying, "I don't like music, I don't like being in places that play music, and I don't like watching people jerk when they listen to music."

I leaned on the broom and looked up into her face. "You don't know how to dance, do you?" She pointed her finger at me as if to speak but faced with the truth, she just turned and walked away. When she wasn't looking, I smiled.

It went on that way every minute of the day, but she needed an extra hand, and I needed Joe's key, and we both knew it. I kept the key in my pocket. Sometimes, when my heart beat too fast or I got mad or scared, I held it in my hand and ran my fingers over the ridges. I had them memorized.

Edna's place had a few tourists at lunch and a few drinkers at night but nothing like it used to. The redhead became something of a regular. Her name was Agnes and she said she was from New York, but you could look at her and tell that wasn't true. You could look at her and tell a lot of things, but they were all sad. Sometimes she sat alone at the bar, and she let out little sighs and didn't smile.

Occasionally, Lolly Eden came in to get something to eat. She would talk up a storm to Edna about one thing and then another. It amazed me. Both of them being mean and quiet, one so big and one so tight, but there you had it; they chatted easily between themselves about little things like the weather and the price of sugar.

The only thing Lolly said to me was, "How much longer you staying?"

I shrugged my shoulders.

"Rates going up soon," she said. Then she was out the door, and Edna looked at me without raising an eyebrow because she didn't have to. Her point was in the pudding of her eyes. I put my left hand in my pocket and felt the silver edges as I wiped tables with my right.

During the day tourists find their way onto the island to drive through and explore. They think they're playing Swiss Family Robinson, but there's really nothing for them to see. No markers that tell them anything about Toliquilah. No ancient battle ruins or scenic overlooks. Hungry and slightly disappointed, they find the diner and come in for something cold to drink and hamburgers for their kids. Sometimes, tourists want to make small talk, but Edna doesn't know anything. And I won't tell.

At night the fishermen arrive tired and thirsty, but they don't get loud.

*

All in all Edna kept me busy. I guess I kept Edna busy too. We had developed a simple understanding. I cleaned the front and she cleaned the back. She turned Joe's office into a bedroom. Now, it held a single bed, a dresser and had no pictures of anything or anywhere, nothing that connected Edna to where she came from. Once, when she went to Clark

City, I went through her room, looking at all the things that weren't there. Then, double checking to be certain she hadn't pulled up front, I opened the closet.

It was the same one that Joe had used for supplies. Tape for the registers. Toilet paper for the bathrooms. Extra canned goods. Old tax records. Joe's little safe. But all it held now was six dresses, huge canvases for Edna with one short sleeve and one sewed up shoulder. On the floor were four pairs of ugly, flat shoes. I had more personal belongings in my car than Edna had in her whole world.

Little by little, I began to understand her more and more even though some days I liked her less and less. She was made out of red Georgia clay through and through and it showed right down to the color of her skin. She should have been out of place on Toliquilah because there wasn't anything saltwater about her, yet there was something right about her being here in spite of it. In the end, when I'd had time to think about it, her taking Joe's diner had never taken it away from him. Edna had simply come along and stood the ground he walked on as a quiet protector guarding the space until Joe could make it back from a long trip, smiling with stories of his adventures.

Edna and I sat up late one night after closing, just the two of us. She was in an exceptionally good mood. You couldn't tell this by looking at her, but she didn't unplug the jukebox when I plugged it in and that was a telling sign. We sat in the corner booth, which was now taped again and drank cold beer. She let the music keep playing while we talked, pretending it wasn't there.

"How long you gonna just hold that key?"

I started to ask her, *How long are you gonna go on missin' that arm?* but I decided to just answer straight forward.

"I guess until it feels alright." *all right*

"It ain't ever gonna feel alright."

A part of me wanted to argue, but then a part of me knew she was right, so I kept my mouth shut.

"I can go with you," she offered.

Although the house legally belonged to Edna, the memory of it belonged to me. And it was that part I had to possess when I turned the key.

"You should cook fish, Edna," I said changing the subject, and we talked about what people ate, what they wanted to eat, and the difference between the two. Edna wanted to cook food from Georgia. I pushed harder, "How about tomorrow we drive over to the docks together and just look at the catch?"

Edna took a sip of her beer without answering, twirling the bottom of the bottle on the tabletop until it made a ringing sound. I ran my fingers over the duct tape on the seat and started picking at the edges. We paused a lot in conversation because we didn't have anywhere else to go. She hadn't once been to the docks, and when people came around to sell fresh fish, she turned up her nose and turned them away.

"Maybe we'll go tomorrow," she said, but I didn't believe her. Edna would cook or not cook whatever she pleased. I ran my fingers over the edges of the key again and thought, *Maybe tomorrow.* Or maybe not.

The next morning I was awake before the sun had broken the water's edge. I usually slept until it was well into the sky and the sound of children or slamming motel doors woke me. When you wake up early for no reason to no particular noise, you have to lie still and quiet and wonder what you're going to do next because you don't know.

Edna and I had fallen into a routine. She opened, and I didn't. By late evening, Edna's feet were belligerent about walking. When they reached that point, she would sit on a stool by the cash register, and I would do the walking for her. We now stayed open until twelve on Friday and Saturday nights, but Edna said it was just to keep me from sitting and getting drunk. The fact was, I hadn't been drunk since the night she gave me the key. Edna needed an excuse for change.

I once knew another woman who didn't want change. She sat on the same stool in the same bar every night and told the same story over and over again. The story was about how her husband had left her for another woman, but the other woman had turned out to be a man, and so her husband had shot himself and none of it made a bit of sense to her, and it was a terrible waste because he had been a good mechanic for twenty-something years.

"We never had a bit of problem with our cars," she said. "Because he kept them up so well. Henry had pride. You could trust him. He really wasn't a liar even though it might have looked like it in the end, but I knew him real good and no matter what people thought later, he wasn't a liar." She sometimes added that she would have forgiven him if only he would have asked, but he didn't, and now he was dead. "Ain't it a shame?" "Sometimes you just gotta accept people bein' dead," I told her, but she just shook her head, looking up at me through the tops of those red-rimmed hound dog eyes.

*

The light on the beach was painfully bright because there was nothing to stop it. The sand caught it and threw it back in my face, so I had to squint my eyes and shelter them with my hand. The light became softer as I drove through the grove because of the trees and the shelter of the moss blocking out everything but what grew from underneath. Then the beginning of the swamp came up and the sun in my eyes didn't seem to matter so much anymore. I took the fifth dirt road to the right and drove slowly to the end. The sawgrass had grown up thickly on both sides of the road, and it scratched the sides of the car. I parked a good twelve feet from Joe's house. It looked almost the same.

I smoked three cigarettes, staring through the dusty windshield. Then I opened the door, the hinges squeaking in protest, and closed it before I could change my mind. The nights I had lain in bed at Lolly's motel and felt Joe's key pressing into my palm had filled me with an expectation and prepared me for finding things as they used to be. Closing my eyes and picturing Joe among the swampy interior of the marshy grasses and alligators, his laugh echoing across the water and his mother's gentle nature spilling through the house and out across the porch. And somewhere in that part of my mind, I had believed I could simply climb the stairs and, by using the key, bring them back into this world again. Nothing unmoved. Nothing unchanged. But the moment I pulled up, something different had settled in my stomach that changed my perceptions from false expectation to a hard rock of reality.

An abundance of cigarette butts littered the yard. Beer bottles were scattered at the top of the stairs and across the porch. Joe's rockers that had held us in slow, rhythmic comfort on hot summer nights, were missing. One glass door was broken, and the screen hung loose, ripped from the sides. I didn't need the key, but I squeezed it tighter in my hand as I stepped through the broken glass and saw the way things were. Someone had been here. Or several someones. Beer cans were strewn everywhere. Sofa cushions were cut and thrown to the floor. Old trash had been left where it was dropped. The pungent odor of rotten food and rats permeated the one place that had been my safe haven.

I picked my way to the door of Joe's room and thought about my father's gun in the car. Now, it would have felt good in my hand. Joe's bed was ripped, the mattress cut lengthwise at regular intervals. A picture of him sitting on a sleeping gator was still tacked to the wall, but everything else lay scattered or broken. His mother's mattress was stripped bare and cut as well. It had been common knowledge that Joe trusted banks about as much as he did the ocean, believing both held scavenging monsters in the depths waiting to devour the innocent. Someone had gambled on Joe's having sewn money in the mattress, but Joe was never one for sewing. The things people didn't know about Joe were the most important.

I hadn't planned on a single thing that was coming, but here I was, sweeping up glass in a dead man's house with my mind considering motives for murder. I spent the remainder of the day burning rancid trash in Joe's barrel. Without my knowledge, the smoke hit the sky with a message that said, "Someone's come home."

Later that afternoon I drove back to Edna's for something to eat with no intention of saying much of anything, but Edna leaned her one arm on the counter, propping her head in her hand and said, "So?"

"You haven't done too well looking after your investment."

"You're fixing it ain't you?"

I looked down at my smoky hands, spreading the fingers apart where they were blistered and black. "Yeah, I'm fixing it."

"I done just fine."

That night I turned Joe's mattress upside down, covered it with my sleeping bag and lay down on top. The frogs were croaking on and off, on and off, as if they were crying for rain, then changing their minds, then crying again. They went on like that until I drifted off to sleep smelling like smoke and more exhausted than I'd been in a very long time.

CHAPTER FIVE

"What is it you wantin' with me?" Esther turned her head slowly towards me but looked straight past with milky white eyes that saw nothing.

Esther was a snake milker. Word on the island was she got anywhere from thirty dollars to three thousand per gram. Then of course Redbeard said he knew, "for a fact," she once got twelve thousand for one gram of sea snake venom, and if anybody was going to come close to the truth it was Redbeard. She made more money than everybody on the island put together and always had. Nobody cared. They wouldn't want her job and were afraid to come after her money. The only question I had, from the looks of the place, was what in the world did she do with it?

"Whatchu be comin' back for now, girl, after bein' gone so long now anyway?" I wondered if Esther could understand Lemuel. I had the idea she could and suddenly pictured them having intricate conversations into the gray hours of the morning. Esther and Lemuel. It was a strange thought.

She moved across the tiny room quickly, like a snake with a purpose. I had only been to Esther's twice, and this was the second time. The first had been when my mother, in her pitiful attempt at a rose garden, was bitten by a rattlesnake. Not a huge one mind you. Just one big enough to kill her. I was thirteen, Joe fifteen, and neither one of us could drive very well. We happened to be at my house, or the snake would have had his day and been well gone before we found my mother breathless and white.

She had come in through the front door, her face pale and frightened. Beads of sweat had broken out on her forehead and upper lip. She never said a word, only pointed to the marks on her chest where the fangs had pierced the skin. Black Jack was gone, and Mom's car sat outside the house. I grabbed the keys and Joe drove into the heart of the swamps, even farther than his house, to where Esther lived. We had driven fast from the panic of knowing everything rested on whether we made it there and back again in the nick of time.

Joe did the talking, and I stood with my back against the walls listening to snakes slitherin' and hissing in their boxes. Then Esther was with us in the car, with me in the back seat and her sitting fearlessly next to Joe.

My mother had fallen across the floor near the front door, unable to move any part of her body except for her two forefingers, which she struggled to raise and drop repeatedly. I guess she wanted to let us know she was alive, fearing we would sooner bury her than check for a pulse. Esther took full charge of the situation, and the rest became a blur in my memory. I remember thinking whatever prejudices my mother had against race, color, or Toliquilan's in general, she momentarily traded for a greater, more tolerant scope of humanity in the hope of preserving her own life. My only deliberation over the years had been to replay the events of that day with a different ending: one that involved no blind, snake-milking Esther on the island; or no car keys readily available; or one with Joe and I crashing into a cypress tree just hard enough to stop us in our tracks. I'd play it out all the way to the end with Mom being dead and Black Jack alive and me never having left home. Everything would have changed. And somehow the new course of events would even bring Joe back to life.

"You be comin' for something to be botherin' at all. You not be comin' to talk 'bout the moon last night, that's for certain. You not a moon-talkin' girl." Esther moved back across the room and looked me straight in the face with her white eyes. "I got good eyes to see what you don't know about." And she blindly stared at the space of me for awhile. If I hadn't been raised in the whereabouts of Esther, I would have been scared to death of her.

"Have you got good ears I don't know about too?" I asked.

She moved off at arm's length to a cupboard she called a kitchen and poured herself a cup of tea. Her finger stayed just below the rim until it hit her skin. "Maybe so, maybe not. What chu be needin' ears more'n yours for?"

"Like you said, I've been long gone. There's nobody here anymore that I know."

"You don't know me so good now do ya?"

"How long have you been living on Toliquilah?" I asked her.

"More lifetimes than you spent running to nowhere."

"That's good enough for me."

Esther took a sip of tea, nodding to herself and lowering the small frame of her body into a ladder-back chair by the table.

"I don't know who kilt your Joe."

"Didn't expect you to." I pulled a chair out next to the table but stood silent until she motioned for me to sit. "But something, somewhere, happened. Something went wrong." A snake hit the side of its box, rising up and striking for no apparent reason.

"That boy in the box be comin' from Africa. He mad now 'cause he locked up in a strange way."

"Have you heard something from somewhere? Any little thing? Somebody hiding, maybe."

"They always been people on the island that not wantin' to be found." She turned her eyes towards me repeating. "Always."

"Yes, yes. A smuggler now and then."

"And before that, the bootleggers."

"Who do you know that might be hiding now?"

"And I be thinkin', they still bein' a bootlegger down in the swamps someplace low."

"There's no bootlegger I'm interested in."

"Somebody hidin' low, lookin' for the right person to be buyin' what he be sellin'."

The snake raised up and struck the side of the box again.

"You ever seen a snake the likes of him?"

I had to be patient with Esther because I didn't have a choice.

"Nope."

"Neither has this woman. Course, I not be seein' him, girl, like you do. You be studying on his colors, the rings that bind his body, the quickness of his black forked tongue or maybe the length of him. I not be lookin' on these things. They not be matterin' so much to me when I has to grab the back of his head before he puts his bite to me." Esther, we guessed, had been bitten a thousand times. Her blood alone should be worth money as an antidote. "The obvious things not be the ones of the most interest to me in a time like that. I never heard a snake move like I hear him move. Never heard one throw himself against the inside of the box. I be lookin' on the inside of him." The snake threw himself against the box again. "Yessss," she smiled.

Esther's "s" came out in long hisses, and I began to see the reptilian influence in her movements and the texture of her skin. Perhaps, Esther had spent too many hours in the darkness among her snakes.

"By now he should've done give up the good game. This snake be one way, maybe the other. Either very dumb or the smartest snake I ever gonna touch." Esther cocked her head to one side, her ear in the direction of the box. "I've not made my mind yet to which one."

My feelings about the snake were the same as Joe's about the monsters from the ocean; I didn't like 'em. They all looked the same to me. No matter what type or how many rings. They were all the color of white sheets pulled over dead faces.

The snake threw himself against the box again and shook it with his body rolling over and over in wide ropy circles. Esther actually smiled then. "I'm believin' he only be thinkin' one thing. And thinkin' it very hard. Now, when I get ready, he won't be."

My patience was wearing thin. I was tired of Esther's new snake and the hissing of the rest of them. She must hear them hissing in her sleep. Or maybe she hissed in her sleep herself. I looked at the side of her smiling face. She had a tiny pointed nose with black nostrils you could easily see. Her white hair was pulled tight to a bun and perfectly matched the whiteness of her eyes. And her skin was the smooth coppery color of Black Jack's but with wrinkled lines that were darker and looked like the shadows of scales. For a moment I wondered if we were somehow related, but I thought of the snakes and decided not.

"I moved into Joe's house."

"I seen the smoke goin' up."

I looked down at my hands where the black burning was still evident under my nails. Then I thought about how Esther couldn't "see" anything but left it alone.

"The place wasn't in good shape."

"Whatchu be expectin' there after gone so long?"

"Something different than what I found."

"You be expecting the boy come walkin' to meet you on the road maybe?"

For a slight moment, I wanted to slap her. "I be expecting his beds not to be gutted wide open and his house overrun with rats."

"Somebody lookin' most hard for something?"

"Somebody looking for Joe's money."

"Well then," she leaned the chair back until it was balanced only on its hind legs, rocking slightly back and forth, "seein' how you may be the only one know where the Joe boy's money be, they be lookin' in the wrong places." She dropped back to the chair's front legs and leaned in over the table, "Should be lookin' for you."

I could have denied knowing what I did, but to this thing in front of me called Esther, it wouldn't have worked. Her mind moved as fast as her hands.

"In my book, whatever once belonged to Joe still does and always will."

"Maybe Joe not be feelin' that way about it, girl, but that's not for me to tell you. You got a long way to go yet on the whole thing."

She rose up from the table and put her cup in the sink, and I knew it was time for me to go.

"But chu did the best right thing comin' back home. Now it'll be made right."

"Nothing I do is gonna bring him back."

"Everything's gonna be made right from this point goin' on."

The African snake threw himself against the box again, and Esther laughed with her mouth half open and her face full forward. It was obvious she had determined if he was so smart or so dumb, and it was neither one. He was simply set on only one thing: escape. Now all Esther had to do was tempt him with the one hand and seize him with the other. It was wise to know in advance the purpose of the thing you planned to capture.

CHAPTER SIX

Edna's eyes were following me across the room. Black spotlights held in the sky of Edna's head with tracking determination. They had been like that all day. I moved to the bar, pulled a stool out, and, lighting my last cigarette, sat down.

"What, Edna, what is it?"

"You mean to tell me that woman lives out there with all them snakes?"

"She does."

"And she's blind?"

"She is."

"And you say she grabs them by the back of the head and milks the poison from them not seeing a thing."

"That's right."

"Ummmmph."

I leaned back and smoked and watched Edna's face as she tried to get through something by herself.

"Edna, why don't you pull me a beer?"

"It's nine in the morning."

"Then pour me some coffee."

"Pour it yourself."

Things hadn't gotten any easier between us. And they hadn't gotten any worse. We had reached the pinnacle of our ability to communicate to one another. On good days it was just this side of easy friendship; on bad ones it was just the other side of hateful irritation. We both tried to walk the fine line that had developed between us: a private understanding we shared during moments of kindred perception.

A small group of people had become regulars to Edna's.

Agnes regularly made the rounds, usually later in the evening. Sometimes she came alone. If she could help it she never left that way. Surprisingly, one night when she had arrived late, dressed to attract something and smelling of loud perfume, I had been moved to tell her, *It's alright. You don't have to be so desperate,* but as she flipped her hair about her shoulders, casing the room with the peripheral vision of a lizard, I only said, "What'll it be?" and left the rest to circumstance. Something told me what little I cared was more than anybody did.

A few weeks ago, Redbeard "Red" Mahoney had shown up and settled himself in like the ancient days. He had pushed through the door as if a gale force wind had brought him in, but there was no wind, just the full life of him coming into the room. It seemed as if it had been a thousand years since I'd seen him, but there he was, looking more weathered and larger than I remembered him.

"Red Mahoney."

"Mary Contrary."

"Where've you been?"

"Up to the Louisiana coast. Fish was good. Swamps 'bout the same."

"Whatchacomehomefor?"

"Don't know."

"Me neither."

It felt good and right to have him back. He had been one man that I could say was a friend of my father; otherwise, Jack stayed to himself and preferred it that way. Red was solid as a rock and known to be a man you could turn your back on, even if he didn't like you.

Lemuel had developed a habit of coming over after he closed the store and sitting in the booth mumbling to himself. Edna saved him whatever was for lunch and sold it to him for dinner at half price. Or at least it had started out that way, but now, most of the time, she didn't charge him at all. I vaguely wondered when this had occurred without my noticing it, but my mind stayed preoccupied with the mysterious somebody who was looking for things that belonged to Joe.

"How does she do it if she's blind?" Edna was still thinking of snakes.

"She is blind and I don't know. I never watched her."

Edna rolled her eyes to the ceiling. "Take me out there."

"Why?"

She shrugged one shoulder, and paused for a second, then looked away and said, "I don't know."

Esther didn't know anything about Joe's death, and Edna was lying. Neither one of those elements fit into what I knew to be the truth. Esther lived in a world separated from other people by both choice and darkness. Still, information on the island found its way to her as if its final destination had to be Esther's ears. Yet, when it had come to something the size of murder, she knew nothing. And in the two months I'd known Edna, I had searched for answers to her past and what had come undone there— including her arm—but Edna had nothing to say which was one thing. The no saying. The other thing was this: Edna didn't say wrong. Edna didn't lie. But she was lying now about something so simple as wanting to see a blind woman milk a snake. The curiosity was understandable. The lying was not.

It made me think of someone else. Someone that was truth walking.

"I need a few hours off."

"You just got here."

"I need to visit an old friend."

Edna cocked her head to one side, "Alright then, but try to get back before night."

Any time I had spent in Clark City aside from school was only passing through to get to Toliquilah. I didn't like the place. I never had. It had the continual air of decay and represented everything the island wasn't. False order. Masked faces. The unique existence of Toliquilah faded the moment you crossed the bridge. By comparison, Clark City was as cold as a blade with an extra-sharp edge. I had one friend in the entire city, the janitor who worked at city hall. His name was Moses, christened so at birth by a grandmother who believed he was destined to escape the bondages of poverty that had held the inhabitants of Clark City captive. Particularly those of the darker persuasion. Moses was half black and half Spanish, but most people didn't know about the Spanish. We had gone to school together, and—aside from the steady presence of Joe—Moses was the only other person I really knew. He had an easy voice and an affable manner, even in high school, and I trusted him.

The courthouse steps leading up to the less-than-stately brick building were dirty. They were riddled with cigarette butts and tiny strewn pieces of trash. The flowers and trees were wilted in the heat and had turned brown on the edges. There was a seal above the entryway that said, "In God We Trust," and my first thought was, *No they don't.*

If the outside was forsaken, the inside told a different story. The corridors were quiet and cool. A most welcomed relief from the blaring sun. The stairway banister was polished to a fine sheen. The tile floor, a giant reflective pool. In the distance, I could hear the patient sound of a floor buffer, and upon turning the corner, I discovered Moses, his hands wrapped around the handles with earphones plugged into his ears. He looked up and, smiling, removed the earphones. I hadn't thought he would recognize me, but right away he had.

"Mary, whatchu doin' back in this place?"

what exactly it was I thought.

"That, maybe, if you didn't look, it would go away."

"Maybe so."

"Nobody thought anything much about it over here."

"Why's that?"

"You're from over the No-good bridge. You know how the stories go. About what goes on over on that island."

"Most of it's not true."

"They don't know that. Truth is, they were probably afraid to kick the rocks around too much. Afraid something might turn up and they'd have to deal with it."

"Did you ever overhear anything suspicious? Any gossip that sounded as if it might hold water?

Moses leaned forward and laid his hand on my shoulder, dropping his eyes level with mine, "Do you know how long it's been?"

My heart beat double-time so that the blood rushed to my neck and I couldn't breathe.

"A while."

"Three years, Mary." Moses squeezed my shoulder under his huge hand. "He's been gone three years."

The amount of time tried to register, but it didn't quite make it. Three years. It was supposed to be a long time, but I didn't feel it. Moses' bulletin board hung on the wall behind his head. There were pictures of his family. A child's drawing of home. Someone's blue ribbon for winning. Where had I been? What had I done? All the years I'd spent running and nothing to show for it. A face floated up in front of me and said, "Ain't it a shame?"

"I just want to know what really happened, Moses, that's all. He deserves that much."

"You deserve that much," he said, and then he changed the subject and we sat talking about old things, forcing one another to remember

"Moses, the truth is I don't know."

"Well, now ain't that a thang?" He drug the word *thang* out with a wink of his eye, stood the buffing machine up and leaned against the handle, one foot propped on the base. He had always been big for his age, and now, it had settled around him well with extra weight and gravity.

"I want to ask you some questions."

"Uhuh. C'mon, I'll buy you a cup of coffee."

Moses escorted me to the basement café where he had absolute jurisdiction. He picked up a large Thermos from the tiny gray table top that was command central for Moses and poured coffee in the top and passed it to me. He drank straight from the thermos. For a few minutes we didn't speak. Then I noticed the band on his finger.

"You got married, Moses." It surprised me that life had progressed for him in a way it had not for me.

"Got a beautiful woman. And … look here," he raised up and pulled two pictures down from his bulletin board, "got these two angels that come along with her."

"You have children."

"Well, yeah, they were already born when we met, but they're mine just the same, you understand." I looked at the pictures of the smiling faces of the girls. The oldest was missing her two front teeth. They didn' look a thing like Moses, but I imagined their smiles had been develope by his presence.

"Pretty girls." I said passing the pictures back over. He looked them himself again before putting them back up in their place. Mo picked up the Thermos and leaned way back in his chair. I leaned forwa and he poured me another cup.

"You know I'm not here for a social visit."

"Oh, I know why you're here. I just wondered what took yo long."

"I thought…" I paused, looking at the floor trying to deter

what each of us had forgotten. After awhile, there was nothing left to say. We made our way to the elevator, and once we were inside, Moses grew silent. Then he reached out and pushed the stop button.

"If you want to see the file, Mary, come back Friday 'round ten o'clock and wait by the back door till I let you in."

"You can't get caught foolin' around with that stuff. You've already put in a hundred years here."

"On Friday everybody's been paid and they're long gone."

"What about the guard?"

"He sits down front watching T.V."

"Ten then."

"Park on a side street," he said, and he pushed the button again.

When we walked out on the first floor, he smiled and said loudly, "It sure was good to see you, Mary. You drop back by anytime."

As I walked down the long tiled corridor, passing the secretaries with polished lips and tiny heels, I heard the motor of the buffing machine pick up where it had left off.

CHAPTER SEVEN

Edna was a master mathematician. She could calculate the precise amount of time I spent staring out the window, or leaning at the bar making conversation with someone she didn't particularly like, or precisely how many minutes I might have been late. These were great moments calculated in the resource of Edna's mind. What she never seemed to calculate was the equal amount of time I spent scrubbing, or the hours I worked overtime because I knew her feet hurt, or the small fist of tips I took home and called pay. It was all very one-sided, but then so was Edna.

I was being punished by Edna's silent looks and mathematics, but I could bear her mood easier knowing Friday night was only days away. She was sullen now on two accounts: I wouldn't take her to see Esther, and I was going to be gone Friday night.

In between Edna's sullenness and swollen feet and me just being myself, we genuinely shared an insider's look at the lives that had begun settling with frequency at Edna's. We had a particular view of them as though we were looking through a window into their lives without fully participating.

Lemuel was such a fixture now that we referred to the booth on the wall by the window as Lemuel's. As in, "Where does this order go?" "To Lemuel's booth," although he wasn't there. More peculiar than Lemuel himself was the comfort I began to take in his mumbling. It provided me with a security he neither offered nor had the power to remove. It soothed some part of me, and if we weren't busy, I would sit one booth away smoking cigarettes and leaning into the shadow of Lemuel's presence as though listening to the lullaby of my father. Between mouthfuls of creamed potatoes, Lemuel would look out the window and point his fork and speak. Or he'd wave it in arcs above the booth, making explanations for one unknown thing, then another. Then, with whatever oratory speech he had purposed in his mind completed, he would rise and move away.

Agnes continued to come in just about every night with a loud voice and layered laughs. She would hold court sometimes like a comical queen perched on her throne of the bar stool and flirt majestically with one man and then another. Then there was a night of exception. It had been overcast and cloudy with showers pouring down on and off all day. Agnes rushed through the door under what remained of a drizzle. When she made it as far as the bar, the last rays of the sun suddenly burst through with great determination, at once cutting through the blind slats and catching Agnes off-guard. Their shadows slapped her across the face as though a prison searchlight had caught her in the act of escaping. She drew a sharp breath and threw up her arm to shield herself from the attack, yet the sun held its position and Agnes, caught in the blaze, held hers, frozen there with bars cast across her face. I knew then that Agnes was imprisoned in a cell of her own making. Lie upon lie, layer upon layer, Agnes had trapped herself. And now she was caught and exposed. She spent the rest of the evening drinking solemnly at the bar, and when someone passing through tried to strike up a conversation with her, tears came to her eyes, and she looked away.

The next time I saw Agnes, she came in well after dark when there would be no threat of the light of discovery. Her lips were painted in a deeper shade of red—a swatch of blood across her mouth. Her eyes were heavily slitted with eyeliner. She held court that night and vamped her best with her dyed hair pulled tightly up, her eyes becoming more slitted as the night wore on.

Our conversations were limited to her ordering and me refilling her glass. She had once asked me, "Are you whole Indian?" right out the blue. I never answered because I didn't have to. Then she offered, "I don't have nothing against Indians." And then looking down with the most honest tone I had ever heard her speak she said, "I really don't."

Red would come in from fishing to sit quietly in my booth by the wall so I could visit with him in between tables. He was quiet, like my father, and sometimes we would simply sit together without saying any words. Then again, sometimes we would say a lot with very few.

"You know it won't ever be the same." Red spoke with a toothpick bobbing in his mouth.

"No." I ran my finger over the taped vinyl. "Never will be."

"That means it'll be something else," Red held the toothpick steady, stared me square-in-the-eye, and said, "if you let it."

The tape was warmer than the vinyl it covered. Funny the things you notice when your aren't looking. "You gonna stay, Red?"

"Maybe we make a deal chere," and he stepped up his well developed impression of a cajun accent, "you no try to fly with broken wings, I not be thinkin' so fast to sail away. No?"

I reached over and tugged a handful of his beard, "Maybe, someday, I fold my broken wings and sail away with you, my friend."

Edna started clocking minutes in her mind. So did I, but of a different kind. While her eyes grew cloudy with the frustration of inattention, mine grew empty with raw realization. Red was right. Things could be different, but I hadn't asked for a different anything. Joe laughing. His mother cooking. Black Jack fishing. Those were the things I wanted, and they were all gone. Forever. Different was not a comfort for me. It was just a thing that filled the empty places of what should have been. But Red had a wisdom that I respected, so I allowed the tiniest of seeds of his advice to sink inside the depths of me before I had the chance to dig it out and cast it into the rocky ground of stubborn pain.

*

There were two kinds of rain that came to Toliquilah. One came on top of the heat, sitting down upon us with torrential downpours, pressing with a heavy hand, locking in the heat like a cap screwed on tighter and tighter. Tempers grew in times like these, irritation running high for no reason. Lemuel's mutterings would take on jagged edges with sharp hooks as if he fought invisible demons without pause. The second rain brushed lightly across us, seeming to come from heaven itself bringing cooler, drier air, lifting the lid that locked us so near to the ground. Then our horizons soared higher and wider, and Lemuel's prattle became more of a melodius chant. Edna's mood lifted, dancing across the diner on lighter feet. She slapped people heartily on the back, cracked jokes with the tiniest encouragement, and became downright jolly with Lolly Eden, the two of them wrapped in a cocoon of conversation. Lolly would sit with her skinny arms propped on the bar drinking a cold draft and Edna telling stories, comically stretching her arm up and out to describe how far and wide a thing had once been in her life. Then she would nod to me with a private understanding. These were times when our eyes saw in unison and stood in agreement. There was then an air of laughter that filled the diner with the disjointed sounds of life, big and full. Regardless of how short-lived the good rain might be, it was a welcome relief from the heat, and we drank it in with big thirsty gulps hoping it would never end. But finally, as the temperature increased, the oppressive looks of Edna's judgementalism returned as her feet swelled beneath her.

All in all the days and months had been passing without my counting. Without my marking them in great X's that led nowhere. I existed to be home again, and in the mediocrity of the basics, the rituals of living, the daily plodding of my feet forward—coupled with an ever-present question of Joe's demise—I was slowly emerging a different creature than the one that had crossed the No-good bridge five months ago. Without my noticing, the seasons had changed.

CHAPTER EIGHT

Friday morning I stopped in at the diner to help Edna for lunch. She looked up from her one-handed slicing and was, I knew, grateful but acted stubbornly unmoved. I went behind the bar and poured myself a cup of coffee and then held my hand out for Edna's knife.

"I got it."

"Edna, I need the diversion."

Edna had a hard time accepting a free offer. It had to be boxed in a way she found acceptable.

"Couldn't sleep, huh?" she said, passing me the knife.

"No."

"Don't know what you expect to find."

"Me neither." I lit a cigarette and kept chopping. "But," I pointed the knife at her, "I know I care more than anyone, and whoever covered the case found a dead Indian from Toliquilah, and that was the end of it."

Edna nodded in understanding.

At 9:48, tired of chopping, I took a beer from the cooler and walked over to the beach sitting down behind Lolly's motel, taking advantage of her chairs, wondering how long it would be until she discovered my presence and would be standing over me with her lip pulled back and her gums showing, and her saying, "Them thar's for paying customers, and you know it."

The sand was already warm beneath my feet. It felt good. The waves were up just high enough to make crashing sounds as they hit the shore in perfectly timed sequence. I closed my eyes and counted between them. One thousand one, one thousand two, one thousand three, one thousand four, one thousand five, crash. One thousand one, one thousand two, one thousand three, one thousand four, one thousand five, crash. Perfect order. That's the way it was supposed to be, I thought. Everything perfectly ordained. Then someone killed Joe and sent the plan spinning out of control. That wasn't in the plan. Now something had to happen to catch the spinning dial and set it back on its appointed course. One thousand one, one thousand two, one thousand three, one thousand four, a shadow fell across my eyes, and I stopped counting to look up.

There before me stood a dark eclipse of a man. His outline was visible. The face of him remained a shadow.

"Hello."

I placed my hand over the cap of the sun but remained silent.

"I see you are smoking. Could I trouble you for a light?"

It was hard to refuse, although I had always been wary of speaking to strangers along the beach. Toliquilah was my backyard. The people I didn't know, intruders. I watched the brown hand reach out and take my cigarette and, lighting his, kneel to return mine. Then I saw his face, and he smiled. He sat at once on the sand beside my chair with a comfortable persuasion, at home in his own body. His body at home in the world.

"My name is Manuel Garcia Rodriguez." He extended his hand.

"Mary."

"Ahhh, the name of the Blessed Virgin, the saint that she was and still is, as well as the name of my blessed mother, God rest her soul." He made the sign of the cross above his bare chest, and I sensed a danger running along the corridors of his lilted accent and captured in his watchful eyes. But the danger wasn't directed toward me, and I was not afraid of him.

"This," he waved his open hand across the gulf's expanse, "is very nice."

I nodded but remained silent. Suddenly, a dolphin breached the water, riding backwards on her tail, facing us, and speaking across the water as only dolphins do. Then she flipped to her side and was gone. Manuel Rodriguez laughed a great laugh with his head thrown back and the whites of his teeth showing. He was a handsome man. I didn't trust handsome men. "It's my girlfriend. She has caught me here with a beautiful woman, and she is letting me know that if I do not behave, she will leave me for another."

"That is a lie."

"Truly, I swear it. We are, or I should say, we were engaged."

"She would never leave you. They mate for life."

"Ah yes, this is true, but we were never mated, only engaged to be. So there. She's free to start all over."

The dolphins rolled and dipped beneath the waves, three of them. An odd number. Occasionally, I had swum with them in the warm waters of the gulf. They were creatures of great intellect and respect. Powerful, yet gentle to the point they did not kill me, even though I fully realized they could. When I had slid into the water, I was immediately shocked at the immensity of their size and became aware of their abounding grace towards me and surmised that much like God they possessed mercy. I believe this to be true because Lolly Eden is alive, and if I were God I would have struck her dead just because.

Manuel Garcia Rodriguez was studying me without blinking.

I took a sip of my beer and looked back. In a few hours I would be in a dark office with an old friend and a flashlight, looking for a ghost of a clue, but now I sat looking into the eyes of a ghost of a man who turned to look away and out to the water. A scar began at his eyebrow, curved along the side of his face, and reached below his jawbone.

"Although I am a liar," he lost a twinge of his accent, "because of your name I will tell you mostly the truth. I have no reason to lie to you, now do I?" He seemed to be convincing himself of this fact. I had seen this before. Even the most adept con artist occasionally becomes lonely for the truth. It is rare, but it happens. He went on. "We are strangers on a beach in the sun with the dolphins swimming before us. We have only now, nothing more." He took the last drag on his cigarette and flipped the butt out before him. "My name is Manuel Garcia Rodriguez. I have fifty-three dollars and forty-two scars, the deepest of these from my father who was the meanest bastard I ever knew, but I only knew him for a moment. Then he was gone."

And so I entered into a day with a stranger on the beach of Toliquilah. The hands of Manuel Garcia Rodriguez were the color of brown sugar, and watching them was like drinking from a fountain. They orchestrated his words, lifting the heavy air and rearranging it with rapidity. In the beginning most of his time was spent asking me questions about myself that went unanswered. But later, he described the details of the diverse shading of his fellow man and his encounters with them. This would include the intricate details of outlaws, including himself, who barely escaped being apprehended. Or of medals he had won, "In wars in my countries," for he claimed them all, "where there is always a battle within easy reach."

The day stayed heavy and thick upon us, and Manuel Garcia Rodriguez bought us beer from Lemuel's which I calculated left him forty-some-odd dollars. We drank without changing position, and I laughed more at his odd stories in one day than I had in the previous year. Then the sun fell into the water and left us growing silent. It had been a good day. Later, the stars would come out to find me curled asleep in the chair and Manuel Garcia Rodriguez gone.

When I awoke, it was 8:34. My night had just begun.

CHAPTER NINE

The street lights were blurred by a fog so heavy it threatened to extinguish their pale yellow light. I walked quietly down the back streets around the tiny park dedicated to some ancient statesman of the city. Now, it was home to the vagrants who took solace sleeping there at night. This night, only one lay curled on a park bench, mumbling in his sleep in a tone something akin to Lemuel's.

Just as I crossed the last corner, a small gust of wind stirred the dust in the street. The backdoor of the courthouse faced out onto the park. I looked across to make certain the vagrant was still on his assigned bench and placed my hand inside the pocket around the handle of my father's gun. I had lived a long time along the corridors of back alleys and was neither afraid nor naïve. It was almost a quarter till ten. I placed my back against the inside wall, where I could watch the park, and waited. "No one is watching," I told myself. No one knew I was here. No one could care less about a three-year old homicide file on a dead Indian. Yet the hair stood up on the back of my neck and I checked my watch every few minutes.

At one minute till ten Moses opened the door. He didn't say a word, just motioned for me to follow. The corridors were dark. In the distance I heard a television playing, and in my mind pictured the guard in front of its flickering blue light, arms folded, gun in holster, eyes falling shut.

Moses led the way down a corridor past marriage licenses, the property tax office, and driving violations. At the end we turned left and went to the end of another corridor. Here Moses pulled the keys quietly from his belt and opened the last door on his right. Large block letters reading, "Records" were plastered across the glass. We stepped into the darkness, and he closed the door behind us.

Apparently old records were not of major significance. A graveyard of information, they were located to the back of the room, against the wall, and simply stored in cardboard boxes by date and year, then by case number. I didn't have the case number, so the date would have to be the beginning.

Moses silently moved me towards the wall, then he pointed to a large one with "1997" across the front. The rest was up to me. He passed me a small flashlight and took his position by the door.

I took a deep breath and opened the box. September had over fifty files. I pulled #10237 and began searching. Arson: Suspect Female; 45 #60734. Burglary of a downtown pharmacy. No money missing. Only pharmaceuticals. #502397. Stolen Monte Carlo. White, red pin stripes. #622783. Forgers of government checks. #827654. Destruction of private property. Tenant/Landlord dispute. #423984. Homicide. Joe Tompica. Bile rose up from my stomach. For a moment I couldn't remember why I was doing this. What purpose did it serve? He was gone. Nothing here would bring him back. I tried scanning the first page of general information. Time. Place. Description of vehicle. Identification and address of the deceased. Investigating officer. Jimmy Cusler. I clutched the file as I fell forward, dropping the flashlight in an effort to steady myself against the wall.

Moses whispered, "What's wrong?" through the darkness.

For a moment I didn't breathe. Didn't think. I simply held the file, and felt the blow. Jimmy Cusler. Investigating officer. Man in charge. Silent enemy of Joe Tompica. My mind reeled. How could this happen? Why hadn't I known? Why hadn't someone told me? Then I thought at once of Jimmy on top of me in the car, of me and Joe, and that night outside the pool hall, of Joe tossing Jimmy's hair into my lap. We hadn't told anyone. About any of it. And without a doubt, because of pride, neither had Jimmy Cusler. Trying to read the rest of the information was pointless. I was stuck on one thing.

"I have to take this," I whispered.

"No."

"Moses, I need more time. . . ." Footsteps cleared the corridor as the beam of a flashlight caught the window in the door. I lay down against the tile, my eyes focused upwards toward the glass door. The footsteps stopped outside the door, the guard's shape visible through the glass panel. In a flash Moses did something that surprised me into pressing, if it were possible, farther into the floor. He threw on the lights.

"I got you now you hairless, long-tailed, demon." And with that a great amount of banging and rabble rousing ensued. The guard slowly opened the door.

"Moses … is that you?"

"Did you see him, Ed? I said, 'Did you see him?'"

"Who?"

"That prehistoric-sized rat I been trying to catch for over a month. Eatin' papers and records all over the place. This is his favorite room."

"No kidding." Officer Ed didn't like rats. Moses knew this. Actually, he couldn't abide them, and with Moses' news he tightened the grip on the handle of his gun and rolled his eyes left and right as if his feet itched to get back to the safety of his chair.

"Old papers. Loves old papers. If you see him he's about this high, stands two feet off the ground on his hind legs."

"Oh, you don't say." Officer Ed turned a paler shade of white. "Stays back here mostly, does he?"

"Yeah, he doesn't like it up front. Too much commotion."

"Well good luck there, Moses, with everything."

"You could help, Ed. You get on one end of the room, and I'll get on the other, and we'll rush him in the middle."

"Love to, Moses, love to, but got to get back to my post. You understand."

"Yes sir."

And just that quick he was gone to the safety of his box.

"Don't get up, yet."

"You're a genius, Moses."

"Just well-informed."

It was after midnight when Moses and I pulled into a bar on the other side of town. Two guys were playing pool. The only other person was the bartender. She looked ready to go home. We ordered a couple of beers and sat to the side in a table against the wall. I spoke with my head lowered, keeping my voice between me and Moses.

"Copy what you need. Get it back to me, and I'll slip it back in."

"Thanks."

We sat quietly listening to the pool balls clack and roll and fall into their pockets.

"I don't know what good you think it's gonna do."

"Neither did I until I saw that Cusler was the investigator."

"Know of him, but I don't know him." Moses reached around, and rubbed his shoulder. They must have been buffed weary. "Word has it that he collects dirt on everybody in the department just in case he ever needs it."

"Doesn't surprise me."

"What's the history?"

"An old story. I'll just say if he ever truly hated anyone, it would have been Joe."

The tallest player leaned across the table eyeing the surface from the table level. "Six ball, right pocket." The six ball rolled into the right pocket. Straight shot.

"Why's that?" Moses asked.

"He was afraid of him."

"That'll do it."

The fact was, Joe was half the size of Jimmy Cusler. But he was twice the man. And Jimmy knew it.

"How do you want to get this back to you?"

"Through the front door. We'll go downstairs."

The short one limped his way around the table, sighting his prospects and weighing the odds. From where I sat they looked against him.

The bartender sat on her stool lighting one of the night's last cigarettes and said, "Last call for alcohol," like a clock on the wall.

The pool players ignored her, concentrating on who would be champ.

"Eight ball in the left corner pocket, number two in the side."

"No way."

"Yes way."

"Bet me."

Then their concentration turned to how much of a bet it was worth.

"You want another beer, Moses?"

"No, gotta get home, but promise me something."

"Anything."

"You don't look at the pictures. Not from the scene."

"I may have to."

"I prayed that you wouldn't, and that's the end of it. Understood?"

Moses wasn't a fool. And he wasn't one to fool with. He had done me a huge favor. I didn't want to see the pictures. I had thought about it all week. But I was willing to do whatever it took to uncover the truth. Moses believed that when he prayed God answered. It was as simple as that. I decided to take him at his word and keep a promise.

"Alright."

"Good. Let's go home."

Just as we walked out the door, an unbelievable shot was made by a small man with an awkward limp.

*

The No-good bridge had been built one summer by the Hutchinson brothers after the state had decided during a post hurricane destruction discussion that it didn't have the funds to allocate for a strange bridge, leading to an even stranger place. Basically, they believed Toliquilah was more trouble than it could possibly be worth in revenues. The Hutchinson brothers had stayed drunk through the entire building process. It had taken awhile before many people would trust to cross it.

Old Percy Falls had started running a ferry boat back and forth across the bay channel, and they trusted Percy more than they did the No-good. But as time wore on, people forgot to be afraid, and Percy grew old and when the ferry stopped, all that was left was the No-good.

I stopped now in the middle of it, leaving the high beams on, and walked to the side. The water was slowly moving underneath. A brackish mixture of sea and swamp in no hurry to get to its final destination. Sixteen years had passed since the night Joe and I had stopped here. Sixteen years. And I could still remember the smell in the air that night, as if it had been charged with an electric skin of its own. But the sky was clear now. No clouds. No lightning. No Joe. Only a canvas of endless stars. And I felt very, very small in the midst of, not only an infinite universe, but one filled with an interminable amount of time.

I lifted my eyes and offered up a silent prayer. It consisted of only one word: *justice.*

CHAPTER TEN

"Meet your new roommate."

Edna was standing behind the counter, pointing with a spatula towards something that sat at the bar. I was too stunned to say or think anything, then my mind returned with one thought.

It wasn't a good one.

"Excuse me?"

"Roommate. New." Edna turned and walked off to the kitchen. The person at the bar said, "Kallie," and stuck out her hand, then added, "from Alabama."

I shook something round and firm saying, "Uh huh," and followed after Edna. There arose, then, what I believe to be the single loudest argument ever had between a Toliquilan without a leg to stand on and a one-armed woman from Georgia. It began with me clenching my teeth and speaking through whatever space was left.

"I don't live with nobody."

"You do now." Edna flipped a burger twice attempting to stay too busy to stop and face me as I followed her step by step around the kitchen.

"What's the point?"

"She's gonna work at day like you do at night. Same deal. Different hours."

"I'll pay you rent, just keep her out."

"You don't make enough money."

"Then pay me more money!"

"Not enough to pay."

My mind reeled with a thousand trapped questions as I tried to think. Joe's house, Edna's house, my house. My house.

"I can buy it from you."

She stopped dead in her tracks, stared at me and said, "With what money?" I looked back and opened my mouth considering the answer for myself.

"Even if you had it, it's not for sale."

Edna plated up the burger and walked out the door. She set it down in front of Kallie who said, "Is there a problem?"

"Yep. But it ain't yours." Edna stared hard at me and walked off.

I found my cigarettes and lit one examining the bulk at the bar and trying to determine what my options might be. Limited was the only word that came to my mind. I could pack my things and camp in the grove. Or pack my car and leave entirely. Then I thought of Joe's file and Jimmy Cusler, and I knew leaving couldn't be the answer. I could hang out with Red for a few days on his boat, but that space would get tight. I looked again to the bar, at the small bundle of woman that sat there, still looking at her burger without touching it. Then she looked at me.

"I'm not hard to get along with."

"I am," I said, and poured myself a cup of coffee before pulling up a stool alongside my new roommate. She was dressed in a long brown flowered thing that looked untimely. Old. Her skin was as white as kitchen flour but you didn't notice right away because of the freckles. They covered all the showing pieces of her to the point they bumped together. She wore a sun hat that looked as if it had come off a scarecrow I'd seen passing through the back roads of somewhere flat. This she took off now, as if my looking at it had reminded her that it sat upon her head. She shook her head and let her hair fall about her shoulders. Then smiled and laid the hat on the bar. She was younger than her first impression.

"What did you say your name was again?"

"Kallie."

"What kind of name is that?"

"Mine." She said it without malice, like it was the only true answer available. The most consoling thing I could think of at the moment was the fact that although I hated roommates, I didn't hate her. I looked toward the kitchen and thought of someone who, for a little bit, could have elicited that response.

"What are you doing here?" I asked her.

"Gonna eat, then go to work."

"No, what are you doing on Toliquilah?"

I looked at her bag on the floor. It almost matched her dress. She even smelled old. It was as if everything about her had come from a bone yard.

"Granddaddy died." She stopped for a moment, and swallowing, took a sip of her Coke. "His brother come along and took the house and farm and everything with it. Said it rightfully belonged to him, and there wasn't a will. So here I am."

And that both summed it up and skipped a thousand things at once. At this point I didn't care. I hoped all her conversations would be just as short and to the point.

"How long are you staying?"

"I reckon till it's time to go."

I poured another cup of coffee and hoped "time to go" would show up early.

"Is that all of your things?"

"Nah, I got what-all out back in the truck."

"What all," sounded suspicious and suddenly goats and chickens came to mind. At that point the best I could manage was a "S'cuse me," and I went to my booth, lit another cigarette, and tried to think, but mostly I just smoked and shook my head. At some point, Kallie finished her burger, and Edna began showing her around the kitchen where everything was kept.

Later, I managed the courage to take a look out back. The truck was, at best guess, a '70 something Chevy, faded blue, and strapped to the gills with what I guessed was the leftover life of Kallie from Alabama. On top of a covered pile was a rocking chair that looked like it had been around awhile. I didn't mind the rocker, but what lay underneath looked imposing.

When I went back inside, Edna was quick to suggest we take a ride to the house to get "Kallie settled in" and turned her back before she could see my painted expression. I could tell from the way she looked back and forth between Edna's back and my face, this situation wasn't her fault but a matter of circumstance. This Kallie person had been booted off the farm and ended up on a forgotten island in my dead Joe's house, which now happened to be owned by a mule-headed, one-armed woman from Georgia who let me stay there for free in exchange for slave labor. It could happen to anyone.

Red walked in and looked at me, taking his regular seat in my booth.

"Hold on a minute, can you?"

"It don't matter none to me." Kallie shuffled her weight and went back to her seat at the bar. "You go on do what you got to do."

I'm gonna do just what I got to even if it kills me, I thought, but I didn't say it.

"What's that?" Red jerked his head sideways and pulled the toothpick from his mouth.

"My new roommate."

"Well now."

"Yeah."

"For how long?"

I breathed in and out and raised my hands. I surprised myself and managed to smile.

"It'll be alright," he said.

"Yeah." I wanted to cry and laugh at the same time. He could tell. "Want something to eat?"

"In a minute. You go on," Red stretched his arms and legs and seemed to grow three feet before my eyes, "then catch me up later on what's going on." Then he winked and said, "I might give Edna some cooking tips while you're gone.

"Go right ahead. Give 'em to her good."

*

Kallie stood on the porch surveying the swamp water but thinking of Edna. "What happened to her arm?"

"I never asked her."

"How come?"

I shrugged and tried to adjust to the presence of a stranger standing on Joe's porch. A thousand flashes of life, laughter, porch parties, and the smell of brush burning filtered to the surface, overlapping the present. I closed my eyes and heard Joe's voice saying, "Listen, Mary, listen," as he pointed out the sound of a baby gator crying one night. I held out my arm and grabbed the porch railing to keep from falling forward. Then I opened my eyes to the Alabamian watching me with clear, pooled eyes. I looked past her, trying to focus. The cypress trees were standing like guards along the water. And we stayed frozen there for awhile. Me and her and the trees forming a perfect triangle that held the past, and the present, and some invisible future. The seed of Red rolled within me and I heard, "It'll be different, if you let it." But I didn't want different. I wanted to find a magic place where I could crawl backwards, a sudden entrance to the past, a portal, or a gateway that would get me to where I truly wanted to be. But as much as I hated it I was still alive, and life was perpetually pressing forward, carrying me on a wave towards the future without my desire. I looked at Kallie, who'd never taken her eyes from me.

"You want to see the inside?" I asked to change the focus of her attention.

Even though it was larger, I offered her Joe's mother's bedroom. She said, "Are you sure?"

"Without a doubt," I said, and we left it at that.

Then we went about unloading a strange assortment of goods. She had brought a whole corner of the state of Alabama with her. Kallie talked incessantly while we walked quilts, pots, canned peaches, and a case of Mason jars up the stairs.

"They're for canning," she said.

"There's nothing to can here," I told her. But she said "Oh, you never know."

All I could think of was gator tails, and I could see them somehow pickled and lined up in her jars along the shelves.

Occasionally I would take a smoke break and lean on the porch railing, surveying the back of her truck, weighing it all in my mind. The load didn't look as if it was getting any smaller, but Kallie's room was getting filled with pictures of dead people, quilts that had belonged to her grandmother, kerosene lamps, and various one-hundred-year-old junk.

"What is this thing?" I asked.

"Trunk full of food."

"Trunk full of food," I repeated thinking that in all my travels and travails, I had never come across a person like this.

"Potatoes and Vidalia onions, flour and corn meal. You know, just some basics."

"Basic." I tested the weight. "Grab this end." We carried the trunk to the kitchen. She wasn't the type to pry, and for that I was more than thankful, although, once out of friendliness, she paused at the door to my room. I showed her the picture of Joe with the gator and simply said, "Joe," before putting it back on the wall.

"This was his place?"

I nodded, but that was all. She looked around the room awhile. There was nothing to see. A bed, a small table, a dresser.

"Where's your things?"

"My what?"

"Don't you have," and she paused because she didn't really know what to call them, "your things." I thought of her room full of quilts and keepsakes, and I understood.

"Oh. In the trunk of my car." Then she looked at me and just said, "Well, I reckon that's a safe place for them," and went on back to work.

It had never occurred to me to unpack anything. Everything I owned had been in one car trunk or another for fifteen years. So I sat on the bed and looked around the room and considered the novel idea of unpacking.

Later, I sat in Kallie's rocker with my feet up on the porch railing, pushing back and forth while she fell into a rhythmic silence peeling and scraping potatoes until smells emanated from the kitchen that had long since been dead. I had an image of Joe's mother frying cornbread and laughing, chasing me about the kitchen, trying to pat my face with her meal caked hands. Kallie made coffee by boiling the grinds in the water, straining them out, then pouring in lots of sugar, and I sat strangely contented thinking, *What month am I in?* And the word *June* rolled up before me, but I couldn't capture where the time had gone since I'd been back. I finished my coffee, and we moved the kitchen table outside to eat where the air was cooler away from the stove.

Kallie had cooked potato soup, cornbread, and, as she put it, "the last of a good batch of collards," which we ate with pepper sauce she had "bottled with green peppers that I grew myself. Some hot and some sweet so it's just right." But we didn't talk more than that; we just ate and watched the herons at the water's edge, occasionally hearing the slow splash of an alligator move from the bank into the water. I could have told her about the gators and Joe, about where she was, but she seemed content to eat, and take it in for herself.

It was late afternoon now, pushing into evening and I knew Edna would be looking for me to be back again. Kallie yawned and stretched and started to gather the plates, and I realized she must be tired beyond measure. The road kind of tired I knew so well but hadn't felt for awhile. I washed the dishes even though Kallie said, "I got 'em." "Rest awhile," I said. So she poured herself a cup of coffee and went out to her rocker while I finished. Then I went out and joined her and sat on the railing, smoking and watching the sun get lower behind the cypress trees while I put off facing Edna.

"In Alabama," Kallie started speaking not really looking at me but out over the railing at the water, "Spring rolled up on us smelling like dirt. It's a sweet smell when the rain on the air meets the dirt halfway. My granddaddy plowed with a horse, not a mule, and her name was Maude. When I was way little he would set me up on her while he walked the plow from behind, making long even rows. He was big, tall, and wide, and he wore a wide-brimmed hat when plowing to protect him from the sun. He wouldn't plow at noon. I loved spring with everything, and I would set bareheaded baking until I looked like brown sugar. I guess if they'd have let me I would have stripped out of my clothes and rode naked." Suddenly, she cut her eyes my way. "That would have been a sight, me sittin' like brown sugar on an old horse named Maude. It's a very neat business, long straight even rows. One after the next. Then again. And again. I would ride like that till my head dropped down a notch or two, and Maude's head would be down a notch or two, as if we had been on a thousand mile journey crossing desert sands. The truth was, we had both had a little lunch, and where the dirt was still coming up cool from underneath us, the sun came down warm and rocked up into forgetting all about winter. As if spring would eventually push into summer and then drop us off there, forever. Barely able to hold my head up I'd turn to see if Grandaddy was still around or if me and Maude were plowing from habit. But he'd be there. The sun low and following as he stepped forward, nothing but a big man's hat and a big man's shadow. At times like that he looked like an angel of the Lord come to give a message, but I could never get the message 'cause with every step he took, I got further away. Those were great spring days full of corn, and peas, and my granddaddy becoming an angel."

I watched Kallie, whose eyes were now closed, her hands resting in her lap, and I wondered what *thing* had come upon me. I felt the weight of her move, and the relief she must feel at the stopping. Edna hadn't done a bad thing, she'd just done it a bad way. The truth was, I was full and felt as if a part of Joe's mother had walked back in and begun fixing things. The kitchen smelled like real food, and the light inside was growing yellow, as if the rooms had begun once again to glow. Funny. I'd been here all these months, carried and burnt trash, nailed boards together, spent my time rebuilding, but this was the first evening that had felt like home.

Quietly, I left the porch and the Kallie from Alabama asleep in her rocker, and gathered my things together. I went to my room and pulled the police file from under the mattress. With the most current events of Edna's surprise, I hadn't had the time to begin looking for something, anything, that would bring truth to the surface. I stood a moment, filling myself with the new sights and smells the house held, and then made my way down the stairs leaving a stranger in my place behind me. It didn't feel half as bad as I had thought it would.

CHAPTER ELEVEN

Fortunately, the night had been slow which meant Edna and I didn't have to speak to one another. I sat at the booth and got up to wait on customers, but once they were satisfied I went back to Joe's file. Edna wanted to be curious, but under the current circumstances of our not speaking to one another she was at a disadvantage.

I pulled a yellow envelope from the file. It was marked photos, but with relief I found it sealed. It made keeping the promise easier. I ran my fingers down the cover page. Time, place, date. Over and over again. Investigating officer, Jimmy Cusler, and my mind stopped there. I scribbled on a piece of paper. Pure scribbling.

"He was very well the one that killed him." I'd told Moses last night in the parking lot of the bar.

"Don't start out there, Mary." He had been shaking his head, then lifted a finger, pointing in my direction, "You start out there, you'll end up there. Right or wrong."

And he was right. I was having a hard time believing Jimmy Cusler hadn't been the one that fired the fatal shot. And if something else lay on the other side, I was currently blinded to it. I got up from the table and pulled a draft beer and sat back down. I knew Edna's eyes were looking at me and disapproving, so I didn't look back. It was a couple of hours until closing and I was drinking, but she didn't say anything. She knew when to choose her battles. I chewed my pen and stared off into space.

I wished now I had talked to Joe before he died for more reasons than one. I missed him, and in all our late, long talks I had never told him what he meant to me, how empty growing up would have been without him. He knew it, but him knowing it and me saying it were two different things. The other was, I didn't know about any recent particulars concerning his life. No ins and outs. Had somebody new shown up? Or somebody old? Had he fallen in with the wrong crowd of people? I thought harder on this and considered Joe and decided against it. He was too right to fall into wrong. Still, in a parking lot after midnight on the wrong side of the No-good . . . my scribbling had turned into one large question mark that I now traced over and over, indenting the page. The report listed no witnesses to the crime, no leads. I felt dead-ended. And stupid. And stuck.

Then the door opened and Agnes walked in. With Lemuel. Two things occurred to me at once. The first was, I hadn't seen Agnes for a month, and I hadn't missed her. The second was, Lemuel? They moved to Lemuel's booth and sat down across from each other. It was exactly the icebreaker Edna and I needed. We were forced to look at one another with not hostility but humor.

Edna shot up an eyebrow and silently asked me, "Well, what do you think of that?"

And I shot back, "You can never tell," with a shrug.

Agnes spoke and Lemuel leaned his head in as if he were listening closely, which was something for Lemuel who never listened. Then he actually said something. I knew this by the way his lips moved then stopped as if one word alone had come out of his mouth. I put out a cigarette and went to take their order. Agnes was as painted as ever and no less prowlish.

"Haven't seen you around awhile."

"I took a little trip, didn't I Lem?"

Lemuel nodded at me, then quickly looked away.

"We'll just take a couple of beers for now."

I stood for a moment wanting to hear Lemuel speak to see if somehow his speech had changed, but the moment got too long and he looked out the window even though it was dark and changed, and Agnes gave me a sticky smile so I walked away.

"What're they doing?"

"They're drinking beer, Edna, is all I know." Then I added, "She calls him *Lem*."

"Hmmmm."

So I carried a couple of beers over and Lemuel still didn't look up. Then Edna and I leaned on the bar and tried to be inconspicuous.

"How is she?"

"Painted as ever."

"No, the girl."

"I left her sleeping."

"I didn't mean anything bad by the whole thing."

"Skip it." I sat back thinking about Kallie and her rocking and talking to nobody. "She's nothing but strange and tired."

"She didn't seem so strange to me."

I looked at the side of Edna's massive head and her big cow eyes, and the lost arm, and the whole picture of her and thought, *Of course, she doesn't seem strange to you.* But I realized I'd gotten used to Edna, the bulk of her. She didn't seem strange to me anymore neither. And I counted the months again and thought of how numb I'd been when I first showed up. I remembered sitting on Joe's porch a lot. Not thinking, not feeling, not remembering.

"It seems to me they're talking."

"He's always talking."

"I know that, Edna, but looks like they're talking to one another."

She turned her head sideways, then shot her eyes almost out of the side of her face to try to see what was going on. Peripheral vision didn't work for Edna. I don't know why, but it made her look crazy.

We grew semi-bored with Lemuel and Agnes, and finally, after another round of beers, they left. Edna had debated on whether or not to serve Lemuel his usual leftover lunch for dinner but we decided in case he was on a date it would be better not to. I began clean-up for the night and Edna started counting the money. We both had our minds on other things and were tired from being mad at each other and getting over it. It had been a very long day. I was emotionally spent from jousting with Edna and physically spent from moving part of Alabama up into the house. We locked the doors early with tired goodbyes, and I got ready to drive home, then sat behind the wheel as the car changed its mind and drove to the docks instead.

*

There is nothing in the world that smells like the docks. It's a mixture of salt and seawater and fish and men. I loved it. It reminded me of Black Jack and all good things. Red's boat was at the end of the dock. There was no light on inside, and I thought about how late it must be for Red who woke in the night and left before dawn. Surely he was sleeping. I wanted to ask him questions, although I didn't know exactly what kind. More than that, I wanted him to have the answers. To see something that I wasn't. I got out of the car and walked towards the boat.

I felt myself being watched before I saw him. Leaning on a dock piling, smoking and watching me with an unearthly stillness was Manuel Garcia Rodriguez. He wore white pants and a white shirt which stood out against the color of his skin. With all our laughter and beer drinking, he now appeared a distant stranger and something more. Something hard to focus on. Then he called, "Mary," in a slightly hushed voice.

I said, "Yes," but didn't approach him. There was a good twenty feet between us.

"What brings you to this place at this hour?"

I pointed a thumb towards Red's boat, "A friend."

"Your friend is sleeping. He went in hours ago."

"I'll see him tomorrow." I turned to leave.

Manuel Garcia Rodriguez held his position against the piling and said in a serious tone, "Join me for a drink of rum. It's the best."

But the way he said it and the distance he kept made me say, "Not tonight."

"I'm never certain of another one," he said, and the scar along his face stood out under the lamplight.

I thought of Joe and said, "Who is?"

"I am," Red stepped out on the dock, "I'm certain of all the days that lay before me."

Then he looked at me and said, "It's late," with something close to disapproval.

"I had something to show you."

Red looked at Manuel Garcia with an expression I had never attributed to him because I had never been privy to seeing it. It was aggressive and demanding. "Show me now," he said.

Manuel called out, "Maria, maybe tomorrow I will still be here."

I stood looking between him and Red and felt strangely at a loss for words, so I simply nodded and passed ahead of Red into the galley door.

"How do you know him?" Red made us instant coffee and now sat awake and slightly irritated. A mood, which for him, I was unaccustomed to.

"I met him on the beach. Yesterday." *Yesterday* came out impossible. I thought of meeting Rodriguez, me and Moses, moving in Kallie. Suddenly, I was very tired.

"Met him how?"

"He bummed a light, we sat and talked. No big deal."

"Have I ever told you what to do?"

"Why would you do that?"

"But have I?"

"No."

"Well, I'm telling you now." Red turned and looked out the galley window. Manuel still stood leaning in the darkness. "Stay away from that man."

"Red?" My voice was filled with questions.

"What you do, Mary, is your business, but if your father were here he'd tell you the same thing." Then he paused and added, "so would Joe."

We sat quietly then, studying our cups. I could understand his feelings. Strange man, strange scar and forty-one more somewhere I hadn't seen. Suspicious character. But I was a big girl and had been around a long time.

"I came to talk to you about Joe, not the drifter."

Red leaned in towards me, "He's not drifting, he's determined." And that statement held weight because I could see it was true.

I caught Red up to date on Moses, the file, and Jimmy Cusler. He got over irritation, made us another cup of coffee, and listened like I knew he would. Then he stretched and took the file and began quietly pouring over the details himself. I got up from the table and stood in the doorway for fresh air. I didn't return until he called me.

"You've got to go see this man."

"Who?"

"This Cusler."

I shook my head.

"Mary, he was the investigating officer. If he wasn't who he is, would you go?"

I thought before answering, "Yes."

"Of course you would. It's the starting point, and you can't let the past keep you from starting in the right place."

"Why not? It's worked for fifteen years." I smiled when I said it. Red allowed himself to smile back, but it was painful. I realized then he didn't joke about the past. Remembered it, respected it, but he didn't cover it up with humor. Then again, he didn't have to. Fishing. A simple thing. One solid, simple thing that carried him through. Funny, in all my love of Black Jack, I'd never caught on to it. I loved the boat ride, the smell of the water, the dolphins surfing the wake home, my father's tawny back bending and stretching over nets and lines, a living painting of a man at sea, but the catching of the fish, it wasn't in me.

Red was flipping through the file again, one paper at a time, absently scanning for anything.

"Stop."

"What?"

"Go back. No, let me see this." I took the folder and flipped through to a single sheet. The sheet was nothing in itself. It was a detailed description of the contents of the car the night Joe had died. However, stuck to the backside was a tiny pink slip of paper. One of those that said someone called while you were away. This one was marked to Officer Cusler and had a check in the box 'Called while you were out' and another next to 'please call.' Below, in handwriting that looked like teased hair and tiny heels read, "Woman says she has information on murder of Joe Tompica. Lives on the island. Name is Esther. (Talks funny!)"

Without a word, I slid it over to Red.

"Well, what do you know? An old bone floats to the surface."

CHAPTER TWELVE

"What you be sitting outside my house all night in car for, girl?" It was daybreak. Esther looked wide-awake.

"What you be knowin' everything in the world except what I ask you?" I was tired from the last two days, had slept roughly in the car in front of Esther's house, too mad to go home and too mad to go to her door. But it was coming back now. Residual anger on the rise.

"It's mighty early, girl."

"It's three years too late." This time I pulled up a chair without asking and sat down. Esther paused by the door undecided, then relented and closed it and came and sat beside me.

"I told you I didn't know who kilt your Joe and that's the truth."

"Right. Now let me hear what you didn't tell me."

"What I didn't tell you is you are stubborn." She took her cane and hit the side of my chair. Hard. "Stubborn, stubborn girl."

"I got stubborn for you, Esther, but she's back at the diner and begging to come see you milking your snakes."

"That one-armed woman got no hard thing I haven't seen on you." She hit the chair again. Harder this time. If she hadn't been old and blind and snaky, I'd've wrestled the stick away from her.

"And how you know 'bout a woman you haven't seen?" Esther pulled her stick in then and sat with her lips sewed tight together. The snakes started hissing in their boxes. Then, I pulled the pink paper from my pocket. "Look what I've got." She turned her head sideways from habit to listen. "It's a note, three-year-old note. Say's there was a phone call made to one Officer Cusler on the mainland about information regarding an Indian boy that had just been murdered. Does that ring a bell?"

I held my breath and waited. She was wily and stubbornly stiffnecked herself. I couldn't imagine getting anything out of Esther she wasn't willing to give. She might not want to answer, but I wasn't leaving until she did. Then out of the blue, she said, "That boy never did no thing to nobody."

I thought of the partial scalping of Jimmy but said, "No, he didn't," figuring that one thing didn't count. Everybody needed just one thing that didn't count.

"And it was a breaking to my heart when I heard this bad thing done. It was on a Saturday. In the morning."

"Who told you?"

"I forgot who bein' brought me the news, but it hurt me, didn't sit right with me you bein' gone."

I turned my head to avoid the blow but it was too late. Esther hadn't meant it that way, but I felt the imprint along my face. "Go on."

"Wasn't nobody here. No good person to be sayin' what about him. Shot down like a lost child. Nobody even to see to what was left of him."

I thought I'd pass out if she didn't shut up, but I'd wanted her to speak, and now she did. Without stopping.

"What was I not to say? I call the man to tell him Joe done no wrong." She moved to the kitchen and poured us both a milky glass of green tea. She brought mine close enough, held it out and sat down, "That and the one other thing."

"What's that?"

"That somebody maybe been after Joe's money. And that's what you done come to me sayin' girl. What's new for me to be telling?"

"You told them somebody was after his money."

"Thassss right. Drink up."

I squeezed my eyes and looked from the snake boxes back to Esther. "What made you do that?"

"Drink," she repeated, and so I did. "Cause of my smellin' desperation."

"Desperation?"

"And fear. The two usually be addin' up to somethin' for money, and only two places on island money be," she put the cane between her legs and leaned on it with both hands, "the money be with Joe boy or the money be with me."

"Then why didn't they kill you?"

Esther leaned back and cocked her head half to the ceiling, half towards the past, thinking. "I don't know. Maybe on account of them." She waved the cane wand-like over the boxes. The mice scurried in their cage, throwing themselves into a huddle.

Feeding time, I thought but kept my mouth shut. Again, her face blurred, losing definition then emerged again just before she shed her skin. It was hard to imagine my nose ever tracking something like Esther's could, but right now it was working better than my eyes. "I got nothin' else for you, girl." She pointed her cane towards the outside world, "The rest of what you're lookin' for is out there."

Then the strangest thought occurred to me. "Esther, where do you keep all your money?" She laughed with her head thrown back, with her body thrown forward tapping her cane up and down on the floor, a minuet of applause. "Where no man gonna be looking." Then she leaned in with wide, blind eyes, "In the belly of the snake."

I could still hear her laughing in my tired mind after I had closed the car door and driven down the road.

*

The road to the house was weighty. My head seemed too heavy to carry. I was surprised when I walked in to see the new order of things. Then I remembered another person lived there. A new person full of things. She was gone. I supposed it was her shift. Long live Edna, creator of a balanced world.

I was too tired to sleep and opted for Kallie's rocker. Then I realized I was out of cigarettes, had smoked them all last night watching Esther's house through an angry haze. Esther. I had no idea how old she was or where she'd come from, but she was something the likes of nothing else I'd ever seen. But then, recently, everyone seemed that way. Even Red, that jolly giant of an old friend and fisherman had taken a strange turn. Protection? Instinct? Jealousy? He was a good man. Black Jack trusted him; therefore, I trusted him. Yet he was younger by a decade than Jack had been, maybe more. It was hard to tell beneath the sun-dried skin, the abundance of hair. Still, the thought seemed ludicrous and the last thing on my mind. But his advice on seeing Cusler was what I had expected. Clear and to the point. He could see the big picture. I was too close.

I decided to at least keep moving until exhaustion reached the point that sleep could reach in and take hold. It was eleven o'clock. With the house in its new Alabama order, the only thing left for me to do was unpack what things I might possess from the trunk of the car.

I opened it and stood looking. None of it made any sense. It was a strange, twisted tapestry that led backwards over the roads I'd taken. A conglomeration of a tattered scrapbook, albeit one in three dimension. I pulled out a ceramic Indian sitting cross-legged with a full chief headdress holding a ceremonial peace pipe. A neighbor in Kansas City had discovered what she termed "my heritage" and insisted I take it. It didn't look like anyone in my family or anyone I'd ever known or, for that matter, anyone I'd seen from here to the west coast. But for reasons beyond me it was here in the trunk of my car. I grabbed a suitcase that held extra clothes, cold things for cold places. There was a handmade quilt I'd picked up in Tennessee. The mountains had been cool when I bought it even though it was summertime. I'd drunk green apple cider from cold kegs and thought about settling down awhile, but instead I made it out of the mountains and into Kentucky where I got a job at a truck stop off the interstate. On the bottom of the trunk were the old things. A necklace of sharks' teeth my father had made me. I put them around my neck and kept filling my arms, the past rekindled with the touchable memory of things. Silly, inanimate objects that demanded recognition for what they owned, a piece of the past and all it entailed. The sights and sounds beyond the thing of them. *No wonder I kept the trunk closed,* I thought as I surveyed the final remnants, tiny shipwrecked pieces hanging on over the ocean of time to surface back here in this world of here and now. I pulled them from where they lay and made the final trip upstairs.

*

"Are you ~~alright?~~" I give up

I had no idea how long I had been sleeping. I opened my eyes to a Kallie in my face, looking as peculiar as she had the day before. I was sitting on the couch, my arms full of the past, my feet surrounded with more of the same.

"I see you found your things."

I almost nodded. The sleep had finally caught up with the fatigue, and the collision has been total.

"You got an Indian. I almost bought one like that one time, but I didn't get it. And you got a pretty quilt for your bed, even though it's too hot. It'll make your room nicer."

I tried to nod. Words seemed like an option but not a requirement.

"What's that thing?"

I looked down to her pointed out spot. In my arms were the remains of brown and white fur, but there wasn't much fur to it. It really didn't look like anything anymore. Just a used-to-be.

"Nothing." I whispered because I was taken off guard, asleep and exhausted, and because it wouldn't come out any other way. "It's nothing at all." Then I began to cry. I cried because I should have taken better care of the thing and it might still have lion fur. And because I couldn't stop anything from happening. I couldn't stop Black Jack from putting a bullet through his head even though I had known it was coming. Known it the way you sometimes know a thing inside yourself before it happens. And I cried because I couldn't stop it when somebody killed Joe the same way, as if they were trying to punish me for not being there the first time. And I cried because he'd died alone and been buried alone because they couldn't find me.

To Kallie's credit, she didn't try to talk to me, she didn't try to hold me, and after awhile I was vaguely aware of her moving away. At some point, she brought a cup of coffee and set it next to me. But I sat numb, unmoving, unthinking in the corner of the couch. Eventually I must have dozed off to sleep again. I heard a car start and realized it was Kallie's truck and it was late, and I knew she was going back to the diner to work for me because she was made out of the good stuff. Better than most people, including me. I got up then and went to bed and slept, crying on and off, until the next day.

CHAPTER THIRTEEN

Lemuel was silent behind the counter, which I found disconcerting, as though somehow I was being robbed. Agnes sat nearby on a stool sipping something fruity. "Hey Lem, did you hear that? They're gonna get married. What do you know?" She was painting her nails "El Torro Red" and watching a fuzzy picture of a soap opera. It was more radio than picture, so she reached up with a red pincher and tried to adjust the aluminum foil on the rabbit ears. It didn't hold and she let out a little sigh and then said under her breath, "Married."

Lemuel looked at me out of the side of his eyes, but I pretended not to notice. He started writing something down, and for a moment I thought it might be a note, *Help me! I'm being taken against my will.* But it was just a sign that said, *Vodka. On Sale.* And he propped it up in front of a stack of cheap bottles.

"Gimme two packs of Marlboros," I said and almost added, *and a bottle of Black Jack,* but decided against it and walked out the door.

I drove to the docks, but Red's boat was gone. I wasn't surprised. Fishermen had to leave in the dark just before dawn. My father had done it all my life. I used to get up with him in what I considered the middle of the night, and we would drink coffee outside the house where we wouldn't wake my mother. We'd talk in whispers so low that even the birds would still remain asleep. My father's voice was deep and rich and a good thing to hear before the sun made its way through the sky. I usually never finished my cup but held it in my hands, happy to have this time with him before he was gone. Then Black Jack went off to the docks and his boat, and I went back to bed and stayed there until my mother's shrill voice talking to herself made it more preferable to get up and go to Joe's.

The boat Manuel Garcia claimed as his was there, though. In the daylight I could now see the name painted in scrolling, black letters. It simply said, *Maria.* I watched through the dirty windshield for awhile, then out of curiosity got out of the car. The docks were quiet at this time of day. All the fishermen had left. The few boats that remained behind were supposed to be for the simple pleasure of being on the water, but as Toliquilah did not boast a population of the wealthy or idly rich, most of them belonged to regular families and were in a constant state of repair. I recognized another boat belonging to a storm-chaser named McGurty. He had walked into the diner a week ago. "Lots of work for a man after a 'cane. Can get quick work and he can name his price too." He took a sip of his beer and repeated to himself, "name his price," as if to convince himself his fortune was just around the corner of the next catastrophe.

The *Maria* was silent. No sounds. No movement. I looked through the windows and was surprised. Unboatliness. I was trying to figure out the difference; then it hit me. Money. The boat had the look and smell of money. Odd for a man with only forty-two dollars.

I had other things to think about, I told myself, and washed my hands of Manuel Garcia, his boat, and his money.

*

The courthouse seemed unusually busy. I didn't like it. The island had a rhythm of its own, but Clark City ran on the rhythm of man's invention, the clock. People lined the walls, filled the benches waiting on loved ones, waiting on court to be in session, waiting on court to be out of session. They were all haggard looking, tired, and full of struggle.

Nothing had come easy for any of them. At least not for a long time. Most likely, nothing ever would.

I didn't hear the buffer and didn't know exactly where to look for Moses. I stepped outside to smoke a cigarette hoping by the time I got back in he would have surfaced. But there was still no sign of him. I considered riding the elevator to the basement but decided it might be risky, so instead I found a phone book and looked for the name *Jimmy Cusler*. He was the only one in the book, 1204 Pinetop. I bought a cup of coffee at a diner next door and set out for Jimmy's.

The neighborhood turned out to be an unkept one where bikes were laid over in front yards and balls lay where they fell when the last game was finished. I pulled over and parked a few houses away where it appeared, and I was hoping it was true, that no one was home. A few kids skateboarded past, beating on the trunk and the hood as they went by. 1204 sat silent. No more junky than its neighbors. A football had been left in the front yard. I still had to fight down the belief that Cusler was the bad guy, but the fact remained that there was a bad guy, and unless he had been run over by a semi-truck or met his death in some other manner, he was still out there and running free.

A screen door opened and a woman came out. My first thought was that she looked almost normal. Pony tail, tennis shoes, incredibly pregnant belly. I hadn't counted on that part. Not even Jimmy having a wife. Or a life. But here was his house with its unkempt yard and bikes and a basketball hoop against the garage. I didn't recognize the woman. Not that I would have. I had never paid a lot of attention to anyone in school, or all of Clark City for that matter.

Then the door opened and Jimmy Cusler walked out. He had on his uniform. Seeing him in it made me feel ill. He wore sunglasses and stopped to look both ways. I slid down lower behind the wheel. He pulled his cap off and ran his hands over the top of his head. To my delight, the famous Cusler curl was gone. Permanently. Only a few strands remained, and he knelt beside his mirror and tried to comb them artfully over a vastly receding hairline. A boy of about four ran out of the house screaming, followed quickly by one similar in shape and size, but obviously older. The mother put her hand to her back, reached out and slapped the older one on the head as he ran by. He stopped running and held his head. She turned to finish talking to Jimmy, and I watched as the older boy walked over and hit the younger boy on the head who then started screaming "Mom," over and over again, so she hit him on the head as well, and the older brother doubled over in laughter. Then Cusler got in the car and backed out of the driveway and drove down the street. It seemed he took an incredibly long time to clear the corner. Then I watched as the mother took the boys back into the house.

I waited a few minutes and got out of the car and crossed the street, carrying a notebook, a pen, and in case anyone was watching from the window, I tried to look professional. I had no idea what I was doing, but I was doing it anyway. I walked through the clutter of the front yard and knocked.

Mrs. Jimmy Cusler opened the door.

"Excuse me, ma'am." I tried to sound all business. "Our company is taking a survey in the neighborhood, and I was hoping you could answer a few questions." She paused, rubbed her belly.

"What kind of survey?"

"A toy survey, ma'am. It's real simple. Won't take up much of your time. We always follow up by mailing you some nice gifts for the children." The boys ran behind her screaming at full tilt. This time the older running from the younger who had something large in his hand.

"That's a good-looking family you have there."

"Righttt." She said it with an sardonic edge drawing it out. Then, "C'mon in. Watch the cars, watch the cars. Boys, get these dang cars up off the floor, or I'm throwin' 'em outside and I mean it!" From the looks of the yard, I believed her. "If you gotta write something, come to the table."

I followed her to the kitchen as Mrs. Cusler picked up a stack of dishes and started piling them in the sink.

"It's always like this. Jimmy eats at such crazy hours 'cause that's the way he works." She rubbed her stomach again and took a deep breath. "What I'd give for a cigarette. You two get out in the yard!" she screamed at the boys then gave me a serious look. "It's enough to drive you crazy."

She slowly sat down and leaned way back. "Now tell me, what sorta toy company you with, Mattel, Disney, Hy-bro?"

I couldn't decide so I said, "All of 'em."

"How's that?"

"Research and Development."

She let out a little, "Oh."

"They make you think they do it all but they don't. Everything begins with us. We look into what the kids like and don't like. What they want that they're not getting."

"Uh, huh."

The boys ran through the kitchen asking for a coke.

"No. I said no! Put that back Jimmy or I'll—God, let me live to where I can chase that boy again."

"Mrs. Cusler, I'll just go ahead and—"

"How'd you know my name?"

"Research, ma'am. We know everything."

"I guess with all them computers these days it's pretty easy."

"I don't know how they do it; they just hand me survey sheets. I check the names off."

"Well, I'm really not Mrs. Cusler." She emphasized the *Mrs.* portion. "You got that part wrong."

"How's that?" I asked.

"I am a Cusler. I guess I'm a Miss Cusler or even maybe a Ms. Cusler but I ain't really a Mrs. Not anymore."

From the looks of her condition it looked like a Mrs. would be in order. I didn't know what to say, so I waited.

"Me and Jimmy was married, and had Jimmy Jr. and Clyde, but we ain't married now.

"See," and she held up her ring finger for me to witness that it was bare. "I still got it but I ain't wearing it again unless we get remarried. We got divorced last year on account of, well, different things really. Then come to find out, I got another kid on the way, and so he moves back in. Made it real sweet and easy for Jimmy without changing a thing and the only thing changing about me is I'm getting bigger every day. God, I wish I could smoke. You got any kids?"

I shook my head.

"Imagine that. No kids, and you're working for a toy company. Ain't that a silly thing?"

"I guess it is."

"What you want to ask me?"

What *different things* means. If your husband, ex-husband as of last year, talks in his sleep. What he was up to three years ago when a certain homicide took place.

"How long ya'll been married?"

"The first time three years, but we didn't have any kids then, and the second time eight, and there sure wouldn't have been a possibility of a third, if it hadn't been for this thing." And she patted her stomach. "The good news is it's a girl."

"So you know."

"Oh, they can tell you everything now except when it's really gonna pop out. That's still up to the baby."

There wasn't a lot wrong with the double-ex Mrs. Cusler. Except for one thing, and that one thing was a big one. I wanted to say, *Why'd you marry him*, but I remembered there was no such thing as *why* and besides, it wasn't part of the survey.

"You know what bein' married to a cop has taught me?"

I shook my head even though I could have filled in a few thousand blanks of my own.

Ms. Cusler stared out the window and squinted her eyes. "It's taught me how to spot a liar a mile away."

Cold busted. I could see it now—arrested for something akin to stalking. Entering on false pretense. Lying.

"It should, 'cause I'm married to a cop that lies." Then she smiled in a serious way, "*Was* married."

"I'm sorry."

"I didn't recognize you at first, but then I saw a part of you I remembered."

"What part was that?"

"The Indian part."

I nodded my head understanding.

"I don't remember you."

"I was behind you and Jimmy by about three years. He didn't know me then either. But you were different. You stuck out. And I always thought you had pretty hair."

I ran my hand over my head and felt at a loss for words, real or made up.

"You cut it."

"Yeah," I said, "I cut it," and at once saw my angry reflection in a bar mirror one night when I'd first cut it off. I'd borrowed someone's knife to do it. The man that had owned the knife had only had one ear. It was all I remembered about him.

"Why'd you do it?"

"I got mad."

"No, why'd you come here like that? Making up stories."

I wanted to say, *I don't know.* I wanted to make up more stories. I wanted to be a long way away.

"Three years ago my friend was killed. Your husband," then I corrected myself, "ex-husband was the officer at the crime scene."

"What's that got to do with me?"

"Probably nothing."

"You know I could have you arrested."

"I know."

"Why didn't you just talk to Jimmy straight up?"

"He doesn't exactly like me."

"Oh, that don't mean nothing." And she looked at me like she knew something. "Jimmy just don't like it when he don't get his way." She got up and walked to the window, squinting her eyes and shading them with her hand. "Can't stand it really." Then she turned to study me. Peggy Cusler was pretty in a way that didn't make you not like her. She wasn't wearing any make-up, and she seemed to have a hard time breathing because there wasn't any room left.

"I remember when he was killed. Me and Jimmy had just made up again. Everything was brand new then. Fresh and scary in a fun way." She looked out the window, but I knew she was looking backwards into what used to be good. "I remember the night he came home. You know, around here there's not much murdering going on, and he had never seen anything like that before. A person shot in the head."

I gritted my teeth and turned sideways. It should've been numb now, that spot that hurt for Joe. It wasn't.

"I'm sorry." She came back to the table and stood and would have touched me but didn't know how, so she sat down again. "I remember Jimmy saying, 'How strange.' And that's what he'd say over and over again as the week went on, but that was about it."

"Nothing else."

"Not that I can remember. Most people in town figured it must have been drugs and let it fall that way."

"And they quit looking and closed the case."

"Sometime you gotta quit," she said. She looked me in my single eye and I knew she meant well.

"I really am sorry for the lying."

"Oh, I'm used to that part, just not from strangers. I gotta go find them kids." Then she pulled herself up and stood next to the chair with widening eyes. Her only words were, "Uh-oh," as she looked down at the floor and back at me. "Third babies come awful fast," she said.

*

As it turned out, Jimmy Cusler was off the radio and out of reach. Peggy Cusler politely said, "Screw Jimmy," and got in my car with the boys bouncing up and down in the seat singing over and over again, "We're gonna have a baby, we're gonna have a baby."

"I really appreciate this," she said. I said, "No problem," like it happened every day. I really wanted to light a cigarette but I figured right now she wanted one more than I did.

At the hospital they put her in a wheelchair and rolled her out of the lobby, and I found the waiting room and sat watching Jimmy Jr. and Clyde who were making a general nuisance of themselves climbing over all the chairs. So I emptied my tip change out of the bottom of my bag and we raided the snack machine for Cokes and M&Ms and potato chips. I found the cartoon channel on the television and they were happy and I was happy because they were quiet and staying in one spot. Then Jimmy Cusler walked in.

You can imagine something all your life being one way, and when it turns out to be the other thing it will always take you by surprise. He recognized his children and looked around passing over my face for one he knew better, a friend, maybe, a relative.

"Jimmy Jr., how'd ya'll get here?" And the boy with all the genius of a hound dog flicked a thumb over his shoulder in my direction, never taking his eyes from the screen. He started walking and talking at the same time, "Want to thank," and his voice slowed keeping time with his feet, "you for," and then he stopped. "How?" He was stunned and the rest of his words were shut up stuck in his throat.

I raised my right hand, palm facing out and repeated, "How."

"Jesus!" Jimmy said, but he wasn't praying. He started subconsciously running his fingers through his no longer-existent curl. "Jesus! She said an old friend brought her here."

"Baby was coming fast."

"It's a girl."

"Yes, I know."

Then we stopped, and I had no way of explaining the last hours of my life to him, so I didn't try. I got up to go.

"Well, it looks like everything is under control. I'm gonna get on back to," and I pointed east toward the Island.

"I didn't know you knew Peg."

"It's been a long time." Then I added without lying. " I never knew you married her."

It didn't seem like the time to ask Jimmy anything about Joe, with his kids sitting there getting stuffed on M&Ms and his ex-wife worn out from childbirth and a minutes old new baby somewhere in the halls.

"I gotta get going. Really."

I could see the shock wearing off and the old Jimmy Cusler making his way to the surface. It was like watching one of Joe's sea monsters rise from the depths. "See you real soon, Mary."

I moved faster to the door.

"Good luck. With the new kid," I said as I tried to breathe steadily. I passed hallway after hallway. My day had crossed over into bizarre. All I wanted now was to get back on the other side of the No-good where things might be odd but were at least familiar. Then I lost myself. I wasn't used to hospitals. I didn't visit them. All the doors and hallways looked the same. The numbers went down, but when I turned the hall, they went back up again. Then I passed by a window as a nurse was pulling open the pink and blue curtain. Arrayed in the finest hospital whites were a new batch of babies, and I paused and looked for the latest addition. She was there at the front, awake with unfocused eyes. The card read, *Angela Lee Cusler, female 8lbs 4oz 19 1/4inches long.* Big enough baby and not the least bit pretty. I had never held a newborn. I put my hand to the glass and hoped for a moment that Jimmy Cusler wasn't guilty of murder. The noise of Jimmy Jr. and Clyde fighting over someone's last M&Ms carried around the corner with one saying, "Mine," the other screaming, "Gimme." Jimmy Jr. remembered me and what I was good for and ran arms out screaming, "Quarters, quarters, quarters," and grabbed the handle of my bag jerking it so hard it fell from my shoulder and across the floor, spilling quarters, a pack of Marlboros, my lighter, a Cover Girl powder compact, and case #423984. I reached to get it but Cusler was faster. He was on one knee in front of me. The two of us down low and looking eye to eye.

"Here, let me help you, Mary," the words came out with a twisted edge. He picked up the file and gave it a closer look. He began to tap the edge of it against his lower chin, and the smile that spread across his face made my stomach turn.

CHAPTER FOURTEEN

"Jesus, Mary, Jesus." Moses sounded like Cusler had a little while ago, but when he said it, it came out "Jazuss."

"I'm so sorry, Moses." I'd been sorry a lot today and was getting sorrier by the minute. "You were in the hospital with his wife's baby?"

"Took her to the hospital to have the baby," I corrected.

Moses sat down hard on his sofa and put his head between his hands, "Jesus, Mary," and that was all he could say for awhile and then, "Maybe you better start again from the top."

So I took it from the top and told him about my first looking for him at work and his not being there. Then about me driving over to Cusler's house. The baby part was actually pretty easy to tell because it wasn't motivated on my part which made me think maybe I shouldn't get motivated to do anything from here on out.

"And I was looking at Angela Lee."

"The baby."

"Yes, the baby, and then the kid ran around the corner and grabbed my bag and dumped it."

"Jesus. And he took the file?"

"What could I do? Jimmy said, 'Well now, seems this is out of place,' and all I could tell him was that I was taking it back. That I had just wanted to see it because of Joe, and he should know that. 'This here's police business,' he said like he was the long arm of the law."

"Jesus, Mary, Jesus."

"Moses, will you stop saying that? You're making me nervous." I looked around for an ashtray or other signs of smoking life but there weren't any. So I didn't light up. I just sat politely and watched Moses shake his head and thought of Norma Raison that used to live in apartment Number Nine when I lived in Number Seven in Lubbock, Texas. When I went over once to borrow matches I'd said, "I like your yellow parakeet." She coughed and said, 'He's white." I coughed and thought, *Not anymore, he's not.* Then I seriously considered quitting smoking, but that's all I did.

"What did he say after that?"

"After what?"

"The criminal charges."

"Moses, he didn't say anything about criminal charges, he said, 'police business.' Then he took the file and the kids started banging on the window of the nursery with their fists screaming. 'We had a baby, we had a baby,' over and over again and made all the babies start crying and nurse Rachet's twin sister came out big and mean and started screaming at Jimmy Sr. and the banging brothers and I got away. Besides that," I started slapping my thigh with open-ended fingers, "I never said a word about you."

Moses looked at me as if he were about to say, *Don't be stupid,* but he didn't say it.

"So he can't prove anything."

"We'll just wait, Mary, and see what happens next."

*

What happened next was that Edna broke her leg. She walked outside, stepped off the only step to the door, slid, twisted, lunged, and fell on the wrong side to catch herself, and the bone popped. Kallie and I happened to be in the middle of changing shifts when it happened, and Kallie said, "Just like the mule." I didn't have time to ask her if she was referring to another farm story or Edna herself. It struck me solid, however, that lying down Edna looked like a continent waiting to be discovered. I'd never seen her in that position, and she appeared even larger, if that were possible.

*

We tore the mattress from the top of Edna's bed and put it in the back of the truck, covered it with blankets, and I went over and said, "Lemuel, we need you," and he came out with Agnes following close behind. Then me, Kallie, and Lemuel hefted Edna by a supreme force of will. We assigned the position of holding the leg together to Agnes because otherwise she was useless because of her nails. When we finally got Edna on the mattress, Agnes said, "Oh, Lem," and deftly fainted dead away as if he were Rhett and she were Scarlett. Kallie said, "It's just like," but I cut her off by telling Lemuel he better drag the fainted Agnes out of the way because we were backing out. Then I remembered something and said, "Hold on," and ran inside Edna's room and grabbed a little brown bottle out of the dresser drawer. When I got up in the back of the truck, I pulled it out to give Edna a sip, and she looked at me in a wall-eyed full-of-pain way and said, "How'd you know where it was?" I said, "From snooping through your drawers," because I wasn't in the mood to lie about anything. I didn't know what was in it but I suspected it was for desperate causes of which I had once been one and Edna was one now.

Kallie drove the truck due east, and I sat next to Edna in the back of the truck because it was the right thing to do, and we left Lemuel fanning Agnes and her red hair and matching nails in the parking lot.

Our arrival at the hospital was an occurrence. A day that the inhabitants of those white coats and arched up shoes would remember for a long time to come. Kallie smelling like the past and her odd way of talking, Edna just as she was but now more broken, and me with my hair wild-winded from the truck ride looking every bit of the half-breed that they had always called me.

"We've got a situation," I told the emergency room nurse who immediately tried to get me to classify my situation. I thought for a moment about just what my situation was. About Edna and Kallie and Lemuel fanning Agnes and Moses and the file and Jimmy's new baby and decided I couldn't exactly classify my situation so I said, " You just better come see."

On the way over, Edna drank too much brown stuff and was now singing, "When we all get to heaven, when we all get to heaven, when we all get to heaven," and I never did get to figure out what happened when we all got to heaven because she never sang the next line. Days later, when the brown stuff wore off, I asked her about the verse she was singing and she said, "How should I know, I ain't never been there," and that was the end of it.

It took four big orderlies to unload Edna off the truck, which made me proud we'd gotten her in there in the first place. Of course I didn't know how much brown stuff weighed. In the excitement, one of the orderlies started asking where her arm was and Kallie said, "She left it back there." Before I could respond that 'back there' was long way away, another orderly hit him and said, "Not the arm, stupid, it's been gone. It's the leg." The largest one, a man half her age, kept saying. "Now *that's* a woman." Even after they had carried Edna back to set her leg, he'd shake his head and rub his hand over his hair and confirm to himself, "Now, *that's* a woman."

By the third time he said it, I told Kallie I was going for a cigarette, but before I walked out the door, I had a second thought and turned down the hall.

I rode the elevator to the second floor and got off and carefully followed the arrows to maternity and asked for the room of Peggy Cusler. She was in 232 but the bed was empty. I warily walked the halls and found her by the nursery window watching the baby. Thankfully, she was alone.

"I was just getting ready to go outside for a smoke," she said. I took the hint and we walked outside. Peggy bummed a cigarette and lighting up leaned back in the sun and blew a trail of smoke from her mouth a mile long.

"I know I got to quit, but I been wanting one of these now for nine months."

We sat at a picnic table in a break area. She had dark circles beneath her eyes but aside from that she looked better. With all the extra room she could lean forward now. It must have been a relief.

"Thanks for not ratting on me."

"You didn't hurt me none. Wasn't no need for me to go dishin' out on you." Then she turned towards me, "He came back asking me more questions."

"I didn't mean to cause you trouble."

"Oh, I been getting around Jimmy for a long time."

She took another drag from her cigarette and looked the other way. "Someday, I'm gonna have to leave him for good."

I nodded, but I knew she wouldn't do it. Not now. Not with a new baby. Things were locked on course. Peggy was as entrenched as if she were at war.

"Thanks for helping with the boys."

I shrugged, but she waved me off. "I know what they can be like. Right now they're with Jimmy's Momma and she'll be crazy by the time I get outta here." Then on another note she said, "You're not a bad person. I can tell that about somebody, but with Jimmy," she seemed to lose her focus and said, "well," and put out the cigarette.

I thought of the boy I used to know. The one that had smiled at me over his homework, and I thought of his curl and I understood how she could be sideswiped in spite of her good common sense.

"I hope it all works out alright for you," she said.

"Oh, I'll find who did it, or I won't. Either way, it's not changing what happened."

"No, I don't mean that. I mean, I hope it all works out for you. All the way. To the end."

And I realized she meant the rest of the river that ran out before me. I tried to follow her wish all the way. To the end. But right now the river stopped with Moses and the file and Edna's broken leg. Everything got chopped off right about there and my future couldn't proceed farther than Edna's big toe.

"You too, Peggy Cusler. To the end." Then we both smiled as if we had been bosom buddies all our lives and had just made a toast.

"You can just call me Peg."

So I said goodbye to Peg, who I would probably never see again, as I walked her back inside and toward her room. On my way past the halls I looked one last time at Angela Lee who was awake now and screaming. *newborns don't have lung power yet* *Feeding time* I thought, and immediately pictured Esther's white mice piled high and shaking in a corner. Everything had to eat.

When I got back to the lobby, Kallie was nowhere in sight but Lemuel and Agnes were in the waiting room, which didn't make any sense. I walked over and stood above him.

"Lemuel?"

"Oh, he was worried about me so he made me come in to get checked." Agnes was fanning herself with a *People* magazine.

I thought if I had to take Lemuel out back and point the gun at him I was going make him start mumbling again, whether I could understand him or not.

"You look fine."

"Oh, I know that, Mary." It was the first time she'd ever said my name. I didn't like the way it came out of her mouth, and I wanted to shove it back in. "It's just you never know about what's happening on the inside." She said *inside* slowly as if she were spelling that out for me also.

Then Kallie came in and said, "I can't even find the moon out there," as if it should be in the parking lot and it was her job to round it up.

"Agnes Turley," a nurse called and she and Lemuel got up to go, but she stopped him, "No, Lem, this is woman's business, Honey," and she followed the nurse as he sat back down.

I watched Kallie wander off down the hall possibly in search of the moon. Finding an opportune moment, I sat down next to Lemuel and said, "Just what do you think you're doing?"

"The Bible says a man who finds a wife finds a good thing, so I'm finding me a good thing wife."

I was content to hear Lemuel's gravelly voice again and just as content that I couldn't understand a word he said.

*

Six hours later Edna was drugged and in a wheelchair with one huge leg in a cast that stuck out in front of her. A nurse was trying to push her, but the chair was barely moving because the nurse weighed about a hundred pounds. I watched in amusement as she turned around and threw her backside into it as if she were pushing a sofa across the room. That's when the "now *that's* a woman" orderly walked in and said, "Oh, allow me."

His name was Wallace P. Ketchum, and he pushed her out to the waiting truck, and the other orderlies were summoned to help with the moving and lifting ordeal. Then he pulled me aside and said, "You're gonna need some help with her," and I told him we always had, but he said, "speaking of the convalescence time." Then he leaned in quiet and serious, "I'm volunteering my services." I suppressed a grin and gave him directions to the diner.

Kallie slowly drove west, and we crossed the No-good with Edna asleep on her mattress and me with the wind in my hair and the moon in full view out over the water.

CHAPTER FIFTEEN

I waited for the bomb to drop. For Jimmy and a gaggle of bad guys to walk in, pull me from behind the counter, handcuff me, and drag me away. But it never happened. Night after night, there was no sign of Jimmy. Moses had driven over twice to say, "Hello," sit at the bar drinking coffee and report no change. I knew because that's what he said, "No change," both times he had come, and it was like a weather report regarding a crucial front that could, at any given moment, push through and permanently affect our lives.

Edna sat propped in a booth with her leg sticking so far out we pulled up a chair for the lower part of her cast. Assisting her in the sitting was her new good friend Wallace P. Ketchum who had changed from his white uniform and wore a striped shirt tucked into the waist of his jeans, along with a pair of cowboy boots. He still wasn't as tall as Edna, but then, who was? The adjoining booth was filled by the Lemuel and Agnes phenomenon. Agnes asked Edna if she wanted her to sign her cast, and Edna had replied, "Get away from me," which was short-tempered even for Edna, and Agnes began to cry and Lemuel began to mumble. Kallie had been in the kitchen cooking while she alternately sang, "Swing Low, Sweet Chariot," and "Sweet Home Alabama," as if they were the only two songs she knew. Edna had not begun singing "When we all get to heaven," but she didn't seem to mind Kallie singing as much as she minded the juke box. I began to apologize to customers for everything, and that wasn't like me, but as I stood at the front door one evening with it propped open for good air, listening to the waves, I turned and was struck full force by the way of things inside. Kallie's voice was in full tilt somewhere behind the stove and Lemuel was muttering and Agnes' nails were weaving like great red-eyed worms in and out of her hair. Then of course there was Edna with no arm and her leg in a cast sitting with a cowboy orderly. I almost wanted to stop people there at the door and say, "Are you sure you're that hungry?" Then Red walked up behind me and said, "How'd it get to this?"

I was about to answer, "I don't know," when Lolly Eden literally knocked both of us out of the way as she skinnied past saying, "For God's sake can a working woman get through to get a bite to eat?" Then she saw Edna and said, "Poor child," and Red and I went inside and sat down.

"You know it wasn't like this before you came back." He was chewing on his toothpick, contemplating.

"How would you know? You weren't around."

"I passed through a few times." He paused and looked around again, "It wasn't like this."

"Are you saying I caused this whole thing?" I asked and swung my hand out cutting the air across the diner.

"Well, did you?" He meant it to be joking, but I thought about the heat wave in Memphis and me thinking it was my fault and vaguely remembering I had once wished Edna would trip and fall. But I had never wished for an Agnes or a Kallie or for Edna to break a leg, so I meant to say, I haven't caused anything, but instead it came out, "It's not my fault." Then Red looked at me seriously and said, "Nobody ever said it was, Mary." Then he changed the subject. "Your friend pulled out today." Then I lied just a little by asking, "Who?"

"Mister Santa Maria."

"Oh." I felt a small disappointment that I attributed to boredom.

Then I looked around again and wondered how I could possibly be bored.

Red was searching for a reaction. "So how'd the talk with the policeman go?"

"Not like you'd expect." I recounted the last few days, and he listened closely, paying attention to details and at one point let out a long low whistle.

"Seems to me you have gotten yourself into some kind of trouble."

"Uh huh. I feel a rope out there dangling, but no one's come to get me." Then Kallie showed up with a different kind of rope.

"I been thinking."

"Yes, Kallie."

"We orda take her home with us on account of her leg."

"She won't want to go."

"She might."

"She won't. Go ask her."

So Kallie, being the kind-hearted thing she was, went to ask Edna if she wanted to come home with us, to which Edna replied, "Get away from me." Wallace P. Ketchum, never changing his facial expression, stared off in the distance until Kallie left. Then he stared at Edna.

She passed the table and said, "You were right."

I didn't say, "I told you so," because it didn't matter. The idea of Edna with her leg propped up at Joe's house was suffocating. I thought of how big she was and how her attitude had turned to rotten and the great dampness of spirit that would settle at the house under the presence of Edna. No. Better to leave her under the care of Wallace P. Ketchum by the single-wide bed in the back room of the diner.

Wallace was what some might have called a man's man. Firm handshake. Not afraid of hard labor. And apparently possessing his own ideas regarding the perfect specimen of womanhood.

Edna seemed to take the new-found suitor in stride, alternately having the patience to speak with him and then having nothing to say. Wallace had spent the night sitting in a chair by Edna's bed. "Why don't you lie down on the floor?" I'd asked. But he assured me he was used to chairs by beds and sleeping as needed from that vantage point. When Kallie came in the mornings, he would look at Edna sleeping, and Kallie would say, "She'll be alright." Wallace would look back over his shoulder before he cleared the door.

Edna never commented on Wallace. She wasn't in the mood to comment on much of anything. One night Red brought in snapper for us to eat, and Edna yelled, "Fish!" at the top of her lungs before we could get it through the kitchen. I walked back and said, "Uh huh, fish. We're eating fish."

"You're doing this because of my leg."

"No, I'm doing this because I've been home for months and still haven't had any fish."

"Fish," Edna repeated and jerked her head sideways so as not to look at me and crossed one heavy arm over her heaving bosom. You would have thought I'd assaulted her. I suspected tears had welled up in her mule-headed eyes, but I didn't want to know, so I closed her bedroom door and said, "Fry it, Kallie."

Kallie shrugged and went about breading fish that came out golden brown and melted in our mouths, but when we took a plate to Edna, she said, "Get away from me, all of you," and so we did. We were happy to see Wallace P. Ketchum come in that evening so that we could shift the responsibility for Edna over to him, lightening our burden considerably.

I asked him one night when he came through to get something to drink, "Wallace, what in the world do you see in that woman?" and he grinned at me. That's all, just grinned and never said a word. I didn't bother asking him again and decided it might be better if I didn't know.

It was almost closing time, and the diner was down to me and Kallie and Red and Lemuel and Agnes. We sat at the table beside the booth and played the juke box, but I had turned it down as low as possible. At the last minute Lolly Eden came over again and, smelling the fish, had looked about and ordered "a decent size plate." I simply smiled and said, "It's not for sale," but before I could derive any pleasure from our positions of have and have not, Kallie offered up, "Shoot no, but we'll give you some."

So even Lolly Eden was there, sitting at the bar gumming snapper while I thought, "Just one bone, all it takes is one bone," watching her eat with great expectation. We were more relaxed knowing Edna was in bed and Wallace was tending to her every need. In the strangest way we were back again to some old familiar place.

I remembered nights of closing with Joe, and now it felt near to the same thing. I was soaking it in for all it was worth and looked from Kallie to Lemuel and Agnes to Red's blue eyes watching me. Kallie was drinking her one cold beer when she said, "White pythons aren't the biggest thing in the world even though they like to say they are." To which I just said, "Uh huh," because I was getting used to Kallie.

Red looked at me and smiled. He leaned in over the table and whispered, "Peculiar." I looked around and listened to Lemuel's mutterings, at Agnes twirling her hair with one free hand and holding Lemuel's with the other, at Kallie talking snakes and Lolly gumming snapper, at Edna's closed door, her propped up in there with Wallace beside her and said, "Yes, peculiar."

A few short months ago I had lived in a different world, one that barely touched its feet to the soft floor of humanity, one which was numbed by the layers of distance I could strap on if I kept moving.

I felt the diner becoming something it used to be and something different at the same time, and in it I felt Joe's presence and his absence. It was sweet and it hurt all at once. I closed my eyes and said, more to Joe and myself than anyone else, "Time does not heal all wounds."

"Whoever said it did?" Red's eyes were blue to his shoes.

"I should have sobered up and looked for who killed him three years ago. Much easier trail to follow."

"What about your friend Esther?"

"I wouldn't call Esther a friend. She's more of an island commodity."

"And her note?"

"Some kind of dead end. She had a suggestion. Thought someone was looking for his money."

"His money?"

I paused. Joe's money. Red didn't know. Lemuel, maybe. Agnes definitely not. I changed the subject.

"Basically, she said she was trying to look out for him."

Kallie rose from her chair and said, "Can I get you something?" To which Lolly Eden replied without turning around, "Yeah, something to drink before I choke to death." Lolly didn't choke but went on to put away another pound of snapper at no charge. Kallie could barely walk because the double shifts were getting to her.

I said, "Go on home."

And she said, "Alright. I will," leaving me to clean up.

Red said something about dawn coming early as always and slapped me on the back in a gentle way, leaving his hand there long enough for me to feel the warmth of it penetrate my shirt and imprint my skin. Then he looked at me as if he felt sorry for me because he did and said, "You may never find out who did it, Mary." And I told him, "Don't you think I know that?"

Lemuel and Agnes left together, and I watched them walk across the road in the darkness. The wind blew her hair and Lemuel reached up, pulling it back for her with one hand and walked that way with her hair tied by his hand. I thought it knight-like, the strange wiry body of Lemuel, the soft roundness of Agnes and him holding her whipping locks, protecting her from herself. I stood by the door watching long after they had disappeared into the liquor store, watching as water from the gulf made its way through the air, dancing beneath the street lamp about

Lemuel's store. I listened to the palms slapping their taut fronds together and to the waves crashing beyond sight in a quick windy precision. Then I closed the door and began to clean, so I turned on Zydeco very low and made certain that Edna's door was completely closed. I sponged the tables until they shined, and I made certain there were no crumbs hiding in the booth cracks. I wiped down the vinyl booths, the vinyl chairs, spray-cleaned the cover to the juke box and thought about ordering new records because they hadn't been changed in years. I swept the floor and mopped with ammonia which burned my nose and lungs so badly that I had to step outside again and wait until the fumes died down. Then I cleared the money from the register and put it in a bank bag and then into the freezer where Edna felt it was safe.

I cracked Edna's door. She was sleeping with a faint snoring sound coming from the bed. The bulk of her was rising and lowering, rising and lowering, like a boat riding the waves. Wallace sat by the bed wearing glasses and reading, *The History of Western Art*. He looked settled, and both of them appeared content within the confines of the little room.

"I'm going now."

"Well, alright then," he whispered so as not to wake his patient.

I closed the bedroom door behind me and turned out the inside lights. Lemuel's streetlight filtered through the blinds, leaving bars traced against the scrubbed surfaces. It was quiet and for the first time I almost had the place to myself. I sat down in the booth in the corner.

I could hear the palms outside the windows. The wind was up, and I could even hear the waves if I closed my eyes. And beyond this, old voices. Pieces of songs. Small talk. Fish stories. I had always loved the diner because it was Joe's and I loved him, but now I realized I loved it in a new way. I loved it because it had been his and was now, strangely, also mine. As if he had, all those years ago, prepared it for me and managed to hold me to the earth when all else was gone or had fallen away beneath my feet. It had provided a good night's work and tired muscles and, although I hated to admit it, under the helmed tutelage of Edna, a sobering shelter from my ever-present desire to escape. I silently whispered, "Thanks Joe, for saving my life." It was the best good feeling I'd had since coming home. I wrapped it around me like a blanket, holding on to it long after I stepped into the warm, wet air, quietly locking the door behind me.

CHAPTER SIXTEEN

The following morning we commenced to planning a wedding. Lemuel came over alone for a change and sat in his booth, alternately silent and then himself again, muttering and waving. Then he motioned for me to sit across from him, and he very slowly spoke words I could not comprehend.

"A man can't live in sin 'cause I tried and it come to a bad end and I'm looking for the good thing for the long road to hoe."

Then he fell silent. I tapped my fingers against my face, my chin in my hand.

"Your friend the fish captain, he can marry, so you talk to and make a date."

I tapped some more. I couldn't understand a word he said.

I pulled a pencil from my pocket and turned over the paper placemat of Florida. I passed the pencil to Lemuel and said, "Tell me."

And so there came to be the story of Lemuel and Agnes. How he was looking for "a good thing wife" and had fallen in love with her the first time he'd laid eyes on that red hair. Of how when she'd left the island, Lemuel had hired a private detective to find Agnes, who had been at the time in, as Lemuel put it, "a special place," which later turned out to be a hospital for a nervous breakdown. But Lemuel had managed to convince her, through the said private detective, to come back to the island and that he would give her a job, which explained the bar sitting, television watching, and nail-painting. I hoped for the sake of the simple, long-time-Lemuel-of-my-childhood that she would be indeed a good-thing wife for all the years to come, and we set about trying to determine a date.

Sunday was appointed the day of days and it quickly approached. Frank McGurdy, the storm chaser, claimed not only that he could play the fiddle, but that he also possessed one, so by default was appointed wedding entertainment. Red agreed to perform the nuptials, although he had never married anyone in his life personally or otherwise. When I told Edna of the upcoming plans, she actually smiled. That meant that because of all the arrangements to be made, I was temporarily forgiven for the fish.

When it came to the doings of a wedding dress, Kallie offered the use of her mother's which she had, of course, brought from Alabama. She and Agnes were round in the same places, and it stood to reason that if her mother had been built the same, the fit would be close enough to count. Lemuel, as it turned out, had his wedding suit in hand because he had ordered it months ago in preparation. Sometimes Lemuel could lock on to something like a well-oiled bear trap, and apparently this had been one of those times.

In a great wave of generosity, Lolly Eden said they could spend a night at her motel on the house, as a wedding present. Lemuel shook his head no, and Agnes explained they were taking their honeymoon in the tropics of Miami. Lolly Eden said, "Suit yourself," and I noticed she didn't offer anything as a substitute gift.

I asked Lemuel who he planned to invite, and he said, "Poppincottin," with big open arms. "Make a list," I said and shoved him a pencil. He wrote down one word, *Everybody*, which I guess is what he had meant.

Red was appointed to invite the fishermen from the docks. I made a note to invite Moses. Edna made plans to bake a cake in spite of her condition, and Wallace P. Ketchum said he'd be more than happy to assist in any way possible. Lolly said we could borrow her beach chairs if somebody promised to count and make certain they got back where they belonged. I would have said, "No thanks" in a hurry, but Kallie again beat me to the punch and said, "Well ain't that a nice thing?" Originally, the wedding was to be held at the diner but as the guest list grew, we narrowed down the places to outside on the beach or up in the cove until Kallie piped up, "We could have it at our place." Then everybody grew silent as I tried to consider a variety of reasons to say no.

Lemuel said, "Courseandsottin."

And Agnes said, "Sure why not?"

And Kallie said, "Alright then."

And it was settled before I had time to think. The best I could do at that point was breathe down Kallie's back, "Nobody goes in my room, you hear me, nobody." And she said, "Alright," sweet enough to make me feel mean.

Lemuel took it upon himself to supply all manner of liquid refreshment. Kallie left the diner early Saturday to get everything ready. I cringed. Wished them both well. Began thinking they should have eloped. Easy enough. Go to Miami, get married, have a honeymoon and come back all in one straight easy shot. But instead I called Moses who gave me the weather report of "No change," and I invited him and his wife and his children to the upcoming affair to be held on Sunday afternoon in the neighborhood of four. He said they'd come on over after church in case we needed help with anything. I could tell he was starting to feel better since some time had gone by and neither one of us were in jail.

I tried to draw a map but it became a muddled picture of incongruent lines and I finally decided if no one knew how to get there, they didn't need to come, so for the most part we just said, Joe's house and that was enough. We scouted out the swamp sisters Mabel and Doris Monroe, who didn't get out much for anything, but we invited them anyway so they wouldn't feel left out. Agnes invited the nurse from Clark City who had examined her. I wasn't sure why except she might be desperate for a friend. Then as the day was upon us we invited a retired couple from Chicago who happened to be staying in Lolly's Motel for the night and two teenage boys who had been camping all week in the cove.

On Sunday morning Agnes was over early squeezing into Kallie's mother's dress. It turned out that Kallie's mother had been tinier than both of them. Agnes held in her breath, panted, fanned herself while I said, "Don't even think about it, Scarlett," and she said, "Don't yell at me today of all days. I'm nervous as a coondog in heat already." Then I said, "I thought you were from New York," and she said, "Don't be putting words in my mouth that I don't remember saying." Kallie said, "Maybe I should make us all some ice tea."

So Agnes squeezed and sweated but did not faint. Kallie made finger sandwiches and talked about all the things she could have made like a good peach cobbler if she'd had some of this thing or that thing but instead she had to make do. Edna baked a big one-layer cake that said, "Forever" across the top and that was all. I thought about mentioning she might want to add the date, but when I found her she was standing with her back to me looking in the closet. I already knew what was in there. The huge dress canvases and the flat shoes, and even those were not worth much now. And it struck me hard what it must be like being Edna. She couldn't exactly clean up pretty for a wedding, not wear a lacy thing if she wanted to. Dressing up had never mattered much to me. I didn't think about it, but looking at Edna's back standing before her meager choices I knew it mattered to her. Maybe it had mattered for a long time and I simply never realized it. Then Edna sighed and turned far enough to see me and caught the full expression of my face. She didn't try to hide hers but said, "What can I do?" and I said, "I don't know, Edna," because I really didn't have any suggestions. Make yourself about a foot and half smaller, grow that arm back, do something really different with your face. I don't know, smile maybe. So that's what I said, "Smile, maybe." And she did, but it was a painful smile that made me want to put my arms around her for what good it might do.

"Looks like they're going to go through with it," I offered, but she didn't comment.

Kallie had picked out the marrying spot on her own accord and strung up a row of white Christmas lights around the porch with a string of paper angels hanging over the marrying spot. I said, "You did bring Alabama with you," and Kallie said, "Look how handy they come in." And I had to admit it, it was getting pretty festive. In spite of myself, I started looking forward to the wedding because I'd never been to one in my whole life except in the movies. The final fact that it was at Joe's house made it more special and I didn't mind us hosting it anymore.

Red said he had to get dressed in something appropriate for performing the ceremony. There was a sweatline above his eyebrows and he kept stroking his beard repeatedly, over and over again, until I said, "Stop it, before you pull it off." Maybe for the first time in his life he was nervous and had no idea what he was doing. Then I realized I had to get dressed and wondered if I owned anything appropriate myself to which the clear answer was, *No*.

Kallie walked by and I actually uttered the words, "What are you wearing?"

"My blue and white dress I used to wear when I sung in the choir," she said and never slowed down on account of her making food until the last minute.

I decided clean blue jeans would have to be appropriate enough. Then I put on my old white workshirt because it was a wedding color and my tennis shoes that weren't so clean and washed my face and dug around for a tube of lipstick and painted my lips, "Pink Flamingo." Then I heard Moses' voice outside and went out to meet his wife and kids. The kids were well-dressed and well-behaved, and I was happy to hear them call him Daddy, and the way he smiled over them seemed to just about break my heart, so I looked away.

Red stepped out of the doorway without his beard and after I recognized him I said, "You finally pulled it off." I had never seen him without a beard in my life. He looked ten, twenty, maybe a hundred years younger. A smooth faced stranger carrying a couple of fresh cuts. "Do you know what you're going to say?" I asked him.

He looked like he was going to pull an Agnes and faint. The sweat continued pouring from his forehead.

"May I suggest something along the lines of, 'Dearly Beloved, we are gathered?' Or is that a funeral? Well, how about, 'Do you both take each other forever and ever, Amen.' "

"I think I'm supposed to have a Bible."

"It certainly couldn't hurt any." I went off in search of a Bible, guessing that one had moved in from Alabama. It was a good guess, but the Bible turned out to be a family heirloom weighing twenty pounds and not handy to hold. As we were trying to find a makeshift podium for the only thing we knew that could make the wedding seemingly blessed, consecrated and of lasting legal nature, Moses began to understand the overall perplexity of the situation and produced a more appropriately sized version of the same. Then upon closer examination of the stuttering Red, he proposed to perform the ceremony, if there would be no objections from the bride and groom.

"I didn't know you were a . . . hmmmmm," I paused searched for the word, got stuck on *priest* and knew that wasn't right, "a God man."

Moses smiled affably, showing all his teeth. "I am a God man, but not the kind to which you may be referring. I'm not ordained for the pulpit. Just happen to be a notary so I can help take care of the church business, board stuff, you understand. However," and he stood tall and proud of the proclamation, "that makes me qualified to perform the civil act of marriage."

Then a conversation of sorts took place between Lemuel and Agnes through the bedroom door where she held fast to the superstition of Lemuel not seeing her until her altar call or in their case, call to the marrying spot. Then after a discussion, half of which I couldn't understand and the other half of which I couldn't hear, it was decided that the sweating Red would join the guests and Moses would take the officiate's stand to perform the sacred ceremony.

Then one of the sisters said, "It's like the blind leading the blind," and I thought of Esther and thought, *Uh oh.*

*

"You're late." Esther stood ready by the door, fully clothed and looking very un-Estherly. "You're all the time bein' late." She wore a veiled hat which almost hid her eyes and held a pocketbook tightly across the bend in her arm. It matched her shoes. Both were red patent leather. The toes of the shoes were sharply pointed, which matched her tongue.

"You're lucky I came at all."

"Are you late, girl, or are you not late?"

"Alright, I'm late."

She let out a clicking sound and pushed past me with her cane leading the way out the door, then she stopped and sniffed the air and headed left towards the car.

*

When we returned, Lemuel was standing in his new suit at the head of the porch. The sun had begun falling behind the cypress trees and Kallie's lights began to show up, at first unnoticeable, almost imperceptible, then growing in power as the darkness grew deeper.

Edna had arrived with Wallace at her side and I was glad I had missed the spectacle of her getting up the stairs. She was seated now, in Kallie's rocker toward the back corner of the porch and Wallace seemed quite content to be standing by her side. I remembered the dress-hunting and smiled at her. She was wearing what she had always worn but had a pink flower pushed into her hair behind one ear. It didn't look comical, not even a little sad, just mostly out of place. Like a rare petal found at the top of a dry rocky mountain where certainly nothing should be able to grow.

Joe's house was overflowing with people. Red stood over to the side, decidedly back to normal.

"Feel better?"

"Oh yes."

I pulled up a chair for Esther and guided her to it.

"Red, this is my . . . Esther. Esther this is Red Mahoney, an old friend."

Esther raised her head, her nostrils flared open, then her head turned sideways and back again.

She didn't extend her hand. "So, this is Joe's place?"

"Yes."

"Can I hear from where I am?"

"Esther, you can hear from a hundred miles away."

McGurdy began playing music, which signified something and Agnes, believing it signified her entrance, came through the door. She was pleasantly stuffed into a white dress with a white scarf lying over her head and she was as close to looking bridal as I could imagine her becoming. Lemuel, by contrasts of anyone's expectations, was not nervous but stood to receive what at some point he had decided would belong to him. As if he were now receiving his long awaited inheritance. Agnes walked alone to Lemuel's side and stood beside him slightly quivering. Lemuel reached one long, extensive arm around her shoulders and left it there for comfort. Or to catch her in case she fell.

Moses cleared his throat and said, "We have come together today to witness one of God's most sacred ceremonies. It was the creation of the both sexes in which God pulled woman from the side of man and made the one, into two. Now you, Lemuel and Agnes, have come before God to be joined once again into one flesh. I urge you today that from this moment forward to look upon one another as only one-half of that which makes each of you whole." Then Moses turned to Agnes and said, "Do you take this man to be your lawfully wedded husband, to have and to hold, in sickness and in health, for richer or for poorer, as long as you both shall live?" And Agnes said, "I do." And to Lemuel he turned and asked, "Now Lemuel, do you take this woman to be your lawfully wedded wife, to have and to hold from this day forward, in sickness and in health, for richer or for poorer, as long as you both shall live?" And Lemuel said, "Egob" Moses said, "I now pronounce you man and wife, you may kiss your bride."

Lemuel kissed Agnes and everyone clapped and Frank played the fiddle. Kallie invited everyone to please help themselves to the food. Lemuel threw his arms open and said, "Sok fod torsport" and Agnes interpreted, "God bless us everyone."

And the night proceeded with the house being filled with the scents of other lives and stories and pasts. The Monroe sisters stayed close to Kallie and asked her assorted questions about Alabama and about her finger sandwiches of which they consumed many.

I kissed Lemuel's cheek and said, "I hope the best for you." Lemuel nodded and hugged me tight which felt funny because we'd never hugged, and he said, "Magoo." Which I truly believed was, "Me too," although I didn't know if he meant for himself or for me. But it didn't matter.

Esther tapped her cane on the floor and said, "Bring me a brandy."

"I don't imagine there's any brandy," I said.

"What self respectin' type of a man be ownin' a liquor store and not be bringin' brandy to his wedding feast?"

So I said, "Be back in a minute," to Red who looked baby-faced naked. I took her a root beer and sandwiches instead.

"What's this?"

"Root beer."

"Not be askin' for no root beer, girl."

"Well, that's what you got."

Red and I wandered off and left Esther to deal with herself.

"This has turned out rather nice." He propped his elbows on the porch railing. I joined him looking down at the people walking beneath the house. As tiny as the house might be, it had opened itself up with a warmth and richness that felt welcoming. Once again, Joe had reached forward from the past and made provisions for the present. This made me start thinking.

"What are you going to do now?" Red turned sideways, locked his long fingers together and leaned on one elbow.

"Do?" From somewhere I heard the screeching voice of Lolly Eden followed by Edna's laughter. I would never understand the easy, simple friendship that had grown between them.

"Will you be staying here then?" He turned again, looked over the water. "Staying home?"

"You know me, I've never stayed anywhere very long."

But silently I had to admit, home had taken on a new feeling. One of forgiveness. Either I had begun to forgive Toliquilah or it had begun to forgive me. Maybe some of both.

Red looked at me, looked like he wanted to say something, then didn't and looked away.

Moses came to stand beside us and I thanked him for the great job he'd done, but I slapped Red on the back in the process. "Not that we didn't have it covered," and I winked at him trying to get him back in a playful mood, "but we thank you just the same."

"My pleasure, Mary. Really, my pleasure."

Then the three of us stood leaning, spectating on everything that went on below and before us from a peaceful distance. Agnes got ready to throw her straw-colored bouquet, and the single women moved to the porch. Lolly Eden said, "Oh, throw the darn thing and get it over with 'cause ain't none of us getting any younger including yourself." I refused to participate. But the motly crew of Kallie and the Monroe sisters, Esther and Lolly Eden, the nurse from Clark City and, finally, the propped-up Edna, gathered with a respectable, ritualistic speed.

Agnes squeezed her eyes shut. Everyone counted to three and she released the dusty missile in the direction of appropriate screams and laughter. The bouquet bounced from fingertip to fingertip, disappeared once in what may have been the clutch of the Monroe sisters and popped up again from the midst. However, its freedom was short-lived as a large red, Georgia hand pushed forward and for all the life in her, Edna grabbed the trophy with a pressing determination. Then she became both embarrassed by her boldness and proud to be the winner.

Esther screamed, "Who got the thing?" but no one paid her any attention.

"I'd of laid my money on you, Mary Contrary."

"Not my style, Red. I never learned to play."

Lemuel declined tossing the garter having decided he was keeping it for himself. Then they cut the cake with each of them getting a piece of "Forever" and us eating around the outside. The bride and groom left by the stairs as Frank played a faster tune and we pelted them with rice for their exit. The boys camping in the cove had offered to decorate Lemuel's car and with great pleasure they had made the thing just about impossible to drive.

So, Lemuel disappeared into the night bound for Miami with his new bride by his side. The rattling of cans could be heard disappearing in the distance at a great speed and we all guessed he'd set a new record in crossing the No-good and would be in Miami well before midnight. Red offered a toast in his absence, "To the conqueror belong the spoils," and Kallie said, "Amen," and the wedding party began to dissipate.

Later, with the guests gone home, Kallie, Red and I sat outside amidst the white lights and made small talk about the evening's events. Edna had offered to take Esther home and she, Esther, and Wallace left together as a hobbling, jerking package with Wallace binding up the middle. Frank McGurdy had drunk until he started playing songs that made him cry and we'd told him there would be no crying at a wedding so he had to go back to his boat. Little by little, the noise filtered down to a comfortable silence. We sat in the midst of it as if we had just ridden an exhilarating roller coaster with the world rolling beneath us and now were still light on our feet with the pleasured certainty that we stood on solid ground.

Kallie rolled her eyes to us from the middle of nowhere and said, "Sometimes the cows do come home," to which I said, "Uh huh," and Red nodded in amusement. "She's special," I whispered under my breath and he said, "Very."

After awhile we more or less moved into goodnights. Red made his way down the stairs and Kallie to her bedroom while I yelled, "Good riddance and good night," from the rocking chair and sat then for a very long time thinking of Lemuel and Agnes, of Edna and Wallace, of Esther, of Joe, of Black Jack and the night I found him. It seemed a far distant dream now and somehow almost safe enough to touch. Almost. Then I thought of Joe's money. Wondered if it was still where we'd left it. Wondered right now, if he were here, what Joe would want to do with it.

"Give me a sign, Joe, tell me what's on your mind," I said. But there was no immediate inclination of what Joe might want at this point. *Maybe nothing*, I thought. *Maybe nothing at all.* Maybe not even justice mattered to him now. But it still mattered to me.

The wind picked up slightly and began ringing the chimes Kallie had hung over the porch railing, a huge old rusted set depicting barnyard animals. A sheep, a cow, a dog, and a chicken. A rooster sat at the very top holding each animal separately from his claw like talons, his wings outspread. I thought, *How strange, roosters don't fly,* and as I drifted off to sleep I could have sworn I heard Kallie saying, "They do when no one's looking."

CHAPTER SEVENTEEN

The day after the wedding the weather changed. I knew it from the moment Moses walked in the door, his face a visible record of some silent attack.

He held up a pink slip in his hands. "It finally happened." I didn't have to look at it to know what it stood for.

"How'd he do it?"

"Blackmail most likely. They didn't have a reason."

"Did he mention it to you? Ask you something?"

"Nah."

"Then they don't even know everything about you."

"He knows. Seen me coming outta payroll after it was all said and done. Leans up against the wall and say's 'Hey Moses, tell your friend I'll be seeing her real soon.' "

"He knows then."

"Yeah."

"Ahhh, Moses." I poured us both some coffee and we sat down at the bar.

"Three years to early retirement, Mary."

"I'm sorry."

"Weren't your fault."

"What do you mean? It was all my fault."

"Well," and he dropped it because it was the truth but he didn't hate me for it.

"I didn't think he'd go after you, Moses." I twirled, twisted, looked for a cigarette, "I thought he'd come after me. It doesn't really make sense."

"He doesn't have the kind of mind one can rightly figure ahead of time," Moses' eyes stared vacantly over the edge of his cup.

"What was their reason?"

"Cutbacks."

"You don't believe it."

"It's not the truth."

"Did you tell your wife yet?"

"Nah." He reached up and began rubbing the right temple of his forehead, "Thought I'd try to figure something out first. Don't want to worry Dolores with all that."

Then we sat awhile and drank coffee and didn't say anything for almost an hour. Just sat together with me feeling guilty and him feeling upended. Kallie came out of the kitchen and sat down next to me. I noticed the whiteness beneath her eyes, the lines around her lips. She was tired and it showed.

"Moses?"

"Yeah?"

"Didn't you say you always wanted to own a restaurant?"

"I don't have the money to be buying a restaurant."

"But you can cook, right?"

"I can cook."

"Then come cook for us."

They both sandwiched me with stares. I looked straight ahead because it was easier that way.

"You could help us at night because Edna broke her leg and Kallie is over-tired."

"I know it would be a drive, but if you could do it just till she's back on her feet it'd help you and it'd help us."

"I'd have to ask Dolores."

"Alright. At least it'd give us time to think about what to do next."

And because we'd reached a point of something possible, which was better than nothing, Moses ate a cheeseburger with fries on the house and went on home. Kallie said, "She's not gonna like this." And I said, "She'll get over it." Then we made a list of supplies we were low on.

I decided to break the news to Edna as quietly as possible so I waited until Kallie had driven over the bridge to the store and we were both propped up in the booth and there were not customers.

"Remember how you moved Kallie in on me."

"Yes."

"Remember how you didn't mean anything bad?" Edna's eyes rolled towards me, starting to get suspicious.

"Yeah. . . ."

"How you were trying to help her out."

"What'd you do?"

"I hired Moses to cook at night."

"We don't have the money."

"We'll get by."

Then Edna stared off into the jukebox but I didn't think she was considering music. For that matter I didn't even think she was considering Moses, she seemed to be on a long journey, past the kitchen and her leg, past the diner and all it entailed. Then she turned around and came back.

"They fired him then."

"Laid him off."

"Same thing."

"That's what I said."

And it was settled more quietly than anything that had been done between us to this point. Moses started cooking the next night and after that the diner was never the same.

A different menu emerged which included fish. He had managed this by an unseen miracle which was accomplished through the closed door of Edna's bedroom. He had mentioned maybe wanting to try a few new things and I motioned with my thumb to Edna's door. Moses had knocked twice and said, "Ms. Edna?" and when she said, "Come on in," he closed the door behind him. I had tried to listen through the door and waited with anticipation for the raised bellowing of Edna's voice but it never came. All I could hear was the melody of Moses' reasoning rising and falling, rising and falling until he had apparently parted the will of Edna like the Red Sea because she rescinded the no-fish policy. The greatest miracle was she did it without an attitude. When the menu changed so did the clientele. For one, the friends and family of Moses showed up in multitude, and I found that refreshing. Then someone came in from Clark City one night and told a cousin about the place, so they drove all the way down one Friday night with their neighbors. Getting by started getting easier. The prices went up on the dinners but the lunches stayed about the same. Kallie took over cooking breakfast and maintained that the best of breakfasts were served Alabama style. The breakfast crowd, which consisted mainly of the fishermen, Lemuel and Agnes, and often Lolly Eden, didn't seem to mind.

Then one Friday morning Kallie brought her Christmas lights and strung them up around the outside, and Moses' wife, Dolores, brought in some old tablecloths for the tables and put candles on them "just for the night time," and Edna and I sat in a booth drinking a beer watching the whole thing like it wasn't really happening.

"Next thing you know," she said, "they'll be wanting to change the name."

And I said, "You're probably right." Then we both imagined the names they would come up like "Alfredo's" and "Josephine's," until we grew weary. Edna seemed good-naturedly resigned to allow them to maneuver around her, knowing none of it was done out of spite or disrespect. The only fear it held for me was one of change. Slowly, the diner wasn't looking like Joe's place anymore. Not the way it always had with Edna. With her, not even the dust had changed. *But now* . . . I bit my lip so that Edna said, "What is it?" I said, "Oh, nothing" and looked for my cigarettes. It was changing, and in the process, I was afraid, it was wiping out all traces of Joe. I said, "What have I done?" aloud but thought I had said it to myself.

Edna looked back at me for a long time and finally said, "Probably saved me from going out of business whether you like it or not."

Edna tapped her fingers on the table, got up and refilled her coffee cup and settled down. Then she began to tell me more about herself than I'd heard since I showed up.

"I wasn't even coming to this place. Was on my way down to Miami. Had a job lined up in Biscayne Bay nannying these two twin boys."

"Nannying doesn't seem to suit you."

"I don't worry about what suits me or doesn't suit me. These folks come through Georgia, stayed at a motel where I was working." She cut her eyes to the side in my direction, "Mostly cleaning."

That explained the cooking part but I didn't say anything.

"One thing led to the next and they seemed to be in need of somebody to control them boys. I guess I looked big enough to control 'em. Fact was they were scared of me so they shut up and sat down when I was around."

That I could understand.

"Anyway, they offered me good pay, a free apartment, and what-all. My husband had been dead a long time. None of it mattered none to me anymore so I says, 'Sure why not?' "

"But you didn't make it."

"Nope. Kinda got lost. Ended up at that No-good bridge and crossed over in spite of myself. When I come up on this place with the sign up across it something stirred on the inside of me."

"Like what?"

"Nothing much. Just a turn. A change in the roads. And I knew it way down on the deep inside of me."

The deep side of Edna had to be mighty deep indeed. She was too big for it to be otherwise.

"Well, I'm from Georgia, don't know nothing about what's going on in this place. How could I?"

"You couldn't," I agreed.

"Except of course what I got from Lolly Eden. Lemuel tried to tell me but I don't know." She let her eyes drift across the street where the sign on the door said, *Gone Married.* "Maybe he talks too fast or something."

"What did you get from Lolly Eden?"

"Dead Boy. Place set empty. Family all gone. Maybe a good deal. It didn't seem like a great deal or a bad one, you know what I mean, and I didn't have nothing to lose. Go in debt or raise some twins. I don't know." She said it again and seemed more than resigned to whatever the future held.

But that future wasn't what either of us had expected. Jimmy Cusler walked through the door in his uniform. Shades on. Lately, he had been the last thing on my mind and now here he was.

"Well, hey there, Mary."

I hated the way he walked. The way he talked. My skin began to crawl. I got up from the booth and walked behind the bar. It seemed safer there with something strong standing between us.

"What do you want, Jimmy?"

"Just taking a friendly drive. Thought I'd drop in. Say hello." He pulled his shades above eye level. Gave me what Jimmy must have believed was a million dollar look. Hair or no hair. "What'll it be, Jimmy?" I slid a menu over in front of him. He looked down with a smile, slowly picked it up and laid it aside. Then he leaned in and lowered his voice watching Edna from the corner of his eye.

"Thought I'd come out and collect on the protection I've been giving you."

His breath smelled rancid and slick. Something like dead eel. "What protection?"

"Mary, don't play dumb with me. You know as good as I do that I could have had you in jail by now for stealing police property. Fingerprints alone. Nothing to it. Sorry about your friend, though. I mean it's not like it can go unpunished. But," he leaned over, rubbed his fingers along the back of my arm before I jerked it away, "I figure it's payback time. What do you say we take a ride?"

"You forget, Jimmy, your wife's a friend of mine."

"You don't owe my wife a thing though now, do you?"

My gun lay under the counter of the bar. It was within easy reach. Jimmy probably would never see me move. All it took was for me to call him over. Beat him at his own game. Whisper in his ear. Shoot him in the head. *An eye for an eye*, I thought and began reaching for the handle as Moses walked out of the kitchen.

Jimmy leaned back a foot. "Now isn't this cozy?"

"Mary," Moses said and put his hand on my forearm, and brought my hand above the counter.

"Is there a problem, officer?"

"No. No problem, Moses. Just stopping by to say hello to an old friend."

Moses stood silent, strength that wouldn't cower before Jimmy's bullying. "Well, that's good. You should have a bite to eat while you're here, but right now Mary's got business to take care of with me. You'll have to schedule a visit with her another time. Kallie, could you please help Officer Cusler with his selection."

Kallie didn't move, but Jimmy did.

"No. It'll have to be another day, Moses. It's time for me to be heading home. Mary, be seeing you." He pointed his finger at me as though it were a gun and pulled the trigger. Then he said, "Ladies," to Edna, Kallie, and Dolores as he turned and walked out the door.

CHAPTER EIGHTEEN

There was no rest for me through the labyrinth of what had happened. Somewhere, I knew, if I dug far enough, hard enough, there had to be a truth that would not escape me. I vacillated between the ranges of hopeful and hopeless and every shade in between. Today I was having a hopeful moment.

"Why did you care so very much what happened to Joe?"

Esther turned sideways in her chair.

"Why you come 'round girl 'cept when it's to please you?" She emphasized the *you* with the force of her tongue. I ignored her. I had thought a lot during the day and then into the night, sifting through old facts and new news. I had questions that needed answers.

"We're both thinking somebody was after Joe's money a long time ago, yes?"

"Yessss."

"Well, if somebody was after Joe's money, why didn't they hold him up at the diner?"

"Maybe you want something to drink?"

"What do you have?"

"What difference to you girl? Either you want something to drink or you don't. Which one it be now?"

Esther's reasoning was pungent. It slapped me in the face like raw garlic.

"Whatever you have, Esther."

She opened the refrigerator, took out a pitcher of what appeared to be green seawater, poured it into two mismatched mugs, and brought mine to me, holding it before my face until I accepted.

"What is it?"

"What you think, poison maybe." Then she smiled a one-up-on-you smile and uncoiled in her chair.

I took a sip and said, "Maybe." The thought of milky snake venom being an ingredient made my stomach turn.

"It's tea," she said, reading my thoughts.

It didn't taste like tea and it didn't look like tea. "Uuummm," was all I managed. "What about the diner, Esther?"

"The diner?"

"Why didn't they rob him there?"

She put her cup down, her elbows on the table, and held her face in the upturned palms of her hands. She looked almost normal and at the same time tiny and childlike. If she'd have closed her eyes I could've almost forgotten she didn't have any.

"Whoever it be, wanted more money than that. Wanted all the money that ever has been. Greeeedy."

"Surely, they didn't think all the money was going to be in the parking lot in the middle of Clark City." The snakes were silent, unmoving, as if they were waiting for something to happen. I looked over toward the cages. Even the mice were silent. "What were they thinking, Esther?"

"Maybe they not be thinking right way to start out. Maybe they not be so good in the head here." She pointed a long brown finger to the center of her forehead. "Or here." Then she pointed over her heart. "Maybe you know somebody like thisss."

"Oh, I know lots of somebodies that don't think good. Me being one of them."

"Not the same no good."

"Maybe you have one in mind."

"Maybe not."

"Why don't you have the right answers, Esther?"

"Maybe you not be comin' round with the right questions, girl."

The right questions. Alright, I thought, I'll ask the right questions. Now, only to figure out what the right questions were. Right and wrong to Esther were like black and white to Esther. Her version existed somewhere in the blackness of her mind. It was there, in some form, but the path leading the way was dark and convoluted, which was frustrating for me. Yet anytime I thought for very long, my contemplations brought Esther's face back, her broken words haunting me. Somehow, she possessed a key.

"You be askin' stupid questions like a machine."

"A machine?"

She slapped the cane against the side of my chair. "That's what I said to you, a machine. Wrong questions over and over again, girl." She slapped the chair again, twice. "You run like a monkey in a circle."

I had never seen a monkey run in circles. Neither had Esther, and I suddenly understood something more about her mind. She put it together herself. Filled with imaginings and the way she believed things must look, the shape of them, the color, the contrast. In Kallie's world snakes could talk and roosters fly. In Esther's, monkeys ran in circles and the way to get to who killed Joe was to walk backward with blind eyes.

"How do you say I should run?"

"You should be runnin' with your heart, girl, not with your eyes. I may be blind here," she pointed two weaving fingers to her whiteness, "but not here." Then she rested her palm across her heart and I believed her.

"I do run with my heart, Esther."

"No, girl, no!" She slapped the cane point to the floor. "You feel with your heart, maybe this is true, but you not be runnin' with it, or this whole thing be locked up tight tonight."

I was tired of Esther not making any sense but I knew I needed her. It was as if I possessed a large puzzle where I fit on the one end and Esther the other and the space that fell open between us was where all the answers were supposed to fill in the gap. They were separate ends of an invisible bridge.

"Esther, you want to get out of this place for awhile?"

"What for I gonna sashay to some no good place to go fallin' down now?"

The lights flickered twice then cut off completely. We sat in the still darkness for a hushed moment.

"Does this happen to you often?"

"What?"

"There is no light."

"You mean from above."

"Yes. We're in darkness Esther, total darkness."

"Welcome to my world, gin girl."

It wasn't a time to argue with Esther about my drinking habits; although gin wasn't one of them. I could barely see my hand in front of my face much less Esther. I could hear the snakes awakening, beginning to slither in their cages. Then a hand was laid across my mouth and I almost screamed.

"Shhhhhhh." It was Esther moving quietly through the darkness, her hand placed across my mouth. "Shhhhhhh," she said again before she lifted the fingers away. They smelled something like lemon, something like medicine. I heard the latch lift on a cage door to my left, a slithering scuffle, heard a squeeze, almost felt a pulse outside my flesh. Outside then, a shoe against shell, the slow cranking sounds of a turning knob, my heart beating in my chest, my throat, my head. Esther somewhere in the blackness, silent. A snake outside its place, moving. The shadow of the moon escaping from outside to inside as the door is opened. A bridge of natural, nocturnal light, a flash of arm, of pants, of man. The quickness of Esther unleashes then from the silence, snapping forward as though she has no feet. A rope lashing out against the bulk. A surprised sniff and a turning. Then the rope thrown forward again, and again, and a cry, and the bulk of the man is gone. Less than a minute has passed. I have not moved, but clutch the seat with both fisted palms. Esther moves across the door, is caught in the stream of light, lifts her head facing out. There are three moons now. The one outside stealing in, and the white orbs of Esther's eyes spilling out. She holds a snake behind the head as his body climbs, coiling about her arm. I will never forget this picture as long as I live. Her silhouette, the moons, the snake. I close my eyes and it burns its way into my brain.

"That one won't be back," she says.

"How do you know?"

"Because he will most surely die."

Esther slowly closes the door, and the darkness circles about us like the snake wrapping its way slowly along her arm.

Chapter Nineteen

The wind picked up Esther's scent and blew it in my direction. She was silent now with her head tilted to one side. We sat beneath a mangrove tree or it sat amongst us. It was old and its branches curled about us, then shot back down, rooted into the ground. In the darkness, they reminded me of Esther's many snakes. An owl called twice.

"An owl," she said.

"Yes."

"I like their eyes."

"How would you know?"

"See how you be thinkin', gin girl. I like that they are open." She turned her head back towards me. "I like that they can see in the darkness."

I understood then. Esther's way wasn't wrong but it was as hidden as Toliquilah. One had to know the secret entrances to get to the tunnels that reached her mind. I was determined to stay around long enough to discover them.

"What happened here tonight, Esther?"

"They shut down the generator."

I waited because this much I already knew. What I didn't know was why. Or who had done it. Or who was supposedly going to die. Or, for that matter, how long this had been going on.

"You know if someone shows up dead, we'll have to—"

"Bury him," she said quickly.

I thought she might be smiling but when I looked back at her face she wasn't. She was looking straight ahead with her eyes closed.

"That's not what I had in mind."

"Doesn't matter. That's the right doin' of it." She nodded in affirmation to herself.

"Have you done this thing before?" I stuck my hands over my ears and half my face. Half asking and not wanting to receive the answer I suspected.

"Only when they come."

"Who comes, Esther? Who is it that is coming?"

She leaned her back against the mangrove trunk pulling her cane up between her bent knees.

"Is it people coming to get your money?" There was a minimal response. Something akin to a snort. "You said you had money in the belly of the snake. I remember."

"Yesssss."

The owl heard the hiss of Esther's *yes*. Called out a *who?* then spread his wings and lifted in the black air.

"So it's the money."

"It is not."

"What then?"

Then Esther in the midst of our aloneness in our seat amongst the mangrove tree turned to me and leaning in my direction whispered. "He's always coming for his children."

"Who?"

"The devil."

I looked at her without saying anything. She couldn't see but must've sensed my expression.

"What's matter with you, girl?" She was forgetting her whisper. "You don't know for the one that lives to make die? The one who spits at God?"

"Spits at God?"

Esther let out a sound that signified both her exasperation and disgust.

"Ohhhh yes," I offered to please her, "the devil."

"Now, you are so smart."

I consented that truly I didn't know so much about the devil, to which Esther's response was, "You should. You have been to him maybe a good friend for long time."

"I swear, Esther, we were only acquaintances." It came out as a joke. Had we been sitting at a bar together I would have reached over and punched her on the arm to share it. Well, maybe not Esther. Or Kallie. Or Edna, for that matter. But Red I could have punched. Esther wasn't laughing.

"Stupid people like you, they look with eyes."

Every time I had Esther talking I suddenly wanted to shut her up again. "I'm sorry. You were telling me what is happening here to you."

"Maybe you would think somebody come to steal the snakes for the money." The owl flew back overhead carrying something in its claws. "It's not for the money. He sends them to steal his children because I take the poison and make it good."

It didn't really matter if it was the anger of the devil or the greed of mere mortals that came after Esther. I knew this much: someone did come.

"How long has this been going on?"

"Since Joe died."

"I don't understand."

There was a screech from either the captor or the captive, I couldn't tell which one. Esther turned her face full length in my direction.

"Neither do I."

*

The journey into Clark City was passed in silence. I didn't attempt to make small talk with Esther. The other kind of talk would involve serious answers like where the bodies were buried. In case there was a definite answer, I didn't want to ask. The idea of Esther wielding a shovel and digging up dirt was a frightening picture. I put it aside and looked at her profile. Her eyes were closed and I thought she was asleep until we crossed the bridge and she said "No-good" beneath her breath.

We were headed for a parking lot, the two of us wandering through the night caught in a web that refused to close. I didn't like the idea of Esther going home alone. Perhaps neither did she, which kept her willing to ride out the night on the skirt of whatever whim came my way. For my part I hadn't been to the parking lot where Joe was shot because there didn't appear to be any reason to see it. But it was late and Esther and I didn't have anywhere to go.

Clark City was under a constant state of urban decay. Anything that was built to be new became old quicker than time and was then left half-abandoned in hopes of more fertile ground only a mile away. The same was true of the grocery store which had at the time of the murder been Motts Supermarket and Deli. It was closed now, but the shadows of the lettering were left firmly bleached into the concrete walls. Strung across the letters was a banner that said, 'BINGO TONIGHT' but it was ripped and shredding. *Tonight* must have been a long time ago. It was a place where details were no longer important. I pulled into the empty lot, to the side of the building away from the street lamp, and turned off the car.

"Is this it?" Esther rolled down her window and sniffed the air.

"Yeah, this is it."

"I don't like it."

"Me neither."

We silently agreed it was a bad place to die. I rolled down my window and the air whipped through, stirring up dust from the dashboard. Funny, Clark City was on the mainland and it could pick up more of a breeze than we could in the swamps. Joe had once told me it was the blanket of mosquitoes that hung in the air. "Nothing gets past them," he'd said, "not even the wind." The palms lining the building slapped their fronds together and looked out over the barren parking lot with us.

"There's nothing here," I said.

Esther opened her door. "Let's get out."

I followed her as she pointed her cane and walked half-steps behind it. Step by step, back and forth, as if she were planting. I thought of Kallie's plowing story, of her neat exacting rows. Esther's were not so neat.

"What are you doing?"

"Be quiet, girl!"

So I was quiet. Standing in the middle of a concrete jungle. Listening to the palms slapping. Esther's cane tapping. Remembering Memphis, and the heat, and my dream. Esther was halfway across the parking lot now. A single soldier marching to war. She reminded me of something I'd seen once but I couldn't remember what or where. Maybe it was a bird. Maybe it was in Texas. When she stopped it was sudden. Like she had rolled up on herself and had to double-back a second. Then she turned and faced in my direction and she didn't say a word. I hadn't known what she was doing, but now I knew what she had done. She was standing in the place it had happened. I wanted to run again. But it wasn't a choice anymore. So I walked, in half-step Esther time, and met her.

"Here?"

"Yessss."

Then we stood in the graveyard of Joe's last presence. His last breathing moment held here. Esther's eyes began to cry. Silent tears that rolled into the creases of her skin and were released again to run down across the raised bones of her cheeks. Here my friend spent his last hour. I wondered at his last thought. His last breath. But my tears had been drained, the rocky bed of my reservoir, dry and unyielding.

Esther rocked back and forth, her cane weaving. I looked beyond us in the dark searching for faces, any unseen witness. I reached out, touched her arm. "What now, Esther? What is this?"

"Ohhh girl. Ohhh girl. I meant to tell …" then she fell to garbled, choking words.

"To tell what Esther?"

"To tell him he was my boy." It came out whispered. Wet and weeping. "What?"

"Girl, don't you hear me?" She slid beneath my hand to the pavement. "He was my boy." Then Esther doubled over as though she had been opened and filleted.

I sat down beside her and laid my arm across her back. Her tiny birdlike bones jutted out against my skin. I was raised with Joe, half-raised by his mother, knew everything there was to know about him. This unacceptable news didn't make any sense. But I recognized the grief of unfinished business.

We sat in the unmarked grave until the sky began turning grey in the east and the mourning within Esther eased with the lifting of the night. By the time we stood, I could make out the outlying shadows of an abandoned plant, a closed shoe repair shop that said, "McGraw's" and a man shuffling in the distance pulling a two-wheeled buggy. He stiffened as we rose, stared in our direction, then picked up his pace, turned the corner and headed East.

Esther pointed her cane in his direction and said, "You need to follow that man to church."

We got into an argument about following some vagrant, and Esther began hitting me with her cane while I was helping her into the car. Things were getting back to normal.

Church Street was made up of empty warehouses and the skeletal remains of an apartment building. Other than this it held a few empty lots that were known to house the homeless who, for the most part, preferred them to the musty broken shelter of the buildings. Ultimately left unfinished by the city planners, Church Street came to a dead stop in weeds at the end of the pavement. The dying of the district sealed its fate to fall forsaken forever.

"I don't see him."

"Of course not. You're too late."

"I don't see what a bum had to do with anything."

"Don't see, don't see, don't see."

"Stop mocking me."

"Stop mocking yourself, girl." Esther leaned her head back on the seat and closed her eyes. I looked in the rearview mirror and saw the blood-red streaks across the whites of mine. I wondered if hers looked partially the same.

"I try to say, follow your heart not head, but I wasted all my breath for no good reason."

"So, your heart says follow the man to Church Street?"

"No! For what I know about Church Street? It says follow the man to church."

"Close enough, Esther."

"Makes no mind now, because you done wrong."

I circled again. The man didn't appear, anywhere. Black coat I remembered, knit hat maybe, two-wheeled backwards buggy. Couldn't tell the real color of his skin.

"No sign."

"Was a sign but now good-bye gone."

"I'm going home now, Esther."

"Go on then."

We drove home in silent exhaustion. This time Esther was truly asleep and didn't mumble as we drove across the bridge.

CHAPTER TWENTY

"Have you heard of any dead bodies floating around anywhere?"

Red had his foot propped up on the boat railing. We sat on the forward deck and I watched as a pelican dove, hit the water like a bomb, and came up with breakfast in his bill. Red's arms were crossed behind his neck, his eyes closed to the sun.

"Should I?"

"I don't know." I looked behind my right shoulder and then my left.

He cracked one eye in my direction. "Seem a might skittish today, Mary Contrary. What's up?"

"Things have been unworldly, Red, that's all."

"Always been that way on this island."

"More unworldly. Even for Toliquilah."

"Tell me." He pulled in his long legs, bent his knees, placed his elbows on them and looked me in the face. "That old swamp woman got you spooked?"

I drummed my fingers on my thigh. For a second the snake was spitting through the air again, the bulk of the man moving backwards, the one moon looking in, the two moons looking out.

"More than that woman. Known her too long for her to spook me too much. Then again," I leaned in and looked back over my shoulders before I whispered, "something's happening."

"What's that?"

"Shooting snakes and two-wheeled buggy men and new mothers being born."

"Mary?"

"Yeah?"

Red stuck his hand out and felt my forehead. "Are you alright?"

"I got a feeling somebody's following me." I stood up, making a circle, "I been feeling it all morning."

Red let out a low whistle. "Mary Contrary, let's go down below."

*

"So she said someone would die. Just because she said it doesn't mean it'll happen."

I leaned my head back against the cabin's wall. "You should have been there, Red, because if you had been you wouldn't be saying that. You'd be looking for the body, too."

"What would you do if you found one?"

I didn't answer because I heard the echo of Esther's words saying "bury it" and somewhere inside me I agreed with her. Besides that, let a dead body show up on Toliquilah and Jimmy Cusler would have me in jail on suspicion for the fun of it.

"Let me put it this way, if you come across a dead body, don't do anything with it."

"Just let it lie?"

"Yeah, let it lie, float, whatever."

"And let me guess. Get in touch with you."

"Probably so." I was trying to imagine a chain reaction. Red to me. Me to Esther. Me carrying a shovel. Esther's cane pointing to the burying spot. "Yeah, that would probably be the thing to do. Get in touch with me."

I looked up at Red. Watched him watching me. I wanted to tell him everything. Roll out a beginning-to-end explanation but sometimes things were too bizarre to tell even one of your closest friends. For all the familiarity I had with Red Mahoney his reality was the wide open spaces of miles of empty ocean. The darker side of the swampy island didn't seem to touch his world and my most recent experiences were definitely rising from their murky bottom. I wanted to tell him everything but in the light of day it seemed untouchable. Surreal. Changing the subject seemed to be a better alternative.

"Why aren't you fishing?"

"El Nino."

"The wind?"

"Bad seas. Late storm moving in."

The skies were clear and sunny, which meant nothing. "How serious is it?"

"Right now, it's only a depression."

Then we recounted a few storms, remembering hurricanes of our past. And for a short time Red relaxed but I felt his eyes still trying to see below my surface as I said good-bye and walked away. I turned and waved before I got into the car and he raised a long arm, palm towards me. For a second I had the funny feeling that I would never see him again.

Things at the diner had taken on a different atmosphere. Edna sat now for the most part just watching as Moses focused himself with the growing business. He was in the process of inventorying, which would be followed by making an order sheet. Edna and I sat in our booth with the ripped vinyl which Moses had fixed with a sealant instead of tape. My fingers ran along the vinyl scar from force of habit.

"That blind woman killed somebody with a snake and said she was Joe's mother."

Edna turned from watching Moses with an uninterested look to face me.

"I get my cast off tomorrow," she said.

"Well then, that about catches us up."

"Yep. Guess so." Edna smiled, and it was one of the few times I'd seen her do it where it didn't seem to hurt her. "Why don't you get us some coffee and tell me how it happened."

So I did. What I couldn't seem to tell Red rolled out in front of Edna like a long carpet I'd been walking on for a long time. The way she listened made it easy. Occasionally she nodded her head like she understood or like the strangest thing in the world was to be expected. Or like she had half-known it would have come this way all along. I trusted Red with the black and white of things. Edna I trusted with things that lay in between.

"You think she's alright out there by herself?"

"I'm not sure." I got up and dug around under the cash register for an old pack of cigarettes. I found a pack with two left in it and, lighting one, sat back down. "She can handle herself in her own special way, like I said. I've never seen anything like I did last night, and according to her, she's done it before. Been doing it since Joe died."

"What could be the connection between him dying and her place?"

"Her place?"

"Did you say they were coming to her place?"

"I did, but I was thinking more . . . " A man who I didn't recognize walked in. He had brown hair. An awkward build. Old shoes. He stopped and watched us for a moment, then walked up to the bar and sat down. Something about him seemed familiar. Moses turned around before I could get up.

"Yes sir. What can I get you?"

The man looked in our direction again, but this time it was directed specifically towards me. There was sweat on his forehead and his upper lip.

"Coffee, black." His voice came out heavy and hard.

He put his eyes to the menu and then looked at Edna.

"What was I saying?"

"Something about her place."

"I thought maybe they were coming after," I paused, looked at the bar, lowered my voice, "her money."

"Her money?"

I motioned for Edna to lower her voice as well.

"She has money. From milking those snakes. And believe me, if she spends a dime it's nowhere to be seen."

"Then she had that before he died."

"That she did." I agreed.

"Then, that doesn't add up."

"She thinks," I leaned in closer and so did Edna, our heads almost touching, "she thinks the devil is sending men to get her snakes. Says they're his children."

"Uhhhuhhh." Edna leaned back in the booth, nodded her head a few times. "I could see that."

The man at the bar dropped his cup to the saucer, which broke in half.

Kallie emerged from the kitchen with a sponge in her hand and said, "Oh, don't worry about it none. Let me get you a refill." Then she looked up and said, "Mister, are you alright, 'cause you look just like my Uncle George the day that python turned up in the corn field and scared him to death." Then she turned to us and said, "And I mean it. He was dead in a matter of seconds." And then she turned back to the man but it was too late because he was already on the floor. Kallie said, "Now, where'd he go?" I didn't move, and Edna couldn't. I had an inclination it was time to get a shovel.

CHAPTER TWENTY-ONE

It was the most interesting employee meeting I'd ever attended. It consisted of Edna, Moses, me, and Kallie, and then from unlucky coincidence Lemuel and Agnes who'd walked over for lunch. Also in attendance was the body of a dead man.

We put up the *Closed* sign and pulled the blinds to. Agnes tried to faint, but I got into an argument with her and when she got mad she didn't feel like fainting anymore. Moses felt the thing we needed to do at this point was to identify the body. It was the second order of business. The first had been to determine that the man was indeed dead and he was. His body was now 'arranged' out of the position in which he had fallen which was most easily described as a heap. The man was large in an old fashioned way. Big and gangly at the same time as if he would have been twice the size if he would have had more to eat in his formative years. Moses put on a pair of plastic kitchen gloves and searched the body. There wasn't a wallet, no form of ID, and only a ten-dollar bill in his shirt pocket. We all agreed the coffee should be on the house and left the ten where it was. Then we considered calling the police but the closest police we could call would be Clark City, to which I looked at Moses and said, "There might be complications." He agreed. We still didn't feel like we were out of the shadow of that other trouble because although one shoe had come off quietly with Moses being laid off, we were still waiting for the other one to follow. The fact was Jimmy Cusler was vindictive, blackmailing, control hungry, and, as Moses had told me, "Unless that man has found Jesus, he's still a bad biter from the pound." I agreed. Having a strange dead body in the midst of Joe's old place at the feet of me and Moses was more power food than Jimmy needed.

I looked at Edna and she looked me in the eyes and said, "I could lie to you, Mary, and say it's gonna be alright, but you don't need a dead man hanging around your neck and you don't need to go to jail because I been there and there ain't no light."

We all looked at Edna who suddenly looked very much like a convict on the run from the great state of Georgia. Agnes started fanning herself again, and Lemuel's head dropped down into his neck, turtle-style, and he eyed Edna from underneath the bush of his eyebrows. I was more focused on the fact there wasn't any light in jail. I felt my throat tighten and wanted to step out for air but now the door was locked. She was right. I couldn't go to jail. As innocent as I might be, the possibility was real. It didn't matter to a man like Cusler what evidence there might or might not be. He'd arrange for anything he was lacking. So the man grew colder as our debate grew warmer over the ethical ramifications of burying a strange man without the proper authorities.

"Toliquilah don't belong to nobody. We make rules to suit selves everything come out good on top just so," said Lemuel.

We all looked at him, each of us trying to discern a word here or there but Agnes stepped in and said, "Lemuel says it doesn't matter on the island because here we make the rules but I think . . ." Then everyone started talking about what Lemuel had said because no one cared what Agnes thought.

"Nothing exactly like this ever come up in Alabama," Kallie said and it meant she didn't have much more to add because any situation she couldn't cross reference from Corn County didn't compute in Kallie's brain. It was a good simple rule of thumb most of the time but these were extenuating circumstances. "Something close one time but not close enough," she added. Then she offered to get everybody something to drink. We all said a Coke would be fine but Agnes wanted "a touch of cherry juice" added to hers. Then she leaned over and whispered to everyone, "I think we should cover him up," and pointed carefully with the painted tip of her red fingernail as if Mr. X could understand what was going on. Moses agreed that would be fitting and grabbed a couple of tablecloths from beneath the counter and did the honors, which made things look more official. We sat respectfully, as though we were a group of sightseers on a local outing, twiddling our toes, tapping our fingers, and twining our hair until Kallie brought the Cokes.

A beige Chevy pulled up to the front door and Kallie said, "Edna, you've got company," as Wallace P. Ketchum stepped out. Although Edna's leg was on the mend and her convalescent period coming to a close, Wallace's attention had not waned but become a staple at the diner. He approached the door, tried the handle, read the sign, and then, cupped his eyes and placed his hands against the glass.

"I think he can see us," Kallie said, then opened the door.

"Why are you closed this time of day . . ." Wallace began. Then he saw the body on the floor and the collective body of what appeared to be a guilty party. "Well now," he said clearing his throat, "appears I've come at a bad time."

It was Moses who took the floor and explained what had taken place and the encumbrances surrounding the situation. Kallie offered Wallace a drink and he said, "Sure, whatever you're having." She asked him if he wanted a touch of cherry juice but he declined. Then, on that most unusual day, Wallace P. Ketchum became our hero. And I believe it was the moment that sent Edna's heart on over to the other side.

Wallace took a sip of his Coke, pulled the cloth back and looked at the body, then covered the face again, detective style. He paced. We watched. He parted the blinds with his fingers, looked up and down the street. We twiddled our toes, tapped our fingers, twined our hair.

He dropped the blinds, turned and faced us. "Best thing to do is drop him off on Church Street. Ambulance makes a spin up through there once a week for sanitary reasons. Can't have dead bodies rotting up the city." Agnes gagged and covered her mouth. "Sorry Ma'am," he went on. "Always a sick or dying soul somewhere on that street. The way I see it," he looked over towards the corpse, "what's one more gonna make a difference."

The light of a thousand days sprung up in my head, Moses' eyes, and Edna's heart. I embraced the freedom I'd never lost and our next order of business was the evacuation of the body. Wallace gave us a few tips on our upcoming duty and said he'd pick Edna up tomorrow. Then he left for work but not before I noticed Edna's newfound look upon him. Yes sir, on that day Wallace P. Ketchum grew a few feet in the eyes of the ex-convict from Georgia, and it seemed to be the final few feet he'd been needing.

Then Lemuel and Agnes went back across the street and the rest of us sat waiting for the covering of darkness. I thought of driving out to Esther's with the news but changed my mind. It was as if the corpse demanded my presence, although I hadn't done a thing to him living or dead. No one felt like eating, and being closed there wasn't much point in cooking, so our time was spent waiting, making small talk.

Kallie said, "Uncle George did fall out dead when he seen that snake," to which everyone nodded and said, "Uhuh," or something close enough to count.

I asked Moses how the family was and he said, "Mighty fine." I asked, "Girls alright?" And he said, "Couldn't be better," and that was about all we could think of in that area for the time being. He offered up that Wallace P. was a mighty fine fellow and everyone readily agreed. I said to Edna, "So you were in jail?" She nodded real slow-like but didn't offer any additional comment. Kallie had to ask, "What for?"

Edna said, "Killing my husband," to which we all looked at our feet, the window, and our hands, but not at Edna. "I didn't do it," she said and drank the rest of her Coke. Then she started crunching on the ice.

A few people pulled up and Moses quickly pulled the body behind the bar where no one could see, then cracked the door and said, "Sorry, we're closed today," and in keeping with his conscience added, "there's been a death," to which we heard the muffled condolences of the parting couple.

Finally night fell, and by unanimous vote we decided Edna, due to her leg still being in a cast, would stay behind. We then brought Kallie's truck around back and Moses rolled the body in a blanket from Edna and hoisted it to the truck bed. Then he rode in the back with the body and I sat up front with Kallie but spent most of my time looking backwards. Halfway across the No-good the mummified body of Mr. X sat bolt upright, and this time I screamed. Moses, by sheer instinct, threw himself against the side of the truck bed and Kallie put on the brakes. She looked in the rearview mirror and said, "Oh, that," and crawled out of the cab. Then she climbed up in the back and pushed the top half of the body back down to the bed and looked at the both of us and said, "It's just gas." I had crossed the No-good all my life but now every time I went across the middle it would mark something I couldn't soon forget.

Kallie got in to drive, Moses moved up front with us, and we continued to the other side. I was thankful for Alabama, which at this moment appeared to be a state that possessed a great source of wisdom regarding practical matters of things one ought to know.

*

At night there was more movement, and unfortunately more curiosity from the lives that found solace in the freedom of Church Street. There were no agendas to keep, no bills to pay, no dates to remember, and, other than the necessities of staying alive, no stress. The real rules didn't apply here anymore than they did on Toliquilah. People shuffled, turned sideways, surveyed the truck. I hoped the body would not rise to the occasion to greet the curious onlookers. We drove to the end of the street, circled back around, parked in a vacant lot, and turned off the lights. We hadn't been there five minutes before a man approached from the doorway of the empty building across the street.

"Heyhey." He staggered just a little when he walked. "Hehhey. Whatshudoin?"

The three of us sat mute. Then I lied.

"We're looking for John."

"Izatafact. Well, hey it's your lucky day on account of," he tried to run his fingers through his hair but missed "cause that's me." Then he stood red-eyed and full of an expression that kept sliding from his face.

Lies. Problem with them, once you get going you can't ever stop. I leaned over the door and spoke to him in my best conspirator voice.

"So you're John."

"Thas right."

"Good, cause we're looking for Mary and somebody told us you could point her out."

"Me?" He took a tiny step back, pointed a wavering finger to his chest.

"Yes. They said, 'Ask John, he knows everybody.' "

"Mary?" He found his head, scratched it twice. "She wear a red dress?"

"Maybe so."

"Got them tiger shades she keeps on."

"We don't know."

"Listen 'ere." He took a tiny step forward again. "She thinks she used to be a movie star. Can you believe all of that?"

I said, "The truth is—" Moses poked me for making the lie worse by calling it the truth— "she is a movie star, John, and Hollywood wants her back."

"Mary?"

"Oh, she was the best. You should have seen her." My lie grew.

"Our Mary Contrary?" My face caved in on itself. "That's what we call her 'cause she puts on them shades and gets meaner than a nest full of hornet bees. And you know what I say to her?" He doubled over in silent laughter, "You know what," and tried to catch his breath, "I say? I say, 'Hey Mary Contrary, how does your garden grow?' Get it? Garden grow?"

Yeah. I got it. I'd had that nursery rhyme sung to me so many times in school that half the time I didn't remember my own last name.

John said, "Garden grow" again and started laughing, then coughing, then gasping until he straightened up and rubbed the water from his eyes. "You wouldn't have a cigarette would you?"

I pulled a pack from my jacket pocket. "Keep 'em."

"Well, alright then. Listen 'ere. You go look in Apartment C, second floor, that'd be Mary's place, but don't tell her I said so."

"Thanks, John."

He turned to go, then staggered back, "And hey, don't go up the stairs on account of 'cause they're ain't any. You gotta go through number one and crawl up the inside that broke wall."

Then he was gone and the three of us sat quietly watching him cross over in front of the building and continue walking down the street. He stopped long enough to offer somebody a cigarette and Kallie said, "Now ain't that sweet?"

Moses and I agreed that it was. Then we decided that Moses moving the body alone might be the least conspicuous. Then we changed our minds and agreed us trying to walk him between two of us would look more appropriate in the surroundings. So we unblanketed the body, didn't look at his face, and Moses got one stiffening arm as Kallie kept trying to drape one arm across me and it kept falling off. Then I heard a loud snap.

"Just like a chicken's neck," Kallie said.

The arm flopped over my shoulder. I felt sick and tried to focus on keeping step with Moses as we made our way across the street to the doorway of the apartment building. Kallie stayed behind and readied the truck.

She later told us we weren't the least bit noticeable. I thanked her for the observation as I tried to wipe the smell of dead from my hands. Just as we cleared the street a familiar shape turned the corner pulling a two-wheeled buggy behind him. I knew we should stop according to Esther's instructions, but we had just dumped a dead body and it didn't seem like the night for asking questions.

Behind us in the dim light of Church Street, Mr. X was leaning against the inside wall of Church Street Heights, and somewhere along its crumbling corridors a different Mary Contrary was walking in shades, making her way back to Hollywood.

CHAPTER TWENTY-TWO

"You were right." Esther was sitting with her face turned up toward the sun, the two of us propped against her southern wall, basking like lizards in the noon day heat. "That man died." A fact somehow was not as frightening with the sun against our skin throwing the shadows into hiding.

"Of course he did."

"I think he was following me," I said.

She made a noise but not a comment.

"What gets me, Esther, is why would the man be following me if he's coming at night to steal your snakes."

"I never say no thing about snakes."

Esther waited while I thought backwards. The fact was Esther had never said anything about her snakes, only the devil's children.

"You said you milked the poison from them."

"Don't be stupid. I say I took the evil, make it good." She tilted her head back further, then to the side as if listening to something I could not hear. "I said he be comin' for his children."

"But that would have nothing to do with me."

"You not be so certain of that thing, girl."

I paused. Pondered a moment. Then shivered as something invisible ran across my back leaving tiny chilled footprints in its path. I was glad it was broad daylight.

"Want to know what we did with the body?"

"Makes no never mind to me."

The dirt was moving in front of my foot. Almost imperceptibly, but moving. Something was crawling just out of my sight. I started to kick the surface, unearth it, flip whatever crawled there into the blasting light. I watched a heron lift off. An opening of wings, a flap, once, twice, then silent flight. I closed my eyes to the sun as Esther did and we propped our heads against the back of the wall and sat half-sleeping, half-awake, feeling time ebb and flow about our feet like the unseen bugs beneath the surface of the dirt. There was the stiffness of time almost coming to a halt and the rush of it beginning again. This continued until I could barely speak but tried.

"Esther?"

"Yessss?"

"How come you said Joe was your boy?" I didn't open my eyes. I didn't look at her. I waited. Time went on.

"Because he was my boy."

"But I knew his mother."

"I not be Joe's mother, he just be my boy."

I kept my eyes closed trying to travel through the tunnels of Esther's mind. Trying to locate the point of her reasoning.

"If Joe be your boy, then who am I?"

"You be the gin girl."

"I don't drink gin, Esther."

"Got nothing to do with the drink."

"What then?"

The tops of the pine trees began to hiss, swaying in the wind. Esther opened her eyes, cocked her head. She turned, faced me, her eyes bold and unrelenting. "That storm is headin' our way."

*

Our tropical depression had become a hurricane, receiving the official name of Ruby. It was sitting southwest of Miami slowly turning in the warm waters and gathering strength.

The waves had picked up. With the great oncoming force they had doubled in size, the surface of them now carrying huge whitecaps. There were a few surfers out on their boards. They would be undaunted by the darkening sky or the increased undertow.

Evacuation had begun in the tropical Mecca of the Keys. The cars biting one another's bumpers. A menagerie of humanity crushed together into a mass exodus with all the belongings they could carry, their screaming children and whining pets. Miles of bottlenecks already were a fact and they would not lessen in severity but grow intensely as the storm inched its way forward. Then there would be a countdown until landfall. When the rain began, the people would curse themselves for having not left sooner. They always did.

I paced the water's edge watching as the waves approached across the darkening water. Now there would be no appearance of the dolphins. No rolling backs, no forward calls, no playful fish. Somewhere deep beneath the growing tide they were rushing full speed to safety.

The waves crashed warm over my feet, the sand sucking away from beneath them as though it wanted desperately to pull me away too. I thought of Joe's disappearing in my dream, the sand eating him alive. And then, I thought of my father's bones lying somewhere at the bottom of the swampy island. There is a great peace in staying behind. And a great foreboding.

At last report, Ruby was a Class Three. Three's were what we considered rideable. You could board yourself down in a strong house and stay the distance from the tidal surge. A large factor depended on whether or not the storm hit at low tide or high tide because at high tide the surge will eat everything in its path.

*

Lemuel's store had taken on supernatural business with bottles being shoved in bags at breakneck speed. Lemuel was in rare form, wearing a chain of smoke and mumbling nonstop questions and replies. No one ever heard him or cared. They kept one eye on Lemuel's television, which was now wearing aluminum foil attached in an exaggerated formation to insure better reception.

"Class Three," the local weatherman repeated for the hundredth time that day. Then the local news switched to the hurricane center which offered the same warnings with more authority. Then they added, "Possibly increasing to Class Four by landfall."

There was a pause in Lemuel's store from people shifting with the weight of decision. Some would leave the island now, making their way across the No-good into Clark City and possibly beyond. The others would wait and see. A three is a three, and a four, a four. Others didn't care and never would. No matter what happened, what classification, they steeled themselves to the fact that they would not run. Some never had, they said, and never would. They would stake themselves out if they had to, they'd exclaim, which of course wasn't true. Lemuel was the only person I'd ever known who'd done so by tying himself to a palm tree. He had survived this thing, stake-eyed tied, chain smoking until the torrential rains had come upon him and everything about his body was soaked beyond his capable craving for cigarettes. Then Lemuel turned his face heavenward with a mumble and rode out a class three hurricane that moved quickly across the island. The speed of it probably saved his life. Battered and exhausted, Lemuel fell into a deep sleep and woke long after the sun had broken through the remaining clouds. He had cut himself from the tree and on shaking, unsteady legs, wobbled back to find what was left of his store. Lemuel had pulled a bottle from beneath the counter, crossed himself and drank it down. With that accomplished he lit a cigarette, sat on his stool and decided never to do that again.

It was Lolly Eden who gave us this jolly report after following Lemuel and sticking her nosy self up against the window.

"I watched the whole thing," she said. She was sucking on a lemon drop and it pulled her face in even tighter than it already was. "I knew he was a crazy man."

"Why didn't you untie him, Lolly?" Joe asked her.

"Cause I weren't sure if he was alive."

And in Lolly Eden's reasoning, that was the end of it.

But that felt like a hundred years ago, and now Agnes stared at the radar on the screen, watching intensely as the white swirl of the hurricane churned.

"Don't you think we should be going now, Lem?" she asked without looking away from the screen, but her Lem wasn't listening. He was pushing cash register keys, the sound of it must have been music to his ears.

I eyed the row of Jack Daniel's bottles, thought of the next twenty-four hours and opened my mouth to order a bottle. Then I clenched my fists, shut my mouth, and walked out the door.

I watched from across the street as Moses worked diligently boarding up the windows, Kallie following step by step with nails in hand. "Worthless," I could have told them. A great effort in futility but Moses was trying to protect a dream. *We're not going to get there from here*, I thought. I couldn't figure out where that thought came from or why.

Lemuel finally turned the sign to *Closed* behind me and I knew with that the evacuation would be complete. The wind had increased, the rain had begun. I looked up at the dark, swirling clouds, felt a gust of wind catch me off guard just as the last sheet of plywood sealed the diner in total darkness. Then Edna stepped out the door and watched me standing in the rain. It was a silent signal that it was time to go. But I wouldn't be leaving. I brushed the water from my face and thought, *Joe's place, Black Jack's bones, Esther's snakes, swamp, cove, mangrove, home.* There was nothing for me now but Toliquilah. There was no other place for me to be. I wasn't certain I could function on the other side anymore but for the first time in my entire life, I knew I didn't want to. I had been through hell and damnation. If the last remains of Joe's life were to wash away with wind and water, so could mine. There was nothing waiting for me but bad on the other side of the No-good. So I did something I was very adept at doing. I lied.

*

"Right behind you," I said with an earnest nod. A large gust of wind hit the building and jerked open the door then slammed it shut again. The eyes of Edna, Moses, and Kallie bore down upon and into me. "I just need a little space. You know," I slapped my hand against the bar with a plastered smile, "for old time's sake." With that, the motley crew gathered a tiny mass of belongings and left to collect Lolly Eden on their way to safety. I watched the rain and wind gusts shift around them as they drove away. I held the door as Ruby tried to pull it loose from the hinges and throw it twisting free across the parking lot.

Then I pulled a bottle of beer from the cooler, the gun from my waistband, and placing both on the table, sat down in my booth. I opened the beer and said, "This one's for you, Joe, while I'm still here." As I closed my eyes I could have sworn I heard laughter and him saying, "What're you gonna do, shoot Ruby's eyes out?"

CHAPTER TWENTY-THREE

I had planned the perfect hurricane-induced suicide, then suddenly remembered someone. Someone I felt oddly protective of. This sense of responsibility. Where did it come from? Especially in me.

The road was deserted now. The rain stepped up a grade and became thicker. Harder. As I pulled away from the diner I was thankful for my great piece of American steel. The car continuously wanted to pull to the right as I forced my way into the swamps and Esther's territory. My hands were fixed to the wheel and fighting the wind. I wondered where Red was and why he had left without a word. That stayed on my mind until I managed to get to the house. I knew from experience that Ruby had picked up speed across the water. The gusts were too strong for her to be too far away. Soon the outermost reaches would begin sweeping their way across Toliquilah's sandy shores.

I entered without knocking. Esther spoke first. "I guess you be thinkin' we should have left by now." The roof rattled. The snakes slithered. The lights dimmed.

"Why do you bother turning on lights?" I asked.

"To confuse the snakes. That way they don't know day from night. Just me."

I said, "Let's go Esther."

Esther put on a coat that looked like part raincoat part life preserver, flipping the rubberized hood above her head. Then she pulled on rubber waders and declared, "I'm ready."

We trudged to the car through the standing water and as my tennis shoes became waterlogged I coveted Esther's boots. I was still coveting as the car tried to start and didn't. And again. The third time the engine turned over. In the back of my mind Kallie was saying, 'In Alabama...' with a sure-fire recipe for starting a waterlogged car during a deluge.

Then Esther said, "Sounds like your alternator's going."

I drove East with a sinking feeling in my gut.

"I don't think this thing be soundin' like a three." Esther's head was bent on listening.

"That's because it's not a three anymore." I swerved to miss a limb lying across the road. The air was alive with flying debris, the wind driving the rain like a river. Even with the windshield wipers on high, I could barely see a thing and drove by memory not by sight.

"The blind driving the blind." Esther was reading my thoughts. I supposed any more time together we'd be dreaming the same dreams. For a little while she was silent as the car fought its way to peace and safety. "Once there was a time," a smaller limb fell on the hood, was lifted by the next gust of wind and blown away, "when I could see something."

I rubbed my hand against the inside of the windshield to no avail. "Yeah, me too, and it doesn't seem that long ago."

"And I remember everything."

Esther knowing and remembering, then being thrust into darkness. I had never considered her any other way.

"When could you see, Esther?"

"Ago."

That summed it up with one word. *Ago*, Esther could see. *Ago*, my life was different. *Ago*, Joe was alive and I'd of tried to get him to swim in the growing waves to no avail. *Ago*, my father would be singing and me sitting by his feet and time would be standing still.

"How far have we come?"

"Not far enough." I answered.

The sand was pouring across the road in great headlong gusts as we passed the deserted diner and Lemuel's store with its hinged sign swinging madly in the air. I wondered where he and Agnes had gone and how far they'd gotten. In this storm, even Clark City would be half-deserted. I could see the waves now and they reached up in monstrous proportions that were fiercely attacking the seawall behind Lolly's cracked motel.

"How'd you lose your sight, Esther?"

"Snake bite."

"I didn't know it could make you go blind."

"It can make you anything," she said quietly.

I put on brakes and we came to a dead stop. A tree limb lay across the road making it impassable. The sand on both sides was deep. If I tried to go around we might get stuck and it wasn't a good time to get stuck.

"What has happen'?"

"Tree in the road."

"We'll pull it."

"You can't pull, you're too . . ." I wanted to say *old* but instead offered, "tiny."

"You still don't know nothin' 'bout me girl. This good body made to survive until done."

So with me leading Esther to lay her hands on the limb, we worked to clear the road. The rains poured against us, and at first we pulled to no avail. Then a pause, a breath between gusts, allowed us the ability to pull until there was a space large enough to cross.

"That's it," I yelled against Esther's ear. "Far enough."

Ruby wasn't just coming in at a four, she was roaring her way toward us, gaining momentum. The car lurched sideways and I pulled hard to the right to counter balance. Then we were almost over, but instead of crossing the No-good, I stopped, rubbed the windshield, then my eyes. Then I held my hand against my mouth.

"What be the problem now, Child?"

I felt strangely abandoned. "The bridge is gone, Esther."

I slowly opened the door and got out. The water had rushed up high enough now that it would have been upon it. Fifteen years ago it would have stood. But the stress from the traffic, the wind, the waves, the time had finally given way and the No-good was no more. Behind me Esther stood holding onto the car door looking out over what she couldn't see. At what was no longer there.

*

Esther sat in the booth Edna and I kept for ourselves. She looked smaller than usual. Tiny and out of place. "I have never been in this place."

"The lights are still working." I readied the matches, lined up the candles. "Are you hungry, Esther?"

"Yessssss."

The beans were still warm to the touch and I spooned some into a bowl for her. Then I put on coffee while there was still power and listened to Esther eating and the wind attacking the building.

"Looks like she didn't want to let us go," Esther said between mouthfuls, her head held low over her bowl.

"Who, Ruby?"

"No. I not be meaning the storm." She paused, looked towards the pounding sound, "Maybe that's true, too, but I was speaking of the island."

"Why would the island want to murder its own?"

"Not to murder, girl, just to keep."

The wind hit the south side, swirled, and sucked at all the hidden cracks in the diner walls. I closed my eyes, imagining the surf line. I didn't want to tell Esther what I thought. I didn't want to argue with her or tell her that chances were good that there wasn't going to be anything left of us for the island to keep. We were trapped and I couldn't think of another place for us to hide out on Toliquilah. The diner was built of concrete. It was my only hope.

"The boy offered to bring me here but I always be tellin' him, *No.*"

"What boy?"

Esther was quiet, laid her spoon aside, listened to the wind. "The Joe boy."

"Then you knew one another."

"I said he was my boy. I meant he was my boy."

"That could mean a lot of things, Esther."

I poured myself a coffee, offered Esther one. She said *No* and began amidst the wind and sound of scouring sand to unravel the veil of her past relationship with a boy I knew everything about and then again, suddenly, nothing.

"Somebody on this place steady to be takin' care of me."

"Taking care of you how?"

"Bring me my food, girl. Sack of rice. Loaf of bread. Check the generator. Carry away what needs be."

"Who then?"

"After my mother died, Percy Falls, on account he be livin' on up past her. Then he come when Percy die. Be surprising me by it too, but I not say not thing to him."

"Who?"

"Your father."

My head spun in her direction.

"Come clean to my door and say, 'Percy send me.' And I say, 'Percy dead.' And he said, 'He send me just the same,' and I don't argue no more with him that day."

"How long did Black Jack do this thing?"

"Back before you was born and then beyond till he was no more."

The vision of Black Jack's truck floated up before me. Then the swamp. Followed by a shot. A scream.

"Who came next?"

"Joe's mother. Then after her, the Joe boy, 'cause he knew about me."

"And you became friends."

"More than this thing, friends. I counted him as my own 'cause he was of a different nature. Like me but not the same." Esther was quiet, somehow looking out over the past. "The Joe boy have a good spirit."

And on this we did agree.

"So you knew my father and my Joe."

"Yesssss."

"Then you knew the best of me."

"You got your own good side, Gin Girl."

"What's with the gin girl, Esther?"

"Listen here," Esther leaned her head back against the booth, closed her eyes, "I'll sing you a snatch of an old song I do know." Then she began to sing off key a familiar nursery rhyme. "Catch me, catch me if you can, but you can't catch me 'cause I'm the gingerbread man."

"Thanks a lot Esther; that really clears things up for me."

The wind hit the diner hard, shaking it to the foundation. Days and nights of drinking the strange teas of Esther's were running through my veins. My eyes blurred, then refocused.

"But they did catch him, now, didn't they?"

"I don't remember."

"Sure you be remembering. And they catch the thing because he want something. Now what he be wantin' so bad that make him stupid?"

"A ride."

"Yesss. See you remember. He got stupid and he got caught in a trap."

"A gin, I said."

"A gin." Esther smiled. The workings of her mind formulated and floated to the surface of my understanding. I was the gin girl and out there somewhere stalked the animal that needed trapping. All I needed to do now was discover the animal and locate the bait. And survive.

"Tell me about your time with my father."

"No thing to tell. He was quiet. Didn't talk none. Didn't lie any. Always come on time. Leave the same way."

"Why'd you save her?"

Esther sat very still. Maybe like me she had looked back over the years and seen what the difference might have been.

"It was what I was born for. What was I to do. Be denying that, girl?"

We sat without speaking while I weighed Esther's destiny and my mother's potential death against my father's wasted life.

"No. I guess not."

I pulled two quarters from the cash register and played K-5, Buckwheat Zydedco, and asked Esther if she had any particular requests to which she replied, "Not today," so I punched A3 then and I made myself a ham sandwich and lit a candle and sat down again with Esther. Three-quarters of the way through the sandwich and halfway through Patsy Cline the power went out, and I ate by candlelight with Esther humming "Crazy" under her breath and me feeling that way.

"You know that boy be lovin' you and always want for you to come home."

"I know."

"I told him you couldn't 'cause of what your father did."

"It wasn't on account of him, Esther." The candle caught wind drafts from the cracks and shuddered, "It was on account of me."

"But you couldn't be stopping what come, Girl."

"I almost did. Fifteen seconds, Esther. I must have found him fifteen seconds before it happened."

"Then you saw the doin' of it."

"It was dark. I came home. Found my mother sitting in the living room. Just sitting. Heard the clock ticking on the wall. Ticking. Second to second. That's when I knew and I ran as fast I could to my car. Drove to where I knew he would be. Saw the truck. It was raining and I left my lights on and jumped from the door and started running. I ran, Esther. Hard. But then . . . " my voice crawled to a whisper.. "Why do you think he'd go on and do it? With me there, you know? With me there?"

"He didn't see you, girl. He done be in a different place. That man never seen you."

"It was sunrise before I let him go. Had him stuck to me—had to pull his head away. Then finally drove to find Joe. Don't remember much for awhile. Except that clock and hearing it ticking and me thinking twelve hours and forty-two minutes ago my father was alive. Twelve hours and forty-three minutes ago my father was alive. That lasted awhile."

"Different day," Esther said. "It don't matter, gonna be the same sad story to no good end."

"No good," I said swallowing hard. Then I thought of the No-good and got up and refilled my cup before the coffee got any colder.

"That Ruby's not goin' to eat you, girl," Esther was reading my thoughts again.

"Who says?"

"You got to be the Gin Girl and make right." Esther laughed.

I paced the floor, placed my hands against the walls, felt the impact of wind. I turned to look at the tiny shape of Esther in the candlelight. She was nothing more that a penumbra. More light than darkness, more shadow than light. I wanted to place her somewhere, a shelf, a corner, a cabinet. Someplace safe where Ruby couldn't reach her. We were in the midst of the hurricane now. And Ruby was raging and letting us know it.

"Who came up after Joe, Esther?"

"That man."

"Which one?"

"The one with the funny talk to him."

"Lemuel."

"No. Lemuel comes as customer only."

"Customer?" I said, raising my brows, "for what?"

"He drinks the milk."

I sat back down with the news. It felt good to be diverted. To be surprised by common talk.

"A little every day. He believes it makes him . . . stronger."

Lemuel drinking snake's milk. Maybe it's why he was able to marry Agnes. He was immune to her bite.

"How could you ever know what he thinks?"

"I listen to him like I listen to you, girl. I just don't be expectin' his words in your order. They come in through the back door."

The secret at last and too late. All the incentive speeches of Lemuel that had washed over me that I might have understood. It was probably better that I never knew, in case those moments of his passionate speaking had been directed in anger towards me.

"Full of venom is he?"

"Should be by now." Esther's fingers shot out in the darkness as though she were catching an insect.

"Wonder if his wife knows?"

Esther coughed twice, made ready to get up, "Only if he wants her to." She pulled from the booth and stood leaning on her cane. "I am tired."

"There's nowhere to go, Esther."

"I know." She walked a few steps, her cane out in front of her, then turned towards me, "They think I know who kilt Joe."

"Who?"

"The ones who did it."

"Who are the ones?"

THE GIN GIRL

"I don't know, but they think I do."

She turned back again and walked toward the door as though she would walk out to leave, but once there she turned and began pacing her way back to me.

"Why would they think that?"

"Cause I told 'em I seen it when it happened."

"Seen it?"

"Over and over. Seen it in my dreams." She reached me, laid her hand on the table, stopped, turned again and walked towards the door. "I got sick of seeing it. I can tell you this thing is truth. Joe driving over the No-good, driving up in that place, waiting on something. Looking at his watch. Waiting. Tapping his fingers on the steering wheel. Looking at his watch again."

"What was he waiting for, Esther?"

She turned back to me halfway there, "I don't know." Then she resumed the path of her pacing.

"Then I seen this body coming up in the dark, off to the side, only Joe's fingers tapping on the wheel and he don't see no thing. This body pulling something from the pocket of its coat." She turned and made her way, cane first, back towards me. The candle fought, flickered, threatening to go out. I started to reach for another one but left it where it sat.

"Then the hand pulled a gun out and Joe's hands were tapping and then—" Esther pulled up at the table, leaned on her cane "—they stopped."

"Why didn't you tell me this before?"

"What chu gonna do with it?"

"I don't know. Did you see the man's face?"

"No. But somebody thinks I did."

The candle died in silence and we stood still in darkness fresh for me and old for Esther, and I understood the intensity of her perceptions. The clarity of all that was real to her. Pure. Unadulterated by the millions of tiny visual inputs that fought for my attention. Esther's vision was one long lucid dream.

"I told the man about the dream. Him and the other one."

"What man?"

"The one on the phone. The policeman."

"Ahhh, Esther. Maybe that wasn't a good man to tell." Then I recounted to Esther the years gone by. About Joe and Jimmy and me. And I went on to tell her about Moses and the file and Peggy Sue Cusler and the baby and all that had happened so far.

"No policeman shot Joe."

"Maybe not," I said, "but maybe he knows who did." And we let this thought hang between us and Esther sat down in the darkness. I fumbled for the other candle and lit it. The building shook again. Somewhere outside something was falling. It was something big crashing in amongst itself and I wanted to look but couldn't.

"I think the water's getting close, Esther."

Then she said, "Me too," and we sat still in the middle of Ruby, listening to her scream, picturing all the while the high tide crashing around and sucking down the motel of Lolly Eden.

"Who's the other man, Esther? Who doesn't speak well?"

"Man be speaking fine, just different."

"Different in what manner."

"Different in his manner of speaking."

She was still elusive when it came to a straight answer.

"Different like what, Esther?"

"I say maybe he be different, like me."

Esther's speech was broken and rambling at times, sometimes I had to think like her to understand and other times it was as lucid as her dreams. Mostly, it was a motley mixture of blended accents from ancient worlds. I never tried to figure her origin because to me it never mattered. Her origin was Toliquilah. Then my understanding of Esther's thinking increased, doubling over itself until eventually in the end my seeing was the way of Esther's. Without looking.

"The Spanish man."

"Yessss."

"Manuel Garcia Marquez."

"Yessss."

"How would he know? Why would he come?"

"He told me," Esther's fingers reached out in a repetitive run as though she were playing an absent piano, "that the Joe boy sent him."

I narrowed my eyes in the darkness.

"But Manuel only docked here this year."

"No. Has been coming."

My mind worked the avenues of Manuel and Esther, his taking care of her, working his way back into the swamps. I tried to remember the things he had told me. They were few and far between.

"He isn't always here."

"No, not always. More times he is here where nobody sees." Esther played the absent piano again with her right hand held in the air. "And when he is not, that other boy come that does not talk much. The sad one."

"Who is this?"

"I don't know but sometimes he is late and then I wait."

The building shook again, the impact more furious. It was a constant rhythm now. By sheer instinct I looked around for higher ground knowing there wasn't any.

"If you hold that snake by the back of the head he can't bite you."

"That's good, Esther." My mind wasn't thinking snakes. It was thinking survival.

"None of them can bite you if you hold 'em by the back of the head like this." She suddenly reached out and grabbed my hand and held it in an iron clad trap bending it up, palm out, my fingers pointed at myself. "Listen here, no matter what they tell you with all their weaving and their hissing, they're full of lies. They can't bite you if you hold 'em tight behind the head."

"Thank you, Esther. I'll remember that." It wasn't the time to tell her I had no plans to be touching her snakes. The water hit the building again harder. I had never seen a tidal surge reach this far. I wanted to rip the boarding from the windows so I could see what lay outside. If the water had hit the glass it would have broken. Right now it was content to be working the south side of the diner, which was solid concrete. I picked up the candle and carried it to the wall. A tiny crack, almost imperceptible, ran halfway up. I put my hand against the wall, felt the dampness and sucked in my breath. At the same time Ruby sucked in hers and the wind died. I turned with the candle in my hand. "The eye."

"Yessss."

Esther slid to the side of the booth as though she might rise but simply leaned on her cane. I thought of the shape of Ruby's eye. I wondered which side we were falling into now.

"Now she be watchin' us."

Esther pushed herself up and walked towards the door.

"Let me out."

"No."

"Open up this thing and let me breathe, girl."

"Ruby's out there."

"Yessss. And I am trapped in here."

It did feel trapped. With the windows boarded it felt like slow death by suffocation. Esther turned back to me leaning heavily. "I am tired."

"Me too, Esther."

Then we stood a fair distance apart waiting for something to change or for something to change us. Nothing happened to alter any course of events we might choose and Esther said simply, "Open." Then she paused and added, "Please."

Partly due to the *please* and partly due to my mounting claustrophobia, I crossed the space between us and turned the silver key.

CHAPTER TWENTY-FOUR

The air outside was thick and silent. Full of secrets and a knowledge Ruby wasn't sharing, as though she were playing hide-and-seek. The palms too were still but not the waves. They were lashed now into a frenzy and still feeling the impetus of Ruby's determination. There would be no sleep for them tonight.

The water had crossed beyond the motel, which in the darkness looked small and forlorn, floating like an ancient ruin set adrift. Only part of the building was visible below the rising water line. Presently, our feet stood on dry ground but a few yards beyond us the water was making its way around the south side of the building.

"She be watchin' us, this Ruby." Esther was right. There was a presence, as though Ruby indeed had a particular interest in our movements and was watching each one of them very carefully. "I don't be carin' what she thinkin', I'm in my place to be here." And she was right. Our standing there in the calm midst of certain destruction seemed the most natural thing in the world. As though we were out for a gentle walk in the evening air. Except for the sounds, which were missing like the moon, everything seemed normal.

"Where did the birds go, Esther?"

"Away."

Esther's head jerked to the side. "Somebody's comin'."

I didn't question Esther but looked hard through the watery shapes.

Then I spotted a figure floating in our direction. Then the figure became a man. Then the man, even from a great distance, became Red Mahoney. No one else could be so tall.

"It's Red Mahoney," I said.

Esther's back tightened along with her lips.

"Why don't you like him?"

"Like's not the point. He's come to carry you away." And she said this with a mixture of sadness at the sound of some unknown wrong in her mind.

"Carry the both of us, Esther."

"Not now, Gin Girl, but farther still." Esther sighed then and relaxed on her cane. The shape of Red was a hard breath away. "You gonna have to choose, and everythin' gonna matter to which—"

"Red."

He was strained almost beyond recognition. "We only have a few minutes," he said between gasps for air.

"How did you know we were here?"

"No time to talk now. Ruby's eye is big but not big enough, if you know what I mean."

I did and the old words of Percy ran through my brain. 'It's the back side of a 'cane that'll kill you.'

"How's the diner holding?" he asked.

"Water's hittin' the south side hard. Crack in the wall."

"Will she last?"

I looked back over my shoulder at the water. "I don't think so."

Esther remained silent as Red pondered the matter, running his fingers through his hair. His beard had been growing back but was just at the ruddy stage. His eyes surveyed Lolly's motel. Then Lemuel's store. Then he locked his eyes on me. "You got a key to Lemuel's?"

"No."

"We don't have a choice but to try to reach the boat."

"Where is she?"

"Back side of the island. She may get shoved up into the swamps so far I can't get her out, but she won't sink."

We both looked at Esther and mentally measured the distance.

"Esther." This was the first word Red had spoken to her, and she slowly turned her head toward him with no expression. "You're gonna have to ride my back."

And so she did. Looking like a small child up on the back of Red Mahoney with her arms wrapped about his neck. Me holding her cane in my right hand and the three of us at a fast jog trying to cover the distance between us and what was probably only marginally better coverage. The sky stayed heavy, watching. We dodged the debris on the road as best we could but it was now like picking our way through a forest. Twice I fell, once hitting myself in the eye with Esther's cane. Red never stumbled but ran like an Olympian carrying the torch. At some point Esther mumbled, "tired" and laid her head across Red's bouncing back and dozed off to sleep.

There was, after this moment, a long awareness as if I were running in the dream. Of sounds which were mostly absent. Of the feeling of Ruby holding her breath and watching all things. The unnatural stillness. The unnatural light. The sense of hurry and forever meeting together. The constant padding of our feet, the constant rhythms of our bodies, Esther's fallen head riding Red without complaint, the swamp side docks rising up in sight. They were rarely used anymore and were worn and unstable. The boat was in view and we were almost there.

Almost. Then the back side of Ruby showed up with an attitude that flattened the three of us to the ground. Red and Esther went tumbling together as though they were a turtle and his shell. I rolled almost in the opposite direction, eating ground limbs and flying debris as I went. The water came back with the wind. It was wet and stinging and what the wind couldn't do to blind me, the water gladly made up in the difference.

"Mary." Red sounded as though he were miles away, not a few feet. "Mary." His hand was a vise on my shoulder as he pulled me into the shelter of his presence and the two of us crawled by inches, lacing our fingers between the pier boards to pull ourselves toward the bouncing whiteness of the boat that lay ahead. It seemed a lifetime before we crossed the deck, sliding on the wetness of its surface and tumbled into the cabin.

Then Red and I lay panting on the floor like wet dogs, but Esther lay silent. Still. I crawled towards her and touched her small frame and realized she wasn't breathing. I lifted the lids of her eyes by instinct but the whiteness that stared back at me in death was the same that had stared at me in life.

"Red?"

He listened for her heartbeat as I tried to find a pulse.

There was neither. Then Red began to apply pressure to the tiny frame that surrounded her heart, but I pulled his hand away.

"Tired." I said and he understood. We sat with the boat rocking wildly beneath us, as Esther lay dead before us. The wind shifted and sent the boat twisting bow to stern over and over again in a three-sixty spin. Esther's body rolled into me and Red screamed, "Hold on!" But there was nothing to hold onto as the boat crashed repeatedly into the worn dock, which gave way and began dropping planks just as the No-good must have. I wrapped my arms around Esther's tiny body as though I could protect her in death from what I could not in life, but the two of us only rolled into one hard surface after another until I heard a resounding crack. Then with a sickening feeling I realized, the crack had come from within my own head.

CHAPTER TWENTY-FIVE

I was walking on great stones atop the water. Spaced so far that with a healthy jump I could reach the next one. They were laid out before me in one direction. An irregular bridge leading to something. Then the stones became the large ridged backs of alligators as they lay smiling in the sun, allowing me safe passage. I jumped from one ancient back to the next without stopping until, nearing the end, there appeared two familiar shapes, those of my father and of Joe. Joe turned to my father and said, "She'll be alright," and my father said "I know," but the voices came from a distant fog reminding me of something, somewhere else.

"Mary."

The voice grew sterner. Closer.

"Wake up now." This from a different voice and my father and Joe were gone and the alligators too, and suddenly the swamp dried up and I was standing in my bare feet, the muddy bottom sucking at my toes.

I opened my eyes to the huge one-sided face of Edna.

"They've drained the swamps," I said. Then I fell back to sleep. At some point in and out of consciousness, the reality of Edna beside me and Wallace P. Ketchum behind my head began to settle itself into whatever membrane might have survived. My right eye was swollen completely shut, my left barely able to open, and my head was trying to rip itself wide open or off my neck whichever came first.

"I'm gonna be sick."

Edna nodded and tried to help me roll to my side. Then she wiped my mouth while Wallace explained in his most medical voice, "You've got a pretty nasty concussion."

"Where's Red?"

"Whittling." It was Edna's matter of fact voice but the information didn't make any sense.

"What?"

"I said he's whittling. See for yourself." Then she pointed off toward my right but my head refused to follow it.

"Esther didn't make it."

"We know."

"You can't take her back." The nausea was rising up from my stomach again and I felt a familiar blackness rising with it.

"Take her back where?"

"To Clark City." Then I heaved but there was nothing left. "No report."

"Don't tell me you want to take her out to Church Street."

"No death report."

The two of them didn't seem disagreeable, yet they weren't commenting one way or the other.

"Promise me."

"That woman's gonna have to be buried." Wallace tried to offer something of rational insight.

"Yessss. But not so nobody knows it." I squeezed Edna's hand for all it was worth. "Some people cannot know. Not yet." And I closed my eyes and left it all in the lap of Edna's mercy and understanding without an explanation because I was beyond making one.

"We're gonna check you now for broken bones," Wallace informed me, maintaining his most medical intonation. Then he inventoried my bones beginning with my feet and ankles, reporting to Edna as though he were the doctor and Edna his trusted nurse. I was more concerned with the pain in my head than anything else that might be broken until they reached my left wrist which seemed to let out a scream of its own.

"I believe we have a break here." Wallace was looking at Edna. "It'll need to be x-rayed." She nodded.

"Not until Esther's buried."

I forced myself to raise my head and will my eyes open. Red's boat lay on its side up against the mud and swamp bushes. A hole had been driven through the side by an old pier piling that was still wedged there. Red sat on the crooked deck, his great legs bent, his knees almost as high as his head, and he was, to the best of my ability to see, whittling. I had never known Red to whittle anything in my entire life. It seemed a funny time to pick up a new hobby. He stopped what he was doing and looked up.

"There she is." It was a salutation of sorts. A crooked way of acknowledging that I was still alive.

"Moses?" I asked Edna.

"He's at the diner." Then she added, "Him and Kallie."

I wanted to ask about the bridge. How they came to be here. How they had found us. But my body wouldn't cooperate with my mental agenda. Then Wallace changed the subject. "This ground's too wet for burying anything." Wallace looked at Edna, then carried his eyes across what looked like burned out ground. "We could tag her unknown," he motioned to the blanketed body of Esther, "hold her at the morgue."

I leaned into Edna's eyes the way a lame friend would lean on a shoulder.

"I don't think so, Wallace." She squeezed the hand with the broken wrist and I winced but didn't yell, "We're gonna have to think of something else."

*

Esther's funeral was scheduled the same day, more for the purpose of getting me to the hospital than for the propriety of the situation. My strongest words spoken were, "If anyone speaks, if anyone asks, she's still alive." And that summed up the best I had to offer.

Moses had cleaned up the best he could from lugging concrete block pieces out of what use to be the south wall as Kallie tried to push the water out with a broom. The tables and chairs had been politely stacked by Ruby against the inside wall. They rose up to the ceiling.

I was lying across the bar out of the way of the water and the salvage process. Moses leaned in across my face with warm heavy breath.

"I'm sorry."

"You didn't do anything wrong," I said.

"I could have waited."

"It wouldn't have been the wise thing to do."

From somewhere I could hear the raspy voice of Lolly Eden, "Ain't nothin' but a scratched-out shell. All the work I put in for nothing."

Moses leaned in closer. "It's a good thing Red got you out."

"Where is he?"

"Outside now." He looked toward where Red must have been standing. "Just staring out at the waves." Then he looked back to me. "I think he's in shock."

From somewhere I could hear Lemuel's mutterings, the voice of Agnes saying "Oh Lem," over and over again.

"If you'd've stayed here all night Ruby would have killed you like Esther."

"Ruby didn't kill her." I put my hand across my face to shield it from the light. "She just closed her eyes."

"Red and I are gonna strap something together to hold her up."

"That's good, Moses." I could see the gators smiling.

"Mary. Mary." He was shaking me gently. "Wallace says you can't go to sleep. Not yet anyways."

I raised my eyebrows to pull my forehead up. One eye stayed closed, the other one lay unmoved by the exercise.

"Sure, Moses." It was an all out lie. Sleep was the strongest thing on my mind.

"Hey, Kallie."

"Hey." The roundness of her came and stood by my side, broom in hand. Her closeness had an odd medicinal effect.

"Talk to Mary to keep her awake," Moses said, then he left.

Kallie stepped forward, propped her broom against the bar and began to ever so gently, smooth the hair from around my forehead, rubbing her fingers along my temples and speaking to me about things back in Alabama that today I could not remember more than this: A woman named Mary, a farm, and a cow called Nellie Bell Bly that decided to come home.

*

The cove was as wet as the swamps but not as muddy. A platform had been fashioned from the plywood that had boarded the windows to hold Esther's tiny frame. Moses read from his Bible. And I, determined to be standing, was held vertical by Wallace and Edna. Gasoline siphoned from the tank of my car was poured over the remains and I questioned if enough pure gasoline was left to start a fire, but even in the midst of what felt like all the wet water in the world Esther's remains held a growing flame and she was put to rest through cremation.

The smoke rose gently at first, then in a fury, making a fist that shook its way high into the blueness of a clear warm sky.

As the last ashes fell we left them there in the wet, wet world and started a peculiar caravan down Hwy 2 toward what was left of Joe's diner. We moved among one another as shipwrecked survivors, both frightened and yet supremely amazed at our good fortune. We were a remnant of a great storm and we were destitute and wounded and confused. Yet, we were thankful for the hand of another breathing soul, even one offered with the same quiet desperation. And we walked the rest of those miles tattered and uncertain and quiet beneath the bright blueness of the sky, each of us smelling like seawater and the smoke of Esther's late perfume. I will never forget this smell: the water, the smoke and Esther all mixed up together. It was this smell in my nostrils, the cushion of Edna's side, the sight of Red's bending back, I last remembered before there was nothing else.

CHAPTER TWENTY-SIX

I felt movement before I could see it. Heard the metallic sound of machines breathing. When I opened my eye, as it were, there was a flash of white. A curtain pulled between me and the breathing thing. I lay hospital-bound with an IV pushed into the vein along the back of my left hand. My head was still splitting. Nothing felt the way it should have. Then my eye turned to find Edna's huge frame forced into a chair half her size.

"How . . ." the words got stuck, my throat a thick foreign entity. "How . . . " Then Edna poured me a cup of water from a plastic pitcher. I tried to take a sip.

"How long have I been here?"

"Two days. You've been awake some. Mostly not."

I didn't remember anything except alligator dreams. Wind, water.

"They wanted to check you for bleeding inside. You picked up some bad bruises. Cracked a couple of ribs. Ruby must of thrown you around like a rag doll."

"Esther's gone."

"Yes. I know."

An unbelievable thing. A snuff of breath. "She was just here."

"I know," Edna said again.

"My father was like that. Here and gone."

"Mine, too." Edna pulled back a piece of curtain, stared down into what had to be nothing but a concrete parking lot.

"He died?"

"He was gone before he died." She dropped the curtain, turned back to me with a smile. "Never saw him again after I was five."

"My father was gone before he died." My throat scratched, broke up. Edna came and brought the cup of water back to my lips, adjusting the straw. "She ate him up."

Edna put the cup down, stared down at me hard.

"Then he let her." I didn't say anything. "Nobody eats somebody up unless they let'em you hear me? You keep blamin' that white woman for him dyin', but he could've left her. Oh, yes, he could've. Don't roll that eye at me. People can make a choice when they got to. You got to cut loose and go on ahead and do what you got to do. Don't tell me 'cause I know."

Edna was breathing down on me like a freight train full of admonition. My brain wasn't clear enough to think. It wanted to drift aimlessly. Stay down low somewhere in dreams where there was no dying. I didn't know what had triggered her anger. Or for that matter, what might have happened while I had been unconscious for days. She sucked in a breath, walked back to the window, lifted the curtain, looked out once and dropped it again in disgust at something that wasn't there.

"Did you kill your husband, Edna?"

"No." She paused, skipped a beat between breaths, "But I could have."

"If you didn't kill him, why did you go to jail?" My head was splitting again. I closed my eyes to shut out the light.

"They weren't sure."

"No, I guess not." Then I thought about Edna and her husband and years of living together. Of cold nights and conversations in the dark. "How do you kill something you've lived with and loved?"

"Now, that's something you should have asked your mother a long time ago."

And with that Edna summed up what had been twisting in me all these years. The unasked questions. Why did you marry him? Why did you hate him?

*

The morning light came through the curtained window. Leaning next to it, as though he might have been looking out over a great Mediterranean pass at sea, was the lanky body of Red Mahoney. I hadn't moved or uttered a sound so he didn't know that I was awake. I lay watching his frame tilted against the wall and the sight of him was a great comfort. It was like Joe's smile. Things that made me feel whole and safe. I didn't understand Esther's feeling towards him. Regardless of what she said, he was my friend. I wouldn't lay that aside. He turned slightly, looked over towards me, then held my one eye good in his.

"Good morning." He stayed against the wall, talking softly from a distance. "You look better."

"Compared to what?"

"Compared to yesterday and the day before."

I started to move my right hand to my face and for the first time I realized I was wearing a cast up to my forearm. I was still good at overlooking the obvious. The IV in my left hand throbbed now beneath a growing bruise.

Red moved to the side of the bed, tilted his head to the right, then to the left, surveying the damage.

"You'll heal up alright."

"Thanks."

"I am sorry about the woman."

"She just died, Red. It wasn't your fault or mine. Now me, you probably saved my life."

"From the looks of you, you could stand saving again."

Then we both laughed, and my side hurt terribly, and I moved the throbbing left hand to cover the pain. The laughing died down and Red grew silent. And serious.

"I can save you again, you know."

"You could save me, if you could find me some clothes and get me out of here."

"Getting you out of here's what I mean."

"Well get me out; I'm more up for a jailbreak than I look. Believe me."

"No, Mary." And he reached out and grabbed the fingers that stuck through the plaster, "I mean," he ran his hand over his growing whiskers, "I am not good at this kinda thing." He said this more to himself and started over. "I mean get you out of here. Out of Florida."

"What?"

"My boat's trashed. There is nothing to keep me here but you."

I looked up at him still not fully comprehending the extent of his explanation.

"What I'm trying to say, Mary Contrary, is this," he squeezed the exposed fingers, "I'm moving to Montana. Come with me."

"Moving to Montana?"

"Yes."

"It sounds like a country song."

He paused, shuffled his long legs.

"I guess so, but it's not, it's the way of things."

"We're saltwater people, Red. You're a sailor, for goodness' sake. What's in Montana that could possibly pull you away?"

"Look, it's not what could pull me, it's what could hold me. I hear that there's wide open space for miles and miles just like the sea and listen, I don't mean come with me, Mary, I mean come be with me. In Montana."

He emphasized the *be with me*, and for the first time the depth of his intentions poured in.

"Red," I paused because there didn't seem to be the right words to tell him what I felt about him, "you have known me most of my life."

"And I would like to know you for the rest of it."

"I have always trusted you."

"Then trust me more. Come with me."

A vision of Montana rolled up before me. Lush green pushed up to the sky. Then in my mind's eye winter set in, and the green became a lake of ice.

"I don't like the cold, Red."

"Neither do I. But then again, I hate mosquitoes. Go figure."

Montana. Lots of air. My eye ran over the caged window. I liked air. In Montana with Red. Someone I trusted. Someone I could laugh with. It wasn't a horrible idea.

"I'm not saying yes, and I'm not saying no."

"Then I'll be waiting." He squeezed my fingers once more and let them go. Then he was gone. I wanted to call him back and say, *Wait, that's too cliché and you're not a cliché kind of a guy and I'm not a cliché kind of a girl.* However, it was an option. An unlikely option, but unlikely or not, cliché or not, it felt good to know someone was waiting. It felt good to have a way out.

*

I continued drifting in and out and remembered thinking, *Drugs.* They must be keeping me on drugs. Or maybe it's just my head. I slept deeply but fitfully with voices of faces that I could not see. Esther was always there trying to tell me something she had forgotten.

I opened my eyes. The face of Manuel Garcia was above me. His scar, an angry stain.

"I don't mean to scare you."

"Edna?"

"No. It's Manuel."

"I know who you are. Where is Edna?"

"The big woman? I have not seen her today."

Today. The word held more significance.

I knew I had been in a watery world of half-existence. I remembered whispers. Pieces of conversations. Needles in my arm. Being wheeled down a hallway. The face of Wallace P. Ketchum hovering over me. Voices in the dark. The dark shadow of Moses leaning by my bed. His head bowed. His hands folded. They were all sketches. More dream than reality.

The metallic sound of someone's machine still clicked on and off through the curtain.

"How is your friend, what is her name, the snake woman?"

"How did you know Joe?"

"We worked together."

"Joe would never do something illegal." Whoever lay on the other side of the curtain never moved, to the best of my knowledge had not muttered a word since I arrived.

"And you think maybe I do?"

"I don't know who you are. I don't know what you do. . . ." My eyes, both of them, began to search for something they could not find. The clicking grew louder. The silent shape through the curtain ominous. The walls closer.

"I am not an illegal man, Mary. I did work with Joe, but it wasn't what you might think."

"I don't think anything bad about Joe because he was not bad."

"Look at me, look. . . . Do I look like a bad man to you?"

I looked at the white scar along his face, the one on his throat, the bullet wound on his hand, another on his arm, the black of his eyes.

"So, maybe I look like a bad man, but you can't judge a book by its cover."

"How long have you lived in this country?"

"But I don't live, I go back and forth. Everyplace you see."

"You should speak better English."

Then Manuel did many things, almost, simultaneously. He dropped his head to his chest, walked to the other side of the room, around the curtain, walked closely to what I assumed to be my roommate of sorts, leaned in over the bed and breathed, "You don't hear a thing in this place, you understand me? Good." And the sound of his voice caused a chill of fear to spread over my body. The final gesture he made cemented the fear until it lay over my bed like a blanket of lead. He walked to the hallway and closed the door. As it slowly swung shut the audible noises in the hallway became muffled almost to a silence. Then he came back to the edge of the bed and stood close to my head.

"Do you remember the day we spent at the beach?"

"Yes."

"I told you I would tell you mostly the truth, did I not?"

I nodded my head.

"Now I take it you want . . . what you call it," he paused, searching for words he already knew, "the whole truth."

I nodded my head again. Oh yes, that elusive weaving web of truth. Reveal it, I wanted to scream. But I lay still. Expecting.

"My real name is Manuel Pasquez. My friends know me as Mike." The accent was almost gone, barely traceable back to the dark genes that gave him his black eyes. "Joe knew me by this name. Some years ago I spoke to him in regards to activities on the island."

"What activities?"

"Illegal trade. Property brought in, property brought out."

"If you tell me he helped you smuggle anything you might as well be dead with him because that would be nothing but lies."

"You must consider, my dear Mary, the other side of this game, to smuggle."

"He didn't do drugs, never touched them, wouldn't buy them or sell them."

"You're not listening to me." Manuel, Mike, whoever he was leaned across the metal bars of the bed railing. "Where there is smuggling, somewhere deep in the dark recesses of somebody's life, there is the hand of the law."

I looked at him hard then. Maybe for the first time. Listened to the clipped, dried pattern of his speech. Watched the way he forced the air away form his body by his very presence.

"You're a cop."

"More specifically, DEA."

"Beautiful. And you say Joe worked with you."

"Oh, he did work with me."

"Well that's where you're wrong, Mr. Identity, because Joe was never a snitch. Not in a million years."

"No. He wasn't. Matter of fact, if there was anybody alive that could keep a secret better than Joe, I wouldn't know who that would be."

I tried to put my hand to my eyes but when I lifted it I remembered the cast. The other one was tied by the tubes to the metal pole. My head was pounding. I began to cry, but I didn't know why. The more the tears welled up, the more angry I became.

"Not a druggie. Not a snitch."

"No Mary," he reached out and stopped my arm, lowering it to the bed, "not a snitch. He was a cop as you say. He was my partner."

I laughed like a person does when something incredulous has shown up to greet them. The man didn't laugh. He looked at me with a straight, unfeeling face.

"Regardless of how it doesn't fit into your memory of the way things were, it's the truth. But maybe it would make you feel better to know that, although you didn't know about me, I knew everything about you."

"I need to—"

"I knew about you as a little girl, I knew about your mother, about your father and the end of him. About your, what should we call it, travels? —What? You want something to drink?" He reached around for the water pitcher, began to pour a glass. "One time so long ago I even saw you, but you don't remember. You had come home to this place to have a nice visit. And you did, I remember, and this made him very happy. He was most sorry to see you go."

"I need—"

"Not water?"

I needed to know the real unveiled truth. I needed Joe's side of the story. And what was now going to become of me. How were we going to get home without the No-good? Was there a home left to go home to? Who was Joe? Surely he would have told me all these things. Surely. The air had begun to grow thin. I was taking great breaths now, my mouth opened wide.

"Maybe I should get you the nurse." Then he looked back over his shoulder from the doorway and added an unnecessary, "You wait here." The door opened and slowly closed on his receding frame.

I pulled the tape from the back of my hand, jerked once hard at the needle and was free. I could hear Manuel's accent return, lilting from somewhere down the hall. I pushed to the window, pulled back the curtain. It was covered with wire like a cage and the air was becoming tighter. I desperately searched for a latch, something to allow me to open the window, but there was nothing. Manuel's fake accent grew closer. A woman's voice. The sound of padded shoes. The shoes cleared the corner.

"Honey, get back in that bed—what?" She rushed to my side.

I pulled at the whiteness of her, pointed to my throat, tried to say, "Air" but there wasn't enough left for the words. Then it grew smaller. And smaller still. Then it was gone.

Esther stood beside my bed, her back unyielding, her cane in her hand.

"That was a mighty big storm, Yessss?"

I tried to sit up.

"Looks to me like Ruby has took a bite out of you. Well, makes no nevermind girl. A bite is one thing and eating something up is another. Besides which," she reached down and pulled a slithering black arrangement of small snakes from her pocket, "God makes an antidote for every evil thing. Oh no, don't try to speak. You not be speakin' now, you just be listenin." Then she leaned in over my bed, put her face close to mine, her eyes wide open. The snakes slithered and hissed. One was the color of an eclipsed moon, red beneath the black. "How long are you to be led by your flesh, Gin Girl, and not by your spirit? Answer me this thing. C'mon, the answer is right there." And she touched the center of my breast bone. "Now be holdin' these for me 'till I get back home." And she squeezed the snake heads into the palm of my hand. "Like this, lock 'em down good and don't be lettin'go." She squeezed the back of my wrist. I opened my eyes and she was gone. Instead Kallie was leaning in over my face, stroking my hair.

"You're awake now."

"Yesssss."

"I been thinking about Edna's arm and I think I know where it went."

"That's good, Kallie. Get me some clothes."

"You can't wear my clothes 'cause—"

"Try me."

And Kallie being the cooperative soul that she was, went down to her truck and brought back an old pair of cover-alls. "For working in the garden" she said, and a shirt that must have belonged to her grandfather.

When I pulled the IV from my hand for the second time she just said, "I don't think . . ." but with one hard look she changed her mind and said, "Well, alright then."

"Where's everybody?"

"Edna went with Moses to shovel out the diner."

"How come you stayed?"

"Somebody always's staying with you, Mary. We just take turns."

This surprised me. A lot. The days had faded in and out and then away.

"How are they getting across?"

"That old storm chaser McGurdy done opened up a ferry service. He's charging to get back and forth."

"McGurdy doesn't have a ferry."

"No. Just his little boat. Then—"

"But to the diner—"

"Then they get in your car, because Moses got it started and they've been driving back and forth to the diner and leaving it there where the bridge is gone."

"Kallie," I refused to cry. "It's more than nice of you, all of you, to try to watch out for me."

"Ain't nothing. Even Miss Lolly come and set up with you one time when we was all tired."

Luckily the cast fit through the big sleeve. "Kallie."

"Uh huh?"

"Don't ever again leave me alone and unconscious with Lolly Eden."

"Well alright but she don't—"

"OK, we're gonna go through the halls together very inconspicuously. Then we're going to get into your truck."

"You ain't supposed to be leaving."

"Actually," I pulled Kallie's hat from her head and fitted it over mine, "I believe I am."

The nurses' heads were bent to opened files and gossip as Kallie and I passed by the desk. I tried to walk faster, and my side complained from the inside out. Kallie brought up Edna's arm again which made it easy to say "Uh, huh," a few times and nothing more especially since I was more concerned with making it down the elevator and out the door at the moment than I was with the whereabouts of Edna's missing limb.

"Don't it seem like we were just here on account of Edna's leg?"

"It does."

"But we weren't cause look at everything that's done happened since then."

"That's true."

We stepped on the elevator as I thought I heard Manuel call my name. My pants legs were rolled up from the bottom. The shirt was rolled up at both wrists. I was moving inside the clothes twice as fast as they were. The elevator doors closed and I leaned against the inside wall. I placed the IV hand that was dripping blood in my pocket.

Kallie looked at the hand, then back to my face. "You're really not up for whatever you're doing, are you?"

"It doesn't matter," I said and stepped out into the freedom of the night.

CHAPTER TWENTY-SEVEN

Outside the sky was pushing purple. Great crimson with blue streaks that caused us both to stop and Kallie to say, "Would you look at that?" It was worth stopping for. The stars were already scattered, and even beyond the lightness of the purple they were visible. I put my hand to my side, caught my breath at the truck.

Kallie searched overhead. "These don't look like Alabama stars, these are from Florida." I didn't have the extra air to tell her the same stars were everywhere. Then she looked me in the eye before she helped me up inside. "You can tell the difference." She looked back up to the sky again, "There they dance. Here they're quieter."

And then I was certain that if I made it to Alabama anytime soon that fact would rest well with me; I could lean into the dancing stars when everything else seemed to be falling away.

By the time we reached Church Street the stars were out in full force and the purple was only a smoky blue haze against the night sky.

"What're we doing down here?"

"I'm not sure." I scoured the street for a familiar shape, a two-wheeled buggy, "Looking for somebody, I think."

"What do they look like?"

"I don't know."

"Is it a man or a woman?"

"I'm not sure. A man I think."

"This might take awhile."

She wasn't being smart. Just Alabama factual.

We slowly drove to the end of the street. A few trees were uprooted. The south side of the apartment building was leaning questionably.

"Do you think they still live in that thing?"

"Yes. Park at the end, Kallie. I don't know what else to do."

And I didn't. I tapped my fingers against the roof of the truck but they felt hot and swollen where the cast wrapped around them. I stopped tapping.

"Alright, Esther, here I am, back on Church Street, what's next?"

Kallie looked at me but said nothing.

Then clear as a voice that calls you awake I heard "Church."

"You say something, Kallie?"

"Nope."

"I didn't think so." I twiddled my fingers across the back of my lips, "Me neither."

"What's that?"

"I said, 'Me neither.' "

"Oh."

We sat in the truck cab, the windows half down. For a little while I forgot everything. Forgot about the storm and Joe and Manuel and Red and Montana. For just a little while, the wind blew through the truck bed, and Kallie's presence was like nothing at all and yet something good to have around all at the same time. For a little while, it just felt good to be alive, to be free and smell the salty Gulf in the distance.

"Kallie?"

"Umhumm."

"What are you gonna do when this is all over?"

"I don't know. Do you?"

I paused, took a breath, held my casted fingers over the back of my left vein. "I'm not sure it'll ever be over, Kallie. Not for me, anyways."

"Oh, everything will be over on account of it's got to die and be born again."

I looked at her profile, smooth and polished like a fine stone. Small nose. Big eyes. Dark blue. Maybe just like the Alabama sky at night.

"Just like planting, you know. Everything's got a beginning and a growin' and a dyin'."

She had the finality of an eighty-year-old woman, a knowledge that reminded me of the secret places of Esther, yet I could see the outline of her eyes, her mouth. I doubted she had cleared the corner on thirty. Possibly not even twenty-five. I wondered what type of upbringing she'd had to bring her to this point, to this place of being the way she was. Then again, I hadn't spent a lot of time in Alabama. Maybe that's the way all Alabamians were.

"Kallie, I have to tell you," I looked out the window, at the shuffling shadows. In the distance they looked like dancing figurines at dusk. "I don't like the dying part."

"Sometimes, it's OK. And sometimes," her voice changed an octave, "sometimes, it can be ugly." I looked back at her face, at her eyes looking at something beyond the darkness. "Then it's not like planting, or harvesting, or dying. It's like a butcher slaughtering your sheep."

An enigma. Everything about her suggested somewhere else. Some other place. Some other time. On the forefront she was the epitome of innocence. Of eyes filled with the dreams of every childhood wish. Of a kindness only to be found in those with simple hearts and minds. A purity. On the backside of her was a hard-learned lesson in some hidden place maybe never to be uncovered. It was a side of her I had left untouched but now a crack had surfaced and exposed a sleeping part of Kallie.

"That's what happened to your Joe," she turned and looked at me with a different set of eyes, "not a good and natural thing at all. But a great lie. Like rotten cotton. From a distance it looks like a great promise. All fields of white are full of promise. But when you get up close, it's rotten to the core. Falls apart in your hands like a flat dream. Not enough substance left to lift it out."

"What are you made from, Kallie?" I had meant to ask her what made her the way she was but it came out right and wrong at the same time.

"Alabama."

"Beyond that. Not where you're from."

She sighed, rubbed her round thigh, looked away and back again. "What's left of all the rest of 'em. I guess it rolled up into me."

"The rest of who?" The back of my hand hurt. It was getting too dark to pick out the shapes of the walking bodies. Besides which, I didn't know what I was looking for, and I was beginning to feel sick to my stomach.

"The rest of all them dead people I belong to."

A knock on the lower part of my window jerked me sideways towards Kallie.

"Heyheyhey. Didn't mean to make you jump."

It was our friendly John.

"Hey. I remember you." He stressed the *remember* heavily, "I do. I remember."

"We remember you too, John."

"Shooooot. And you even remembers my name. Well, hey now ain't that a thang." Then he stuck his head up to the half open window, "Hey. You look … beat up."

"Well, yeah."

"Did Mad Molly get ahold of you?"

"No."

"On account of 'cause she's a mean one, I tell you. Seen her bite a feller's earlobe off, and you know what for?" He staggered back and caught himself with wide eyes and staggered forward again. "They was fightin' over a thang. Wasn't no big deal to me but they was," his voice dropped, breathed in, stayed low, "Fightin' over it. Plenty of blood from that ear. It was every place. Smeared clean over to his nose and back again and Molly, well look here, she must have had a mouthful."

My stomach heaved and I opened the door to throw up, only there wasn't anything in my stomach, so I heaved instead and my ribs felt like they broke in half.

"Well hey, look here on account of . . . awww look here, I give it to you, wanta see, look here. On account you been beat up and got sick and everything like that. Look here. I give something to you."

Kallie passed me a napkin and said, "I think we better get you back."

John pressed a wadded something into my hand.

"I don't even care, 'cause it ain't mine no way."

I opened my hand. Unwadded a moist one dollar bill. Pulled it closer to my face and tried to read by the moonlight.

"Oh you wanta see, look here I got a, someplace I got a . . ." John struck a match and the tiny light shook with his hand as he held it out. "See, it's a dollar. Not much of nothing but it's all I got, and you lookin' like you be needin' all somebody gots 'cause on account of . . ."

And I didn't hear the rest of it as my eyes were fixed on the words scrawled across the dollar in red ink. They read, "Great shrimp! Way to go Joe!"

This time I heaved between my legs.

"Maybe you orda take her someplace on 'cause on account . . . hey, she been drinking?"

"No, she's not drinking."

"You think maybe she needs a drink, 'cause I can take that dollar to Mr. Hopper down there and get a cup—"

"Where did you get this?" I tried to reach out and grab him but the cast wouldn't allow it. He fell backwards from instinct.

"I didn't do nothing."

Kallie asked, "What is it?" But there was no room in me to answer.

"I swear, 'cause on account of it's the truth. I just picked it up."

My first reaction was to chase him down and beat him with my cast to a bloody pulp. The second was to try to talk him back within reaching distance. I tried to make my voice sound kind. Patient. It came out trapped. Tense.

"Look, John," I tried again. "Look, John it's nothing, just a dollar, it's just that," I searched for the words, "it reminded me of something from a long time ago. It's okay."

He eyed me with a rueful suspicion.

"Honest. You didn't do a bad thing."

He started back towards the window.

"Well that's good," a step, "'cause I wouldn't be meaning nobody no bad thing," and another step, "on account of—" I shot my left hand out the window, clutched his throat with a grip fueled perversely with the power of insanity, "Listen here, that dollar belongs to a dead man, and unless you tell me right now where you got it I'm gonna blow a hole in you the size of Texas before you can clear the corner."

"No bad thing." He choked, grabbed at my hand. It refused to let him go.

"You want me to hold him down," Kallie offered, ever the ready worker. I liked her attitude.

"Got on ground." John was still choking and my hand was beginning to remember its condition.

"OK, I'm gonna let you go and you're gonna tell me. If you take off I'm gonna shoot you. Understand?"

He quickly nodded twice.

His eyes widened, and I let go as he started to fall backwards, caught himself and planted his feet.

"I ain't runnin'. See here. Not runnin'."

"Where?"

"Try to give somebody your only thing 'cause on account of how it is and instead they try to—"

"Tell me. Now."

"Molly and that man was fightin' and drop these things. I seen it, but nobody else did cause they was watchin' the fight and the fish, but not me. I seen the dollars fallin'. Got a fistful I gotta tell you straight up, but that was the last one on account of 'cause I spent the others." He paused and took a deep breath. "You don't have a smoke on you, do you? Anyway that's where they come from. Up the street at the Molly fight, but that was a day or two ago."

I had my hands over my mouth trying to count. Trying to stay calm. Trying to . . .

"Fish? You said they had fish?"

"That's what I said. Fish not good for nothing but to look at. Can't eat it 'cause on account of it's what you call a decoration."

"What kind of fish?"

He looked about carefully over both shoulders, "Shhhh." Then he whispered, "Don't say nothin', but I got part of the prize." Then he reached into the side pocket of his fatigues and produced the pointed end of a blue marlin's bill. "I got it 'cause on account of everybody else was watchin' the fight but I know what's the important thing."

"Let me see." He passed it to me gingerly. His prize. Joe's prize. I knew it. How could this be? Me holding the remains of that long dead fish?

"I guess you be wanting that, too."

"Kallie, would you have something we could trade?" She thought for a moment, fished around under her seat, pulled out a box and lifted out a plastic wrapped cigar with a red band.

"My granddaddy's. It was his only vice."

I nodded. Took it and offered it to John.

"Would you be trading? Your prize for a good cigar. Would you John?"

"Shoot yeah, cause hey, it ain't nothing but a thang."

And so in the midst of the late evening at Church Street, John stepped back, puffed out his chest and lit up his cigar. Then we discussed the most recent events. The character named Molly. The location of the fight. The other party in question. All of this as though we were rocking on a southern porch, me offering slow gentle questions between breezes and John politely pausing, considering and answering. Then we parted company and Kallie and I slowly drove down the street as John sat with his back against a palm tree, smoking, considering the stars and his good fortune.

What John hadn't known was that the slow questions were due to my extreme pain and nausea. To appease Kallie's justifiable concern, I returned to the hospital. Later that night from the confines of my bed, I had a dream. One like a person has when she's been tired and hungry for a very long time. When her body is beat up but not nearly as much as her mind.

In the dream, I was trying to get across to the island, but there wasn't a No-good bridge. I was stuck, pacing back and forth until it occurred to me that I could be the bridge, form one with my body. So I flung my body across the chasm, the distance between one world and another, and my hands dug deeply into the sandy dirt along the other side, my feet holding onto the opposite bank but then my feet began slipping, over and over again. I knew there was nothing left for me to do but let go and pull myself up to the opposite side. And when I did this I discovered I had grown. Larger than a man, larger than the cypress trees, into a giant. I could see all of Toliquilah, the waves far out into the Gulf, and with a twist of my head, the swamps, the cove, down by the mangrove trees and back again to the other side where the No-good was no more. Then my feet sank down into the sandy earth and stopped there, hardening, becoming part of the island itself. I was the island and the island was me. As though I was just like the oaks that grew in the cove or Joe's alligators sleeping in the swamp. And I slept too. There in my dream, my great head tilting forward, my eyes coming to a close. After I had slept for maybe a hundred years I felt something crawling up my legs that woke me and looking down found two giant rattlesnakes wrapping about me, around and around and up. Reaching down I seized both of them by their heads and pulled them to eye-level squeezing their jaws until they bled milk from their fangs. And the milk became a great white rain.

CHAPTER TWENTY-EIGHT

Dreams were becoming my reality. Everything milky and from another world.

"Where'd you say you got these things?" Edna was leaning across my bed, the dollar in one hand, the fish nose in the other.

"From an old friend on Church Street."

"How in the world did it end up over there after all this time?"

"That's what I was wondering. Then I figured somebody stole the fish. Then someone stole the fish again. It was making the rounds and ran into the wrong people."

"Unless one of the people that had it was the one that stole it in the first place."

"Unlikely. Couple of homeless shufflers. Not much in the way of transportation, much less making it over to Toliquilah for any reason. No concrete, no benches, no grates. It's a little too primitive."

Edna was thinking. Hard. I was glad because my thinking was watery and shifting every few moments. I had a strong desire to check my ankles, make certain they had not become trees.

"Somebody stashed the fish and the money. Doesn't make any sense. Why would you take something so insignificant and hide it for so long?" She caught my expression. "Not that *you* would think it's insignificant, but you know what I mean."

I couldn't think about the fish for the moment. Let her figure it out and clue me in later. "What about the diner? What's its condition?"

Edna let out a humph of air.

"It's missing the entire south wall, part of the floor. Looks pretty serious. Just like Lolly's motel. Very skeleton."

"Then it suits her."

"One side looks like all is well, go around to the back and it's a different story. The inside's gutted. Insurance man is coming out tomorrow to assess the damage."

"You bought insurance?"

"Thanks to Lolly Eden. At her strong suggestion I picked up a little policy last year."

A pain ran up through my side and tried to split my head open. "You're OK then?"

"Sure. I should get enough. Then there's another thing, but we'll talk about that later."

"The house?"

Edna looked at me tilting her big head sideways. "It's not good."

Kallie rounded the corner walking and talking at the same time. "They say they might let you out of here tomorrow." She was pulling back the curtain from the caged window to let in the light.

I threw up my arm to shield my eyes. "I wish you wouldn't do that."

"You're gonna have to get used to it, don't you think? They also said you could have visitors now. Before you weren't supposed to have any visitors, but we told them we were your family and we were settin' up with you."

"Settin' up?"

"That's what it's called, *settin' up*."

"Settin' up." Edna parroted her with an authoritative nod. Apparently, Georgia and Alabama had some things in common. I had people "settin' up" with me but I had no where to live. The very sands of my existence had finally stopped shifting and begun to settle beneath my feet but now they had been blown away. Erased beneath me. Joe's house was in pieces. The diner half gone. The bridge history. And Joe, how could he have been something he wasn't? Was he secretive? Maybe. Controlled. Yes. A quiet disposition. By nature. Maybe he was perfectly suited to an undercover job. But even if it was the truth why hadn't he ever told me? How could a man like Manuel know about me in relation to Joe's life but me not know about him? It was inconceivable. Our closeness would navigate the most treacherous territory, the most horrible memories. Had he been afraid of my disapproval?

"I'm gonna go down to the snack bar. You want something?"

"No, Kallie."

The door swung shut behind her, muffling the hallway noises. The room was quiet. Then I noticed the room was really quiet. There wasn't a metallic sound coming from the bed next door. I looked through the gossamer curtain. A ready-made bed. No patient. It was an odd feeling. Like an appendage taken for granted then, suddenly missing. Escaped in the night.

My mind tried to sort the pieces. Esther was dead. This part was easy because it was fact. Less fact and more intuition was that no one could know she was gone. People came to Esther's for evil intent on more than one occasion. I once had a dead body to prove it. And I had reason to believe they'd still be coming. Red was moving to Montana. He had never mentioned Montana to me in my entire life. Red had never liked Manuel. Had said he was . . . what was it . . . determined. I could understand that a little better now. He did seem determined, but for what? He had never said. Why was he still hanging around? What was he looking for? And what about Joe? How had our lives become so separated since my father's death that it had come to this? All the years I'd spent wasting away, Joe had been . . . what? What had he been doing? Running undercover operations? Pretending to be a dealer? Manuel was his partner. Knew everything about me. Had seen me once on my last visit to Joe's. When was this? The week had been so low-key. We cooked, ate, hung out. Did basically nothing. Joe was with me the entire time unless he was at work. I tried to think back again to our week. Tried to remember the faces in and about the diner. I closed my eyes. Remembered the smells. Joe's voice laughing from the kitchen. The customers joking in response. Earl's voice dragging out real slow, offering to arm wrestle somebody. Good old Earl. Whatever had become of him? The sound of passing cars. The palm trees slapping. Merle Haggard singing on the jukebox. Someone's feet keeping time. Maybe mine. Then a picture surfaced across the watery distance of time. A face in Lemuel's booth by the window. A shadowy figure between the haze of smoke and people. A face watching. Minus the scar. A smoother skin. Eyes still dark. Mouth unsmiling. Then the mouth smiles but when it does it slides up beyond white teeth, looking predatory. I turn to look for Joe who's standing close behind me at the counter. He nods in the direction of the man and then looks at me with a quiet face. Suggests I go on home in a little while. Says he'll close up and meet me.

If I had a question then about his behavior, I don't remember now. Perhaps I had been too numbed by shots of Black Jack to tell.

Funny how I hadn't remembered Manuel, hadn't recognized him that day on the beach. But it wasn't the face I'd paid attention to. It was the life in him. But the life had been a lie. And all this time I'd hated Jimmy Cusler. Probably still did. But at least with Cusler what you saw was simple.

I looked up at Edna who was sitting stoically on the end of the bed staring out the window. Her face could have been that of a statue. Bronzed. Immobile. Suddenly, I missed the casual bantering we'd shared across the counter. The fights over the jukebox. My ripped seat. The smell of food cooking. Edna's tidy room. The sound of the cash register ringing a sale. Nothing that had terribly impressed me in a day-to-day living. Now they were all part of a very absent presence that might never return.

"Where're you staying?"

"Wallace's." Then she turned towards me with good nature. "He sleeps on the couch."

We had all come to a crossroads. A great invisible transom composed of intersecting lines. One for each of our lives.

"What you going to do with the diner?"

"The way I see it," Edna heaved in a breath, seemed to never let it go, "it's as much yours as mine. Maybe as much Moses' as the two of us. I guess the better question would be," and she leaned in over me a little and patted my covered leg, "what're *we* gonna do with it?"

Well said, Edna. That's what I wanted to say. That's what I felt all the way down to my bones but instead I gave a short nod and looked away. Then Kallie walked in with her prescription.

"I got you a milkshake and French fries." Then turning to Edna, "I had to wait on the fries." And Edna nodded that she understood. All good fries were worth waiting on. We sat in silence while I ate fries and drank a chocolate milkshake through a straw. It was the best food I'd ever eaten in my entire life.

We were still doing this as Moses tapped lightly twice on the outside of the door, then stuck his head inside whispering, "You awake?" Those words began the closest thing we'd had to a meeting since the hurricane evacuation and before the disposal of a body. Moses pulled back the dividing curtain and sat down on the empty bed. It creaked beneath his bulk and seemed to bow up in the middle. Edna pulled up a chair, "for her back," and Kallie propped up next to Moses, and they began to alternately catch me up on the state of the diner, the island, and life in general since I had been, as they put it, away.

"Lemuel got his old school bus running."

"After all these years?" I wondered.

"And you'll never guess who's driving it."

"Who?" I sucked on the straw and felt the cold hit the back of my parched throat and slide down. I made a mental note to drink more milkshakes.

"Agnes." And this Moses offered with a laugh.

"Why?"

"Because before, we had to just about bribe people to get 'em to come over the No-good, but now that it's gone—"

"People everywhere," Edna finished, "wanta ride the boat over. Taking pictures."

"So Lemuel got his bus running and Agnes got a hat."

"She would."

"Uhuh, and she did."

"And she's driving the bus and giving tours."

"Tours of what?"

"Mainly the liquor store since it's the only thing open for business. Except now Lemuel's talking about putting in ice cream and tee shirts and beachwear."

"You're making me sick."

"And sunglasses," Kallie offered, but that was all she said.

"It won't ever be the same," I said, and I knew it was the truth. Progress was like a pistol. One good shot and it could obliterate the past.

"I don't imagine the swamp side of the island ever gonna interest anyone too much. Of course if Joe had been there he could've wrestled gators. You should have seen him because it was worth paying for. . . ." I stopped because it was the first time I remembered speaking about him as though he were dead. "Anyway. . ."and my voice trailed off and fell to the floor.

"Well, like I said," Edna sat up straighter, looked at each of us, "question is what are we going to do about the diner?"

"What's Lolly Eden doing?" I asked. I might not like her but she wasn't stupid.

"She's rebuilding. And adding on."

"Apparently," Moses leaned in, "Lemuel and Lolly think the island's in for a boom. Something about timing."

In the end, somehow, it all came down to perpetual timing. Kallie's sowing and planting and reaping. I was uncertain still of parts, but a picture of the whole began to fill my soul with one solid, resounding fact. It was due season. Harvest time.

CHAPTER TWENTY-NINE

Joe's house was kneeling in prayer. At least it appeared that way. The back stilts were still standing, the front ones completely gone. The windows were blown out. The glass doors missing. I felt guilty that the house had weathered Ruby alone. It was a silly feeling, but a real one just the same. It was as though I had turned my back on a living thing in a time of need. Desertion. Something I had always been good at. I had the number down. Had the experience and expertise that made one not only good at the game but excellent. It hurt less every time you did it. The trick was never to look back.

I sifted through the rubble beneath the house but there were no telltale signs of what might be saved. No signs of what might lie un-shattered in what was left above. I pulled Kallie's wind chimes from the mud. The rooster with the open wings emerged first, and as each piece rose from their grave they began to sing again. One against the other. A sheep, a cow, a dog, and a chicken. I didn't understand the dog. Why not a goat, a mule, or a duck? I looked up over the railing, judged the distance, my casted arm, the soggy depth of the sandy mud. I hoped at least something of Kallie's upstairs Alabama had survived, and I wanted to pull myself into the remains and emerge with armfuls to carry back to her. The sky was light blue, almost white, and there were no clouds nearby or in the distance. The herons had returned in the tops of their trees. Their wings flapped and I closed my eyes and listened to Joe's voice whispering, "Listen, Mary, shhhh. Listen! Hear them? They're catching dreams like yours and mine, and when their wings are full of dreams they fold them very slowly, very gently so's not to break them. See?" And he'd pointed out across the water into the great folding wings among the cypress limbs. "No broken dreams."

He had been twelve and I was ten, and I'd believed him then because he was calm and wise and good.

"Looks like quite a mess."

I turned to see the face of Joe's ex-partner.

"Where'd you come from?"

"Didn't you hear me? I called your name," he turned and pointed, "from back there."

"I heard nothing."

"I'm sorry. Maybe I scared you."

This thought came most immediately to my mind: Black Jack's gun is in the car. "Why are you still here? What is it you're looking for?" I asked.

"Oh, if I knew that," he looked at the white, blue sky, rubbed his chest, "then everything would be so easy."

A speck began in the corner of my eye. Not something you could see from the outside but something I could see from the inside looking out. In it was the seed of truth, and in that instant the seed grew until I covered my understanding.

"You killed him, didn't you?"

"Why would I kill my own partner?"

"How should I know? You're the man, Mr. Manuel Garcia Rodriguez Pasquez." I tried to circle back towards the car. I tried to judge the distance. His power. My ribs. It didn't add up.

"Yes, this is true. I am the man. I always was. This Joe of yours, or should I say of ours," he leaned his head to the right side, smiled factiously, "he hated that. Me always being one step ahead. But you know what, *bella*

Maria," he took one quick step towards me, wrapped a hand behind my neck and poured murder from his eyes, then he whispered hard against my face, his breath leaving an imprint on my skin, "One step is all it takes."

This was a moment I had never expected, but then I don't know what I'd expected. Fingerprints. Simple clues. A clear path unfolding towards a killer. Calling the police. Detailing the evidence. Having a clean conscience. Being able to finally visit Joe's grave and say, "I'm so sorry, but it's been made right. Rest in Peace." But now my ribs still hurt, I was clutching a rooster and being clutched by a maniac. His clutch tightened. His eyes grew blacker.

"Perhaps you can tell me this much, island girl."

"That's gin girl to you, rummy."

"Excuse me?" The clutch became a claw and I said the second prayer I had offered since coming home. It had grown into the silent words, "Help me."

"As I was saying, perhaps you can tell me what is," he laughed, shook his head, "this belly of the snake?"

"What?"

The fingers pressed down on the top of the spinal bones in my neck. Death by a broken neck presented itself as a very real possibility.

"You heard me, island girl. You were Joe's best friend, and now you are spending time with the old woman. I believe somehow there is a great connection. And what they know," he turned my head to face him up close, "you know. Now show me the snake."

On the horizon a black wisp of smoke began unfolding and climbing in the sky, slow at first, then growing by degrees before our eyes.

Manuel saw it and pulled his angry gaze away from me.

"Well now. Looks like the old woman is burning her trash. Amazing how she does it with no eyes."

I could have said, *You just don't know how amazing.* Instead I offered, "Why don't you ask her for yourself?"

"Maybe that is a good idea. Maybe it's time we all have a talk together in the light of day." And he pulled me towards the car. For the flash of a second in passing I thought I saw a face looking out from the glassless window of the bedroom upstairs. But I couldn't turn my head. Not an inch. *How ironic*, I thought. *When I want to look back, I can't.*

CHAPTER THIRTY

Nothing was burning when we arrived at Esther's. Her barrel was half-filled with water and cold trash. But her house was standing. A portion of the roof torn back. Glass in windows missing. Some of her trees torn down, but the bulk of it stood silent and somehow both inviting and accusing at once. Manuel turned his head, turning mine along with it, as he searched the sky.

"How strange," he said. "Then, it doesn't matter. We are here, so we shall conduct business as usual. After you, my dear."

I slowly walked towards Esther's door, stepping over the fallen trees and wondering what *business as usual* meant to a man like Manuel.

Manuel narrowed his eyes in the darkness of the interior. I half expected Esther to step from the shadows and hit him with her cane exclaiming, *So now we see the root of all evil, yesssss?* But instead there was only the sound of slithering. Of great fathomless, hungry bellies. Of mice instinctively rustling in their cages. And the air, some musty feel of expectation.

"Where could she be?"

I shrugged my shoulders although I wanted to say, *With a good wind, as far as Texas.*

"Call to her. Don't look at me like so. I said call to her."

I called her name, but I had never called to a dead person before and it came out rusty and flat like calling a dead pet for the subterfuge of a child.

"Why do you call her from here?'

"What?"

"What is the matter with you? Go to the door and call her. She is not standing in this stinking room, now is she?"

So I went to the door and I looked out, but I saw nothing. Instead, I remembered these things: The bugs crawling beneath the leaves, the herons gently folding their dreams, Joe's mother calling us from a great distance, my father's hands as he fished, Joe's smile. That's when I knew I was going to die. My life unfolded before me in one great uneven song, warbling back and forth between little sounds and large ones, a gun blast, the sound of pine on fire, a tired voice saying, Ain't it a shame? Moses' whispered prayers, Lemuel's jumbled mumbles, Edna's slow shuffle, Kallie's singsong voice, Church Street John rocking back and forth saying " 'cause on account of," and I agreed with him. 'Cause on account of I had answered a strange dream, and now I stood in Esther's shadow about to be killed over the secrets of something I didn't yet understand.

"I don't know the secret." I turned back and told him, "I just don't know it."

"Call her."

I leaned up on my toes and sang Esther's name from the top of my lungs and it felt good. So I did it again growing louder. By the fourth time I was screaming and Manuel's hand clamped tightly around the cap of my mouth forcing me to swallow the last "er."

"I think maybe she heard you." He dragged me back inside and sat me roughly in the straight back chair. "Now we will wait."

So we waited. But there was no ticking during the passing of the time. No mounted clock. No chimes to break the stillness and I sat observing that Manuel was a very patient man because he sat very still and waited without the interruption of hurry. The light grew dimmer, the cages quieter. I grew resigned and even a bit sleepy, which was odd under the circumstances. I was about to be killed by the same man who'd killed Joe. At least in that there seemed to be some strange balance. A scale tipping too far to one side and then back again. It would be even steven. And I'd be guilt free.

"My friends will be looking for me." It wasn't a feeble excuse but the truth.

"Your friends have left the island and gone back by now." He smiled at me, the same smile from the beach, "You see," he slid on his old accent like a comfortable silk skin, "I told them we had planned to have a dinner this evening and that I would see to it that you crossed to the other side with great safety."

"I'm sure they'll believe that. There are so many dining facilities open on Toliquilah this time of year."

"I told them on your namesake, the lovely *bella Maria*, we were to eat and watch the sunset. Such a nice way to finish the day."

Had they believed him or read through the practiced charm? "What are you looking for?"

"The belly of the snake. I told you this. Don't make me repeat myself."

"You didn't tell me why."

"Apparently, it's where all good secrets are kept." He cocked his head to one side. In the dusk I could make out the outline of his nose, the full sweep of his lips but his eyes were in darkness. "But then you already know this, don't you?"

"No, I do not, but," and I swung from the chair to my left, threw out one hand, "try any of the bellies before you."

"Those bellies are not quite large enough to suit my purpose—what are you staring at?"

"How should I know?" I turned back in my seat toward him. "It's almost dark, I can barely see a thing." It was a lie, but a most believable one. Something out of place had caught my attention. Something barely noticeable. The open and empty cage of a snake. One that had originated from the jungles of Africa.

"You're going to kill me also, aren't you?"

His voice was void of feeling. As empty as blank paper with no promise of words. "Yes."

"Why should I show you where the snake is, if you plan to kill me?"

I watched his shoulders shrug against the darkness. "Because if you do not show me I will kill you sooner, and it is human nature to prolong your death to the last possible moment. You can't help it. It is something I believe you call *hope*."

"What happened to you to make you so cold?"

"Don't placate me with psychological stall tactics, Island Girl. You couldn't care less why I am like I am."

"Then why did you kill Joe? *That* I do care about."

"He was simply a part of the evolutionary chain."

"Don't believe in it myself."

"It doesn't matter. Joe fell to its power. Survival of the fittest. The emergence of stronger, more intelligent being. It happens all the time."

We were almost in the dark, then out the window, through the trees, a sliver of a new moon began to rise. It made his scar rise away from his skin, appear to hover an inch above his face.

"You didn't have to kill him."

"You're wrong. It was either him or me." He leaned forward toward me, the scar falling back flat against his face. "I was very partial to me." When he smiled, it stretched an inch, turning whiter. "It appears our friend is not coming. She must know we are here waiting. She has maybe been warned somehow."

"Where did you ever hear about this belly of the snake?"

"From Joe. Only he was not speaking with me but here with the woman. I had followed him. Overheard. Too bad he did not give me the location when he had the chance. But of course, you know it."

"Of course." I said it quickly.

Manuel cocked his head to one side then rose from his chair. "I think maybe you are lying. I think you began telling the truth but now . . . I think now you are lying. I think the only one who knows now is the old woman, and if that is the case," he pulled something from his pocket, opened it slowly and the silver shined between the branch lit pieces of the moon, "I think I can more easily find her alone. Take care of her myself."

"What makes you think so?"

"See, Bella Maria, you do stall for time." He rose from his chair, walked behind me. "They always stall for time."

"You know I can't let you kill her."

It was a strangely familiar voice. One I'd heard long ago in a different lifetime. Scrawny Eddie stepped from the shifting shadows beyond the open door.

"Step aside Mike." Eddie reached behind his back, pulled a gun from his waist, "I said, step aside."

"Well now, aren't you the little hero?"

It's OK. I thought. I'm in shock, but let Scrawny Eddie be hero of the day. I'll make room for him. Lots of room. Then something began climbing in a slow circular motion up my left leg. Death by slit throat. Death by a stray bullet. Death by a snakebite. Options.

"You're under arrest, Mike."

"Don't tell me they gave the snitch a badge. Not after all these years. What would Joe think?"

Eddie took a step forward. The moon spilled through the window and caught him full-length in its light. He looked older. Serious. The snake was up to my knee.

"He'd think, 'Well done Eddie boy. It's about time.' That's what he'd think. Now drop the knife and move to the side."

But the man behind me didn't drop the knife. He threw it with the expert marksmanship of a killer. I heard it fly through the air. Saw it lodge in Eddie's throat before he fell to the floor. Then the hand clenched tightly around the front of my neck forcing the air to a bursting stop.

"Good-bye, *Bella Maria*."

I was aware of the sound of my own heart beating. The texture of the man's hand against my throat. Warm but not sweaty. The coldness of the snake wrapping against my leg. The snake against my leg. Against my knee. Against my thigh.

Bold African boy, I thought, *C'mere*. And with the remaining life of me I reached for the weaving triangle, felt the sharp hit of the fangs break my skin, a burning sensation rush up my arm and I thought *Well, either way I am dying, but now someone's going with me*, and finding the weaving head again, I locked my hands behind its jaws and lodged the mouth against the bending throat above me.

The hand pulled away quickly, the snake was lodged against his neck, hanging now impressively at full length, "What is this?" His voice grew incredulous. The startled voice of an impervious hunter.

I pulled in air. Rubbed my throat. Wondered why I wasn't dead. Then it was Manuel who tried to breathe but instead gasped for air and placed a hand against his heart.

"I believe," I coughed and spit something that tasted like blood, "I believe, Mr. Rodriguez, you are a dead man." He fell to the ground still clutching his chest, his hands pumping the air. "And you know what else? If I could kill you over and over again, I would, but then," I looked over to Eddie's sprawled out body, "as a matter of fact, I can." I crawled to Eddie's side, pulled the gun from his hand. Then I crossed the inches between me and the thing I called *Manuel* and counted the miles he had placed between me and Joe. They were infinite, reaching now far beyond the stars.

I leaned by his side, placed my finger against the trigger, put the barrel to his head. "Is this where you shot him? No, was it lower, maybe here." I slid the gun lower, pressed the barrel of the .38 against his skull. His eyes widened. "Or maybe I should simply shoot out one organ at a time while you are still alive." He clutched harder for air, grabbed at my ankle. "Can I tell you something before you go to hell? I know where the belly of the snake is." I leaned in, pressed the gun deeper into the bottom of his skull. "I always have." The fingers tightened in final protest until, very slowly, they let go and he was gone. Then I felt more than saw, the snake slither across the floor along the back wall towards the corner of the door. With a final flash, his tail receded into the night.

"Mary." It came out garbled from across the room, "I'm not dead."

CHAPTER THIRTY-ONE

"Trust nobody, Mary." Eddie was lying in the same hospital I had just left. Between the two of us, we were giving it a good amount of business.

I said, "Not even you, Eddie?" He looked away.

He was crying, and I pretended not to notice as he said, "I got my good days, Mary, and my bad. But all my days with Joe were *good* days." He emphasized the *good* then he asked, "Do you know what I mean.?"

I said, "Yes, Eddie. I do. I know what you mean."

From the beginning, simply dropping Manuel's body overboard had been appealing but felt wrong. The body of not just any murderer but *the* murderer. I wanted it bagged, tagged, and accounted for. Not that I had any concrete proof he did it because the only proof I had was the word of a dead man and the word of a snitch turned cop.

The autopsy had shown death by lethal snakebite. There had been an immediate investigation held downtown, but the questions came from men in dark suits with lies as thick on their lips as cane syrup. Their concentration was on Manuel's possessions. Did he carry anything with him? Was I sure? A suitcase perhaps? Did he mention anything? A place?"

"Are you DEA?" My questions were met with looks tossed over shoulders which resulted in more questions than answers.

"Why do you ask?" It was the younger one in the grey suit. I suspected he wasn't DEA at all but something else.

"Because the murderer said he was."

"He told you he was DEA?"

"That's what I said. Said he and my friend were partners." I regretted that part the moment it came out.

The older one took out a notebook, began to write something down. "Your friend."

"It doesn't matter. He's dead."

"I see." A look passed between them. I wanted a glass of water but refused to ask for one.

"And your friend's name?"

"You should know it."

"Refresh our memory."

"Joe. Joe Tompica."

"Island boy?"

I didn't say anything. I knew "Island boy" translated to Indian. And I knew whoever these guys said they were, they were not. And that they didn't know the first real thing about Joe. I also knew I'd said more than enough.

I came straight to the hospital, then, to see Eddie and try to get to the bottom of something. I questioned him about his involvement with the man known as Manuel, how he and Joe had fit together.

"Did you know he killed Joe?"

"I knew Joe was supposed to meet him, told me not to come. That it wasn't my place. Would arouse suspicion. I knew Joe went missing. Deal was they never let me see him."

"What do you mean?"

"Never let me I.D. the body. Nobody did. Now what do you think about a thing like that?"

I narrowed my eyes. Thought of Cusler's report. Remembered Peggy Sue repeating him, "Ain't that a strange thing?"

"I mean, there wasn't anybody else. His sister never showed. Nobody talked to you. Who else there gonna be?"

"He said Joe never showed. That's what he told me. He said it like he was really Spanish, you know what I mean?"

"The accent."

"Yeah. He said, 'Eddie, it looks like Joe has blackmailed us and taken off for himself.' Now I can't say to him I got a report to me saying he's dead. I can't blow my cover and admit this thing to him so I just say, 'Ain't that something. For Joe to bail like that?' So Manuel says he didn't show, which is a lie, because I had already gotten jerked in a car and carted off to a hotel room with these guys. That's when they sort of deputized me. Gave me the gun. Said that Joe was dead and they suspected Manuel was the murderer, only they were looking for a certain type of evidence. Said they wanted me to stay close to him. Said sooner or later it had to surface. Only they don't tell me what *kind* of evidence, Mary." I couldn't imagine what kind either.

"Seems to me ballistics would have been enough," I said.

"Oh yeah, you'd think so. So I stayed and stayed and they kept saying, 'Watch him' and I did that too as best I could except when he'd make me stay and he'd go away. That's what happened the night I first saw you back on the island. You were pretty toasted."

"Then that was you at the bar."

"Was me."

"Eddie," I walked around the corner of the bed and leaned into him, "whatever happened to Joe's fish? To the dollars on the walls? Where'd they go?"

"I don't know."

Eddie was a special creature. His face changed features like a chameleon jumping in a fabric store. It had just shifted to cover a lie, but his face was too late and his lie too fast. It took one to know one.

"So, what have they said to you since this Manuel is dead."

"I'm no longer needed. I guess I'm no longer a good guy."

"You almost saved my life, right? That makes you the good guy no matter what. What were you doing up in Joe's house anyway?"

"What?"

"The day Manuel caught me at the house. I saw a face in the window."

"Wasn't me, Mary. I followed him through the woods all the way. When he took your car I was still hiding and then had to walk all the way to Esther's."

"Wasn't you, then."

"Nope. Wasn't me."

"Hm. My imagination." I turned and picked up my bag, "Thanks for taking care of Esther after Joe died."

"Taking care of?"

"Taking her food."

"Mary," Eddie raised one eyebrow, cocked his head to one side, "the first time I ever set foot at Esther's house was the night I got this." He pointed to the bandage over his neck.

"But she told me . . ." I stopped. Exactly what had Esther told me? Manuel came which now I knew was only a ploy on his part to try to find what he wanted. "Never mind, Eddie, must've been somebody else." I pulled the door open to leave.

"Joe was the only friend I ever had."

"I know that, Eddie." I let the door close again, walked over to the bedside and pulled a dollar from my pocket, unfolded it and placed it on his chest, "I also know you stole that fish and everyone of those dollar bills." Eddie pulled the dollar from his chest, held it up and read the inscription. "What I don't know is why you did it or what became of them."

"I just wanted a piece of him. That's all. Just something to remember him by."

"So you took a seven foot fish."

"I was drunk."

"What you do with it?"

"Had 'im in my living room. Didn't even spend the money. Stuck it up over all my walls so it could be like it was supposed to. You know what I mean?"

It was sad, but I did. "So what happened?"

"Come home one day and found my door open and the fish gone. Money gone too. Hurt me bad."

"Why'd you lie?"

" 'Cause I stole them, right? I know what stole is. I mean they weren't mine. By all natural rights, I reckon they should've been yours."

I walked back to the door and opened it again. "By all natural rights, Joe should be behind the bar tonight and the two of us still laughing about the day he caught that thing."

"You got that right." He laid his head back across the pillow, and that was the last we said to each other before I walked out the door.

As I maneuvered down the sterile corridors I knew Eddie grieved for Joe. Had grieved for him for a long time. And in that place, we were standing on common ground.

CHAPTER THIRTY-TWO

There had finally been a change in the temperature. Moses wore a suit, but even with the cooler breeze he still broke a sweat just above his collar line. I stood to the side surveying the waves crashing with whitetops cascading gently in one long roll down the beach. In my hand was a bouquet of baby's breath and peach roses. I held them to my nose and smelled the mixture of salt air and the warm earth smell of something from its bosom.

Nine months had passed since I'd crossed back over the No-good. A lifetime ago. Red stepped up on the newly built gazebo and said, "Are you ready for this?" and I said, "I am if you are." Then we took our appropriate places and Moses cleared his throat and opened the Bible as McGurdy began to play something not the least bit like a wedding march.

Red stood behind the folding chairs and waited as I gathered my dress, tried to remember to stand tall, and held the flowers against my breast. We linked arms and walked the short distance to where Moses stood waiting. Then we turned to watch the bride approach in all her glory. Her wedding dress had been a present from the groom and it was fashioned from an African design, draping one long scarf around her shoulder which fell gently to her waist. There was no evidence of a missing limb and Edna had suddenly become a striking symbol of womanhood. A queen fit to rule by her husband's side. Wallace P. Ketchum stood proud to receive her, and as she laced her arm into his, he placed his right hand atop hers and I noticed something unusual about Wallace. Something I should have noticed before now, so I looked again but there it still was. On Wallace's right hand were six fingers. I know because I counted them several times and through the course of the ceremony was caught up in this fact and the meaning of it. I knew between his excess and her shortage Edna and Wallace made up a whole and in that balance their union would last forever. I was still lost in this revelation when I heard Moses say, "I now pronounce you man and wife," and there was the sound of applause and of Agnes crying and one long, "Hot dog!" by Lolly Eden who had taken on the demeanor of a cowgirl at a rodeo.

We took turns kissing the bride and shaking the groom's hand, and I tried not to look at Wallace's fingers, but I did anyway. Then, we walked among the trees tasting the fruits of Kallie's labors from kitchens on the other side of the inlet.

"What are you going to do now that you know and it's over?"

"Funny thing is, Red," I turned and looked up at him, "I don't feel like it's over."

"How much more over can it be? The bad guy's dead."

"I don't know. Something's," I tried to find the words but I fell short, "something's remembering me."

"Remembering?"

"That's what I said."

"That doesn't make any sense."

"What has made sense out here lately?" I threw my arm up and out across the expanse of Toliquilah and suddenly felt one hundred feet high. Then I staggered.

Red caught me without comment. "Montana makes sense. You and me in Montana together makes sense."

I didn't say anything, but I knew it was true. Something about Red and I together and a long way off in open spaces made the most of sense. A paradigm shift. A new beginning made up of old parts.

"I'll think about it."

Red smiled, pushing a hair behind my ear, "You already have."

"Yeah, but I'm not finished."

Then he grew serious. "I know you, Mary Contrary. You might never decide, but I am leaving."

Lemuel approached, full of good spirits. He, Agnes, Lolly Eden and Moses were a new team of sorts. They were each predicting a boom due to the final demise of the No-good. In only a month McGurdy's boat had become a tourist attraction and now people were clamoring to ride across and comb the beach for shells, driftwood and sightings of dolphins or sea turtles. McGurdy was planning on getting a bigger boat. Agnes' nails were scraped to nubs from cleaning and painting Lemuel's old school bus. They were renovating it for their Island shuttle.

"Goshen sorten some," Lemuel spoke.

I stared at him as frustrated as I ever was and wondered how Agnes could possibly understand a word he said. Maybe they were like Edna and Wallace, made up of minuses and plusses that couldn't be seen by the naked eye.

"Socken fork juci top notch."

Red slapped me on the shoulder and left his hand there for a moment in a silent laugh. "I'm going to get something to drink. Bring you one, OK?"

Lemuel watched him walk away. I watched Lemuel and had the desire to open his mouth and stretch his tongue out to see if maybe it was just twisted. Then his attention was back to me.

"Go forn to bush."

I narrowed my eyes, looked closer to him, thought something made backwards sense. I tried to remember Esther's words, "Listen with your heart not with your mind. Lemuel talks through the back door." I narrowed my eyes tighter and tried.

"Good medicine bite good gone. Snake woman gone say you give."

"Medicine bite? You want the medicine?"

He nodded. "Take good make strong like big."

"I don't know anything about it."

"She there sittin' in dark. I twice knock back forth. Snake woman say you make more good. Not gone."

I didn't do anything with the snakes. I didn't know what to do with them. For the sake of Esther I occasionally dropped furry mice in the cages. Then I slammed the lids and left before I could hear or see a thing.

"Milk good not gone."

"No."

"Milk good not gone."

Red came back holding out a glass of sweet tea. One of Kallie's specialties.

"Care to take a walk, Mary?"

"Yesssss." I covered my mouth and rolled my eyes up to Lemuel.

"Milk good not gone," he repeated.

"What's he saying?" Red leaned into me as we turned away.

"I haven't a clue." I still hadn't made it over that gulch called lying. And I was tired of wanting to hear people speak and immediately wishing they'd shut up. Maybe I hadn't heard Lemuel or understood a word he'd said because I didn't like the inferences he made.

Red kissed me on the forehead, a newly discovered habit of his, saying he had to leave early to get back to the other side. "Travel plans to make," he said and added with a wink, "for two."

I watched him walk away. A long familiar sight. This I knew. I couldn't go back to the blackness of where I'd come from. Not back to empty nights in bars and dreary hotel days.

"No more running," I said aloud and Kallie stepped up to my right side and said, "They ain't nothing chasing you now."

I said, "No, I guess not."

"Nothing ever was except that monkey in your mind."

"What did you say?"

Kallie looked at the white crepe paper blowing from the gazebo, at the bride and groom, then up to the sky.

"I said, it is a good day for a wedding."

I looked over at Wallace's six fingers draped across Edna's shoulder. Lemuel popped the cork of a champagne bottle and, refilling glasses, offered up a toast I didn't try to understand.

"Yes it is, Kallie. A very good day."

*

I got out of bed, walked barefoot to the kitchen and opened the refrigerator. It held nothing but a pitcher of tea. The tea held nothing but tea. Unlike Kallie's sugar water. Unlike Esther's special tonic. It hadn't taken me long to figure out what had saved my life was Esther's special tonic. Either it was her habit to drink antivenom or she'd prepared me in advance.

The light spilled out over my feet. For a slight moment they looked dark and rooted as though they were disappearing below the wood of Esther's kitchen floor, reaching beyond the boards into the soil itself. Then the image passed as quickly as it had come.

I looked up into the trees and beyond where the stars shimmered in the sky. The roof was still torn back in places, and although Moses had promised to come out and fix it, I hadn't pushed him. His heart had been on overseeing the rebuilding of the diner.

The diner was becoming a restaurant. Edna was married to Wallace. Lemuel was an entrepreneur. Kallie was emerging. Red was moving. And I was drinking iced tea at three a.m. staring into the stars beyond Esther's roof.

Sometimes you know where secrets are but you prefer to let them lie there, comfortably tucked in, between the dreams of another world and the wind blowing across them in this one. I could have waited a hundred years without touching those secrets but the hole had grown into a cave and there was no suppressing it now. The empty space pressed in upon me. Demanding. Unrelenting.

It was just before sunrise when I pulled up below the remains of Joe's house. I drove the car up beneath the last two stilts under the roof. Then I climbed up onto the hood, pulled the gun from my waist and began firing at the lock on the chain above my head. My wrist jerked backwards. It still hurt. I pulled at the lock. Nothing. I moved in closer, placed the gun up against the padlock and pulled the trigger. This time the lock blew apart and I slid over the front of the car just in time to see Joe's canoe fall from beneath the rafters and crack my windshield into pieces. I pulled it across the car hood, the aluminum bottom scrapping the paint along the way, leaving a huge snail trail in its wake. The sun was throwing her first streaks across the water as I untied the oar and shoved off between the sawgrass and into the swampy mist.

I could have done this months ago. Could have followed the watery trails of Joe's existence into the back roads of an unmarked world. The water moved before me in a light brown swirl. A heron unfolded his wings as I paddled beneath his huge blue form.

I knew the swamps almost as good as Joe had. Not by choice or desire. Just second hand knowledge. Joe pointing out the way. Always reminding me what the signs were, how to tell where the water had risen or fallen, which left the waterways a maze. A set of eyes surfaced ahead of me and just as quickly receded back below the water's surface.

The cypress stood out on all sides. The bottoms of them far beneath the muddy waters. Some were six feet across on the inside. Great empty caverns. For the most part they all looked the same, straight up and unbending like Red. Occasionally, one or two seemed to be sculpted from a potter's clay. Twisting and turning as though in writhing pain they had bent to the earth and risen again.

Such a cypress lay before me. One that twisted from the bottom to the right then to the left and to the right again. But unlike any other tree this one held secret treasures. I paddled the boat out of the sunlight and into the dark, watery recesses of the belly of the snake.

CHAPTER THIRTY-THREE

Moses was pointing to a pile of rubble and trying to shout above the sounds of hammers crashing into the walls. I tried to shout over the combination.

"I need to talk to you!"

"Come outside, Mary. I can't hear a word you're saying." He pulled my arm towards the space that used to be the door. We walked around to the car and leaned up against the hood. Moses looked at the windshield and the missing paint.

"Should I ask?"

"Not now." I pointed back over my shoulder towards the noise. "Looks like you've got your hands full."

"Do you know how hard it is to get these guys to bring their equipment over on Frank's boat, then drag it down here?" I could see the real truth was that Moses was having the time of his life.

"No more floor wax huh, Moses?"

He crossed his arms over his chest and smiled his biggest smile. "No, Mary. No more floor wax."

I could see then that it was going to work. Lolly Eden and Lemuel were right. Business was going to boom. Moses and Edna were going to be a success. They all were. I didn't fit in the puzzle anymore. My place had been in the ripped booth by the wall, in the dark corner of the diner. The dark corner was gone, was being replaced by tables with white cloths and glass blocks in the walls.

"Look here, Moses," I leaned in the car window, pulled a black book from a plastic bag, still bearing the telltale signs of duct tape, "I need your help."

"Ahhh, here we go again. Where'd you get this thing?"

"Let's just say I gutted a snake."

"Sure. What is this?"

"I'm not even sure I know *about* what it is."

"Uhuh."

"What I mean is," I ran my fingers through the top of my hair, "I don't think you or I need to even know what this is more than the fact that it's what got Joe killed."

"Must be pretty powerful."

"It's got dates, names, coordinates. . . ."

"What kind of names?"

"Our governor."

"The governor?"

"Yes, except this was before Joe died. Before the election. When he was only a candidate. Seems the governor took a few trips. Made a few deals regarding the local waterways."

"What kind of trips?"

"Belize, Cabo San Lucas, Bogota."

"Stop right there."

"What's more, he took them on a certain boat with a man known to us as Manuel Rodriguez."

"And Joe knew?"

"Apparently Joe was there."

Moses ran his hand over his forehead which was starting to sweat. Then he listened to the absence of the sound of hammers.

"How am I going to get new walls built if I can't get the old ones down? You tell me that?"

I smiled. Life was getting better for Moses all the time.

"Don't you think you better contact the F.B.I or C.I.A. or somebody?"

"I think I met some of those guys. Only problem is," I rocked back and forth on my toes, threw my arms to the air, "I can't tell who the real good guys are anymore."

"Maybe Joe was the last good guy."

I looked at my feet. The truth was I had wondered where he fell into the picture. Was he really D.E.A.? There was nobody telling the truth and nobody that could be trusted. Had he somehow turned bad and gone over to the other side like Manuel? I had laid awake at night, thought the thoughts, let them circle like hungry buzzards, but each time I remembered who Joe was, I shot them out of the sky. I might not know the details of how he got into the whole thing, or why, but I did know, like looking with Esther's blind eyes, that the Joe boy had been born with a good spirit and had died with one.

"Yeah, maybe you're right."

"So whatchugonnado now?"

"You been hanging around Lemuel too much. Watch yourself."

"So no F.B.I no C.I.A."

I shook my head.

"Well you could just go put this thing back where you found it, set fire to it, toss it out there in those waves."

I shook my head again. "I can't. Already tried. If it was important enough to Joe to die for, it should be important enough for me to do something with."

We stood quietly watching the waves roll from a distance, listening as the hammers began again, falling rhythmically in time.

"Mary, do you remember that guy we used to go to school with, Robbie somebody?" Moses was snapping his fingers keeping time with his memory.

"Real nerdy guy."

"Robbie Turks was his name."

"Barely. Glasses. Bit of a snitch." A face formed in my mind.

"Well, the snitch is now a writer for the *Miami Herald.*"

"Good job for a snitch." I smiled, "Why don't you give him a call?"

"I think I will."

*

The drive to Miami passed in a flash of toll booths and exits I barely remembered as I turned Moses' car onto Biscayne Blvd. It had been a long time since I'd been in traffic, and I realized I'd spent a year now in the cocoon of Toliquilah. The person that had emerged wasn't the same one that went in. I also wasn't real certain anymore who she was.

A receptionist took my name in the lobby of the *Herald.*

"He's expecting me."

"I'll let him know you're here." Then she looked at me. "You can have a seat."

"I'd rather stand, thank you."

She was displeased with the standing. When Robbie Turks emerged he no longer wore glasses. It didn't matter. He still looked like a nerdy snitch. We shook hands.

"Robbie."

"It's Robert now." He smiled but it was too cocky for my taste.

I decided I didn't have to like him. Liking him had nothing to do with it.

"Moses told me you had a little something I might be interested in."

"Oh yes, Robert. I have a little something." I pulled the black book from my bag and held it before him. "Maybe you have a little someplace we can talk in private."

At the end of our meeting Mr. Robert Turks leaned in close to my ear and said, "You can call me Robbie."

I declined.

*

I had given every good thought I could imagine or reason with for staying behind. With no place where I fit anymore, it didn't make any sense. I had been fighting the inevitable.

Red stood next to a blue four-door rental car. "Don't you have more than that?" He pointed to my one bag sitting in Moses' driveway.

"Do you?"

He laughed out loud. "No, even less."

I searched the sky. "We could have flown you know."

"Ah we'd have missed the excitement of seeing all those relatives on the road."

"My relatives are all dead."

"Then we'll talk about them on the way."

Deloris had packed up a basket as though we were going on a picnic for the day. Moses stood by his carport, his arms folded across his chest, watching me. I walked over to say good-bye.

"You're not ever coming back are you, Mary Contrary?"

"Moses, I've never been able to promise anyone anything."

"Well, I tell you . . . I have never had somebody get me into so much trouble and turn around and do such a good job of getting me out."

"I'm glad it worked out that way."

"I can't believe you are going off while that woman is still gallivanting on her Hawaiian honeymoon."

"I know what I'm doing, but listen, you tell her for me," and I thought, *You tell her she's the most stubborn mule-headed person I've ever met in my life,* but instead I said, "You tell her that she has been a good friend to me." He nodded and I stood on my toes and kissed the side of his big cheek. "Montana's waiting on me."

"I'm gonna warn them you're coming. Hey," Moses pulled me back, looked over my shoulder at Red, "you sure you don't want me to marry you two right now before you take off?"

"Moses, how good can a girl get in a year?'

"As good as she wants to, Mary Contrary."

I waved him off as he shouted, "It's the truth!" Behind my back. I wasn't thinking bad or good but only good-bye and about wide open spaces. Room to breathe. New memories of nothing.

As we backed out of the driveway I looked at Red behind the wheel and thought, *In the beginning* . . . but that was as far as I got.

CHAPTER THIRTY-FOUR

It took eight knocks before the door opened. Lolly Eden stood there in a housedress.

"You're suppose to be in Montana."

"Yeah, well I'm not. Where's Kallie?"

She peered around me, trying to scope out the parking lot. "You dumped him, didn't ya?"

"I told him I'd catch up."

"Then you lied."

"I'm working on that, alright? What's it to you anyway?"

"Kallie," Lolly Eden yelled over her shoulder, "You got some lying company." Then she looked back at me, "Once a liar, always a liar."

I was going to tell her I hoped the sand would swallow her entire new motel, but Kallie walked into the room.

"You won't believe who they just arrested. It's all over television."

"Bet I would. Listen, Kallie, I need to borrow your truck."

"Hey," she paused and stood looking at me, her fists propped up on her hips, "you're home again."

"Yeah, yeah, jiggity jig. Can I use the truck, I need to meet somebody."

"Well, sure, let me get the keys and I'll come with—"

"No, Kallie," I put my hand on her shoulder, "I want to go alone."

"You loan her that truck, you're probably never going to see it again," Lolly raised her voice from the other room.

"If you don't shut up, Lolly, I'm gonna knock those new insurance teeth right out of your head."

Kallie said, "Ya'll are being ugly."

"She's always been ugly, Kallie."

Kallie rolled her eyes, looked at me with a focus of advice. "Well then, you don't want to look like her, do you?" As if my acting like Lolly could make me look like her. Of course, she had a scary point.

*

The Oak Grove Cemetery didn't house the most respectable dead. Anyway, no one who'd had to cancel a long list of social engagements when they booked this one last event. The stones were overgrown with weeds. The grass too high to be considered kept. Vases of plastic flowers lay scattered and as forgotten as the souls that rested here.

I tried to remember the layout. I shined my flashlight on one tombstone and then another until I realized I was totally lost and had to go back to the front gate and start over. It took almost an hour before I found the headstone that read, *Mabel Tompica, 1933-1985. Beloved Mother.* I shined the light to the right. Nothing. I shined it to the left. *John Anthony Silvers, 1913-1954. Always to be Missed.* Back to the right. Nothing. I walked on the ground to the right and placed my hand on the ground as if it could talk, could tell me something. Who would have bought the headstone? Susan? Surely Susan would have bought a headstone. Wouldn't she? Could she have been so greedy? So selfish? I kicked the overgrown grass searching for a three-year-old marker. Anything that at least marked Joe's overgrown grave. Then I thought of something else and went back to the truck.

*

It was the second door I had beat on in the last hour. Eddie finally opened it, had obviously been asleep.

"Were you at Joe's funeral?" I pushed my way inside and closed the door.

"What?" Eddie rubbed his eyes, trying to focus.

"Your dearest friend's funeral? Were you there?"

"No." He pushed his hair out of his face, which made it stand straight up like a cartoon. "When I found out about the whole thing I got drunk."

"Then what?"

"No. I got drunk and *stayed* drunk."

I strung my hands out as if I were talking in signals, "Get a shovel. Come with me."

It turned out Eddie didn't have a shovel, but I was on a mission so now Eddie was on a mission, too. We woke up another friend of his that had a house, and a yard, and a lawnmower, and a shovel.

"You better bring it back, Eddie." I couldn't see the body, only hear the voice.

"I will."

"Yeah, sure. Not like last time. I mean really bring it back."

Eddie threw the shovel in the back of the truck and climbed in.

"You borrow a lot of shovels lately?"

"I don't know if you realize it, Mary, but it is rude to wake a man up in the middle of the night and ask to borrow his shovel."

"What didn't you return last time?"

"His cake pans."

I didn't ask anything else.

*

It was past the middle of night and pressing into morning before Eddie and I had dug deep enough to determine that Joe wasn't buried next to his Mother. All my searching and questions and longing had turned up a big empty hole.

"Who told you he was buried here?"

"I don't remember."

"Mary, what do you mean you don't remember?'

I meant I didn't remember. At the moment I couldn't even remember who had told me that he was dead. I remembered it being a stranger. A cold phone call. A sorry to inform you that . . . death by fatal gun shot . . . happened three months ago. Maybe I had been drunk like Eddie. Maybe I had just lost my mind.

"Mary, can we get out of here?" Eddie was rolling his eyes across the graveyard. The sky was growing lighter in the East but it only turned the graveyard into an ethereal meeting place between us and what lay beneath our feet.

"Don't you think we should shovel the dirt back in?"

"No, let's go." Eddie turned in a full circle checking his back for some approaching unseen monster. "I'm not happy."

I stood looking at the great gaping hole where Joe was meant to be. He wasn't in it. And the flood of this information poured over me like cold water. I reached over and took the shovel from beneath Eddie's arm. He turned and headed for the truck until he heard the first spadeful fall into the empty ground. Then he turned, came back, and took the shovel from between my hands.

"I'm not happy," was all he said again as he began throwing dirt with exaggerated speed.

"It's gotta be this way, Eddie." Then I answered him before he could ask the next question. "There's no such thing as why."

*

Cooper's diner was a run down greasy spoon. Like the souls buried in Oak Grove Cemetery, Cooper's didn't serve the greater socialites of Clark City and cleanliness was not one of the main priorities. I wasn't certain what was, but as I looked at the dirt beneath my nails and Eddie's black streaked face I figured we were in the right place. Blisters were beginning to form on the palms of my hands and they reminded me of the day I'd first moved back into Joe's when they were blistered and covered in smoke. "Joe, you're really keeping my hands dirty."

"What?" Eddie looked up and stopped pouring sugar in his coffee.

"Nothing." I looked out the grease stained window at the pot hole gutted parking lot. Me and Eddie digging graves and eating breakfast. How'd I come to this? By now Red had crossed the Montana state line. Sunrise in Montana. God, I bet it was beautiful. I looked at my hands again and felt crazy. Certifiably crazy. Red had dropped me at a bus stop in Georgia arguing with me that he'd rather turn around and bring me home but I said, "Go on, cowboy. I'll catch up with you, but right now something's calling me back home."

"You're never gonna catch up, Mary."

"I might decide to fly out and beat you there."

"You're never gonna let go." He had said it with a sad eye but a forgiving one.

I had wanted to tell him it wasn't like that. That I could let go but somehow, something hadn't let go of me.

"Made up your mind, yet?"

Cooper's only waitress stood by the table with a pad in one hand, a pen in the other and a cigarette dangling between her lips. I moved the ashtray over to the edge of the table. She thumped her ashes, said, 'Thanks,' and we ordered breakfast.

"Eddie, you said you were the man that could find things out, get information."

"When did I say that?"

"In the hospital. That's what you told me."

"I don't remember."

I narrowed my eyes remembering why I'd never liked him in the first place.

"Either you can or you can't."

"Oh, it's true. Pretty much find what you want. Like an old hound dog. Just gotta point me in the right direction."

"Then why'd you deny it?"

"I didn't deny it. I just don't remember saying it."

I wanted to check his teeth to see if he was related to Lolly.

"I want you to do something."

"Sure, what now? Dig up a real body?"

"As a matter of fact, yes."

Eddie froze with his coffee in midair. "I ain't doing that. One body is enough for me."

"I want you to go find out who was working the night they brought Joe to the hospital."

"Oh sure, the whole hospital staff."

"No, idiot."

"Don't call me an idiot, Mary. Best you be remembering who saved your life."

"Almost." I could have pointed out that in the end it had been me that had saved his, but I didn't. I looked at the welted scar on his neck. At least he tried.

"*Almost* counts."

"Yes, it does, Eddie. I'm sorry. I'm just blistered and tired." The waitress brought over our plates and set them down. "Now listen. Just the emergency room. More specifically, just the people working the night that Joe died."

Eddie shrugged his shoulders, shoved an entire piece of bacon in his mouth. "I can try."

"Try now."

"Mary, I need to sleep."

"I want you to try now."

"Alright. Alright. I'll call a nurse I use to date a while back. See if she can find anything out."

"Fine. Whatever you think's best. In the meantime, I have to pay someone a visit."

CHAPTER THIRTY-FIVE

Peggy Cusler had rings beneath her eyes and a baby on her hip when she opened the door. "Well look what the cat's drug in." She closed the door behind me, and leaning over whispered, "Jimmy's getting dressed in the bedroom."

"It's alright. I came to see him."

She raised one eyebrow, put her cigarette out and wiped the baby's snotty nose.

"Can't imagine what for."

"Old business."

"You still digging up that grave?"

"No. I finished that part." I said just as the every increasingly bald Jimmy walked in.

"Honey, look who dropped by to visit."

He stopped. Looked at me unsmiling.

"I take it this isn't a social call."

"You take it right."

"Some things are better left unsaid don't you think, Mary?" He eyed Peggy Sue and I remembered our last visit but decided an ace-in-the-hole was just that. I looked back with a shrug that stated, "It depends."

"How about I make us all some coffee?" Peggy Sue disappeared around the living room wall but not out of earshot.

"I'm tired, Cusler, and I'm gonna come straight to the point."

"Before you get on your high horse you better remember I didn't have you or your good buddy arrested for stealing police property. Way I see," he reached down and pulled a cigarette from a pack on the coffee table and packed it down on the open palm of his left hand, "you owe me."

"Look Jimmy, it's been a long time. This thing. I should have come to you in the beginning because you were the first officer on the scene the night Joe died. But I'm gonna tell you right now that jail for a hundred years doesn't scare me. Get it?"

Jimmy nodded with the nod of understanding that our positions had changed. Without the threat of blackmail of any kind, he was powerless.

"I need to know the details."

I saw Jimmy Cusler moved by something very foreign to him. It appeared to be compassion.

"No, Mary. You don't."

"Believe me I've got my reasons or I'd be in Montana. When you got to the scene did you see anyone else?"

"No."

"How were you called? Was there a witness? Somebody hear the shot?"

"It was something strange. Had a call. Old lady from over there," he tossed his head towards the island, "says she saw the whole thing." He leaned in towards me, lowered his voice, "In a dream. So I think *sure, prank call number five hundred and five for the night*. Get 'em all the time, only this time—"

"Only this time it's true." I said.

"Yeah, and the spookier part is it's somebody I know."

"You never knew Joe."

"I knew him better than I wanted to." He sucked on the filter of his cigarette, crushed the stub out in the ashtray.

"So you called an ambulance."

"Yeah, and for back up. I mean it was pretty freaky, I'm riding alone and here the guy is with a hole in his head right in the front. Blood everywhere."

"He was shot in the front of the head?"

"No. Back of the head. Nine millimeter. Came out through the front right here." He pointed to his forehead. "Blood was everywhere."

"Jimmy that's enough." Peggy Sue came around the corner and stood looking at me.

"I have to know."

"Well, he doesn't have to throw in all the morbid details." She brought me a cup of coffee and Jimmy one and went back to pick the baby up where it was crawling at high speed across the floor.

"And the ambulance came."

"Ambulance came. Wrecker came for the car. We impounded it for evidence, but as I remember nothing was found."

"Did you hang out afterwards? Look for witnesses? Ask questions?"

"An Indian from the island got shot. Anybody that considered themself worth anything wouldn't had spoke up or wanted to get involved. Figured it involved drug money and kept their distance. The other thing was it happened around midnight down by Church Street. Any loony person down there could have done it and trying to find out the truth from those people is like searching for a rat in a maze. I followed the ambulance. Hung out in the emergency room."

"Twisted sense of loyalty, don't you think?"

"It wasn't loyalty. It was just . . ." Jimmy drank his coffee, stared off blankly out the window, then back to me. I got the distinct impression he didn't know why he hung around.

"See anything out of the ordinary?"

"Yes. As a matter of fact I did. The guys that were waiting around for the doctor. Acted real important but weren't from around here. They flashed a few badges at the desk, stayed until the doctor came out and said he'd pronounced Joe dead. Soon's that happened the guys left."

"Then you left."

"Not right away. I sat there for a little while. Finished a cup of coffee. Thought about things."

I didn't ask Jimmy what "things." Maybe, he'd replayed the night outside the pool hall. Or maybe he just thought about how good it felt to be alive. And how quick somebody couldn't be.

*

It was five o'clock in the evening when the phone rang. I woke in a disoriented haze, looking at the walls, the door, the furniture, searching for anything that would give me a clue as to my whereabouts. On the sixth ring the ringing stopped and a man's sleepy voice from the next room said, "Hello." It was then I remembered I was at Eddie's. That the two of us had waited on a phone call until we couldn't last any longer and had opted for sleep with Eddie saying, "It's been this many years Mary, what's a few hours sleep gonna make a difference?" And I said, "You're right, Eddie. You're absolutely right." Then, he threw me a blanket and a pillow and I had promptly gone out like a light. Now, he walked through the door looking worse than usual. "You might want to scrub that face. We're about to have company."

The company turned out to be Eddie's former part-time girlfriend, Bobbie, who was an attractive woman with obviously questionable taste in men. With her was a tiny L.P.N. by the name of Suzy who appeared nervous to be talking to anyone about anything. I had the impression she stayed nervous most of the time.

"Are ya'll with the police or something?"

"Something," Eddie said, "You might say we're all affiliated." It made more sense than trying to explain the truth.

"Suzy was on duty in E.R. the night they brought him in. She said it got a little crazy."

"How come?"

Suzy rolled her eyes at me, took a deep breath. "To tell you the truth I had just started. Hadn't done nothing but go to school. Worse thing I'd seen was a man that fell across his barbed wire fence and poked out one eyeball and that was enough to make me consider changing professions. I mean studying is one thing and then seeing it up close well, it ain't like dissecting a dead cat. But Momma had already paid for all my schooling and she said I'd better pull myself together, so I did."

"So that night . . ."

"So that night when they brought him in like that," Suzy leaned in to the *that* with both arms across her stomach, she looked like she only weighed a hundred pounds, "well you just don't see nothing like that around here. Miami, maybe, but not here."

I was still tired and getting frustrated.

"Tell me about the particulars, please."

"Well, he was dead."

"Yes."

"Well, no, he wasn't dead first. He was dead later."

"Maybe Suzy would like something to drink," Bobbie said to Eddie. Eddie nodded then went to the kitchen.

"They were working on him all the way from the ambulance into E.R. trying to resuscitate him. With the paddles, you know, trying to start his heart." She whispered *heart* like it was a secret word. "So then they wheeled him in and the doctor kept it up. Must have been over thirty minutes, I know." Eddie handed her a glass of water with no ice. She held onto it but never drank. "Finally, the doctor pronounces him dead. Then he goes out to tell the next of kin, only there wasn't none, just these two guys."

"Suits?"

"That's right. And the reason I remember is 'cause normally family won't leave right away being that upset. They never know which way to go."

"Sure."

"But these guys just leave right away. But the strangest thing is, two or three minutes later his heart starts beating on its own. It was scary. I ran out to call the doctor back in. But the men in the suits were already gone."

"His heart started beating again." I tasted the words on my lips, felt them against my tongue. "How long did it beat before he died again?" I asked this very slowly.

"He didn't."

"He didn't." I repeated.

"No, there were just," she paused, looked at Bobbie and Bobbie nodded to go on, "complications."

"How much more complicated can it get?" Eddie was pacing the floor. Back and forth. Back and forth. On the other hand, I was so still I forgot to breathe.

"What kind of complications?"

"Bullet wound to the head was bad. Went in through the back. Did a lot of damage. Came clean out through the front by the right lobe."

My heart felt sicker than it had in a long time.

"He finally woke up but he couldn't talk. Or he wouldn't. Then when he did talk a little they figured out that he couldn't remember a thing. His name, his age, his address. Nothing. And he wouldn't talk to nobody. I was still assigned to E.R. you understand but I followed him to intensive care, then to step-down, then finally to his room. I'd go in early and visit him."

"Then where is he?" The words came out stilted and choking more to myself than the Suzy creature before me.

"He left A.M.A."

"What is that?"

"Against Medical Advice," said Bobbie sounding much less emotional and more authoritative.

"Then where'd he go?" It was Eddie now asking as I sat on the edge of the couch rocking back and forth.

"Nobody ever knew. One day the nurse went in and he just wasn't there anymore."

She threw up her hands to the open air. Eddie stopped pacing and looked at me but by then I was a thousand miles away, trapped somewhere between worlds. Just like Joe.

CHAPTER THIRTY-SIX

Lolly's motel was rebuilt with two new additions. One was an extra wing on the side of the building and the second was her new partner from Alabama. I had blessedly escaped the details but knew at some point I'd receive them piecemeal, Kallie style. Last month the island of Toliquilah held a town meeting in the newly completed restaurant. The subject at hand had been whether to rebuild or not to rebuild the bridge. Those in favor of the rebuilding became known as the bridgers and those not in favor became known as the ferryers and trying to make peace between the two small factions became a problem. The greatest complaint of the bridgers was that no one could get their cars across the inlet which meant that they had to ride Frank's "stupid little boat" and then catch Lemuel's "tacky" tour bus to wherever they wanted to go. This was offered up by the Monroe sisters who were the most vocal of the bridgers. I was as far in the corner as I could get, feeling out of place in the new building with its glass block windows and draping plants and bubbling aquariums that were still void of any fish. But secretly I considered myself a bridger because I missed the old No-good and because I too wanted to use a car.

The ferryers on the other hand strongly believed that the new business boom on the island was made up by the fact that you couldn't get to it. This faction consisted primarily of the business owners of Toliquilah and Frank McGurdy who was making more money operating his water shuttle than he ever had chasing storms.

I suggested perhaps they might look into Frank getting a real ferry boat so that cars could travel back and forth to which Lolly Eden let out a "Hot dog!" and grinned at me with all her teeth. They made her look like a wild animal with rabies. Lemuel didn't like the idea because of his bus business. Frank said, "No problem, we'll let the locals bring their cars for a discount," and Edna spoke up and said, "You mean 'for free,' " It was said with such authority that Frank saw the error of his ways and said, "For free." Then he added, "We'll just charge the tourists so much they'd rather just ride over and catch the bus." And on that note the town meeting was adjourned with the exception of Moses inviting everyone to the new grand opening.

Over the last months they had tried to comfort me in their own individual way. Kallie told me a story about some dog with amnesia. In her story the dog had a dream one night and in the dream he remembered that he wasn't a dog at all but was really a man.

I said, "So what happened, Kallie?"

"He stopped chasing cats and came home." She said it like it should settle the world for me.

One quiet evening Edna and I had actually had a moment together and we sat, not saying much until she finally offered up, "One day it'll come to an end and that'll be the end of it."

Agnes offered to paint my nails. Lemuel offered me a bottle on the house. Some days I could understand him, some days not, like picking up the right radio signals.

But there wasn't anything they offered that could help. In the beginning I had been filled with ideas of searching. Hiring a detective. Placing classified ads in nearby cities. Poster campaigns with his picture attached. And all these plans had carried me through the shock of realizing he truly might be alive. Then they grew dimmer with each passing day as I realized that if Joe was still alive, he was better off with people thinking he wasn't. And that he also might not have a clue who he was and in that space I had waking nightmares. If he didn't know who he was, then who was he? And where was he?

I never eat without wondering if he has food. Am never warm without wondering if he is cold. And I withdraw more and more into myself because somehow I have to create a world where Joe and I can live. Where the shell I erect around me can protect the distance that lies between us. As if the tiniest of threads, as delicate as hand blown glass, connect us and if I am very, very careful, Joe will find it and follow it home. In the meantime, I practice listening to my heart and not my head believing that eventually, I will follow it to him.

In the mornings I sweep Esther's house, water her plants, watch her snakes and consider setting them free, but I never do. Sometimes I practice milking them in my mind. At noon I sit in the chair propped against the house, with my eyes closed, my face turned up towards the sun. I listen to the scuttling of bugs beneath the earth, to the herons landing in the trees, gently folding all my precious dreams in their great wings.

In the evenings I make a cup of tea and sit in Esther's chair, rocking back and forth, reading books about the mystery of the thing we call memory. Where it is stored and how it is lost and how it may surface in fleeting moments, like puzzle pieces in the fog, then just as quickly submerge, fall apart and hide again. I feel the house grow dim. Then dark. Sometimes, I open the box that holds all of Joe's money, which I knew about, and Esther's which I didn't. It remains in the plastic bags that held it taped inside the tree. I don't bother to count it. I look at it wondering how I might exchange it for what I want the most. Something I can't buy.

At night I listen to the owls hunting. The alligators calling. Sometimes I sleep. Tonight, a great clap of thunder has awakened me. It is the first thunderstorm of the year. I can smell the rain coming before it gets here, and I rise from the bed, pull on my jeans and go outside. Then I sit in the leaning chair against the house. The air cracks with electricity full of itself, pregnant with anticipation. The thunder shakes the windows, the sides of the house, my heart against my chest. The great clouds draw nearer, standing out white against the darkness of the night. When they are right before me I can see them light up blue-green inside. Flashing. Like they are being x-rayed. Like they are phosphorous on a moonlit night.

As the first drops of rain fall, like the rain of resurrection, I close my eyes, dive into the electric current, and pray with all my might.

EPILOGUE

A solitary figure moves along Church Street. He gazes upwards, watching the lightning snake its way across the late-night sky. Behind him, a two-wheeled buggy creaks and strains at the ripped sidewalks, the broken cement. He passes an empty parking lot and turns the corner. Seeking sanctuary from the coming rain, the figure climbs the decaying steps to a lonely church, one with a skeletal congregation. Once inside, he pulls his coat about him and moves toward a pew along the back. From somewhere near the front, a shaking hand lights a solitary candle. The hand withdraws, disappears, and then a voice, much like twilight, is more felt than heard in the darkness as it sends up the incense of a prayer. He focuses on the light, its yellow warmth waning small, but iridescent nonetheless. By some seed of instinct, he reaches out toward it, as if the light itself will offer some Holy Grail of hope. The heavens rumble, the lightning streaks so close outside it swears to burn. A name struggles, fights its way through the great darkness swimming inside his mind. One name forming against his throat, his dry parched lips and with the speaking of it, a life unfolds, returns, *Mary.*

River Jordan's hometown is Panama City, Florida, a place between the salt and sand of the Gulf of Mexico, and the swamps and woods of north Florida. She also lived in Hollywood and Ft. Lauderdale, Florida, where she learned that South Florida wasn't the Florida she grew up in. No sweet iced tea. No ya'll. No Pine Trees. No "Put you're feet up." No "Set a spell." She also lived in Taos and Tucumcari, New Mexico; Kansas City (where a great Bob Seger concert made everything worthwhile); Athens, Georgia; and New York City.

Regarding high school, she says she "Forgot a lot. Was academic. Belonged to no cliques. (Walked among them but not of them.) Had 'friends' from all neighborhoods, (prepsters, dopers, over-achievers, under-achievers, cheerleaders, no leaders, bookworms, teachers) These people still speak to me."

River is a founding member of the West Florida Playwright's Project, an organization dedicated to the production of original works for stage and film, and a founding member of the Honorable F.B. Book Club. She's served on boards for the Bay County Library Foundation and The Florida Network, a statewide organization serving children victimized by physical and/or sexual abuse.)

She fell in love with the theater while studying with Dr. Yolanda Reed, founder and creative director for The Loblolly Theatre of Pensacola, Florida and has had plays produced including, *Soul, Rhythm and Blues, Virga,* and *Mama Jewels: Tales from Mullet Creek,* a traveling show with Amy Bruner who performed for the City of Seaside, Florida and for Calvin Klein International of London.

She divides her time between Panama City, Florida and Nashville, Tennessee and places between and beyond while road-tripping with her husband.